Praise for *Arya Khanna's Bollywood Moment*

"A tender coming-of-age story that navigates fraught friendships, first loves, and the thorny love of family. Avachat is a fresh and sparkling voice, and sure to be a star on the rise."

—Roshani Chokshi, *New York Times* bestselling author of *The Gilded Wolves*

"Avachat's debut is an endearing slice-of-life story that explores how relationships evolve as we come of age: with our friends, our families, and maybe even our rivals. Bubbly and endlessly charming, *Arya Khanna's Bollywood Moment* is a cozy contemporary to warm the soul."

—Jesmeen Kaur Deo, author of *TJ Powar Has Something to Prove*

"Lovable and snarky, Arya is the perfectly imperfect character to follow through the highs and lows of sisterhood, friendship, and romance. Avachat's endearing slice-of-life contemporary nails the energy of a classic teen coming-of-age story while still feeling delightfully fresh."

—Racquel Marie, author of *Ophelia After All*

"Arushi Avachat's debut is a sparkling love story for anyone who's ever had to juggle real life responsibilities and relationships while enduring an epic family wedding. A joy to read."

—Nisha Sharma, award-winning author of *My So-Called Bollywood Life* and *The Karma Map*

Arya Khanna's Bollywood Moment

Arushi Avachat

WEDNESDAY BOOKS
NEW YORK

First published in the United States by Wednesday Books,
an imprint of St. Martin's Publishing Group

ARYA KHANNA'S BOLLYWOOD MOMENT. Copyright © 2023 by Arushi Avachat.
All rights reserved. Printed in the United States of America. For information,
address St. Martin's Publishing Group, 120 Broadway, New York, NY 10271.

www.wednesdaybooks.com

Designed by Jonathan Bennett

Library of Congress Cataloging-in-Publication Data

Names: Avachat, Arushi, author.
Title: Arya Khanna's Bollywood moment / Arushi Avachat.
Description: First edition. | New York : Wednesday Books, 2024. |
    Audience: Ages 13–18.
Identifiers: LCCN 2023033207 | ISBN 9781250895134 (trade paperback) |
    ISBN 9781250895110 (hardcover) | ISBN 9781250895127 (ebook)
Subjects: CYAC: Interpersonal relations—Fiction. | Best friends—Fiction. |
    Friendship—Fiction. | High schools—Fiction. | Schools—Fiction. |
    Family life—Fiction. | East Indian Americans—Fiction.
Classification: LCC PZ7.1.A97325 Ar 2024 | DDC [Fic]—dc23
LC record available at https://lccn.loc.gov/2023033207

Our books may be purchased in bulk for promotional, educational, or business
use. Please contact your local bookseller or the Macmillan Corporate and
Premium Sales Department at 1-800-221-7945, extension 5442, or by email at
MacmillanSpecialMarkets@macmillan.com.

First Edition: 2024

10 9 8 7 6 5 4 3 2 1

*For all my Desi girls,
especially Didi—I still want
to be you when I grow up.*

Act I
Engagement

One
Desi Girls

My sister's hand is gentle and steady at my cheek. Even with my eyes closed, I can feel Alina's gaze on me, studying her handiwork with an artist's precision.

"Hold still," Alina says. She sweeps a gold shadow over my lids, the sapphire bangles Nikhil's mother gave her last night jingling with each movement. She pulls back when she hears me sniffle. "What's wrong?"

I shake my head, pressing the corner of my chunni to each eye to capture escaping tears. "It's just," I say, a lump rising in my throat. "You look so pretty, Alina."

It's true. When I was younger, and Alina was in high school, I thought my sister had to be the most beautiful woman in the world. Years later, not much has changed. Today, her skin is pink and flushed in a healthy bridal glow, and her dark hair falls down her back in loose, shiny curls, shampoo commercial–style. She's wearing Mamma's most expensive and elegant lehenga, a silvery blue set with an intricately embroidered skirt that tapers into a short train at her heels. Swirls of flowery

3

mehndi paint her arms, and her chunni rests gracefully over one shoulder, concealing all but a thin strip of skin above her waist.

Alina smiles. "Thank you," she says softly. "But you don't. Not yet," she teases, tucking a stray piece of hair behind my ear. "So, no more tears, okay? You're going to ruin all my hard work."

"Okay." I give her a watery smile. "No more tears." Sitting straighter on the bathtub edge, I tilt my face up.

For the next ten minutes, Alina works in silence, pressing foundation and concealer into my skin with a damp sponge, dusting on powders with a large, fluffy brush. Something warm settles in my stomach. It feels like before. Alina, back in the childhood bathroom we used to share, doing my makeup just like she used to for every Diwali, birthday party, middle school dance. It hits me in full force just how terribly I've missed this, missed her. Never can I go three years without her again.

"All done," Alina announces, and I stand up, turning to examine my reflection in the bathroom mirror.

"Oh," I say a little breathlessly. I look beautiful. My skin is glowing with dewy radiance, my eyes big and bright from expertly applied shadow and liner. I look to Alina in the mirror. "Thank you."

She squeezes my shoulder. "You look like a princess, Arya."

The compliment makes me smile. I adjust my chunni, trying and failing to prevent it from bunching at my shoulder. "Which princess?"

"Jasmine?" Alina offers, and I wrinkle my nose.

"I'm in pink, not blue," I point out. I open the wooden drawer under the sink, searching for a safety pin to fasten my chunni to my blouse. I find one underneath some hair elastics and hand it to Alina.

4

She secures it in one smooth motion. "A Bollywood star, then. Kareena Kapoor in 'Bole Chudiyan.'"

I raise my eyebrows, surprised and flattered. "That's a very high compliment."

"I'm feeling generous." She grins at me, and I wrap my arms around her waist tightly, kissing her cheek.

"Let's go get you hitched," I say, then stop, correcting myself. "Engaged, I mean. Officially, anyway."

Today is Alina's Roka ceremony, a Hindu pre-wedding event that formally acknowledges Alina and Nikhil's engagement. The shaadi is still a few months away, but Alina and Nikhil will exchange rings today, and the families will exchange gifts. Mamma insisted on following traditions to a T. Alina protested at first, but I know she loves the attention and extravagance that comes with Mamma's way.

When we walk out of the bathroom, we find Mamma waiting for us in the hallway. She's wearing a gold sari and deep red lipstick, the picture of elegance.

My mother is very beautiful. Her beauty has faded with time, but not because of age. Her eyes have lost their gleam. Frown lines crease her forehead. She doesn't smile anymore, not unless we have company. This is how I know her now. Proud, regal, and sad.

She gives the two of us a once-over, and her lack of criticism signals approval.

"Chalo," she says, tilting her head to the staircase. "Guests are waiting."

"I cannot believe," Lisa begins, pushing a lock of ginger hair out of her eye, "that there is all this fuss going on, and it's not even the main event."

I grin at her over a tall glass of mango lassi. The ceremony

5

concluded just moments ago, and now I'm sitting next to Lisa Greenfield, my best friend since fourth grade. She's wearing a borrowed lehenga of mine, a teal piece that looks bright against her pale skin and is slightly too long for her even though she's in heels. We're on the bench by my papa's flower garden, sipping our drinks and watching guests dance to loud, joyful Bollywood remixes.

"It wouldn't be a Khanna wedding without the fuss," I remind Lisa. Last year, I took Lisa with me to my cousin's wedding, where the groom arrived at the venue on a grand white horse.

"True," she says, smiling. "But I won't ever understand it. My parents got married at city hall. Then they got divorced like the rest of America just fine." I swat her lightly on the shoulder, and she giggles. "I'm joking. It was a really beautiful, really emotional ceremony."

"It was," I say softly. Alina and Nikhil had both been teary-eyed as they exchanged rings, and Papa had been openly sobbing for the duration of the Roka.

Lisa sips her mango lassi quietly, and I use the moment to take in the scene around us. It took several hours of hard work, but our backyard has never looked more enchanting. Red rose petals litter the walkways and strings of twinkling fairy lights line our fence. The lanterns I helped Nikhil hang from the magnolia trees last night glint gold in the fading sun. The sky is a hazy indigo, hovering between day and night, and wisps of white cloud float up above us.

Lisa nudges my shoulder. "Where's Andy?" she asks casually.

There's a pause. "I think he's still inside," I say carefully. "He came in late, so he's probably getting food. He should be out soon."

Andy Bishop, a boy well known for his chronic lateness, is the third member of our trio. He moved to town in early middle school, when Lisa and I were already close, and the three of us became best friends after a fateful English project grouped us together. He and Lisa started going out last winter, after years of a drawn-out will-they-won't-they courtship. Just three weeks ago, they broke up. I still don't know the details of their split.

"I'll admit," I start when Lisa doesn't say anything, "I feel a little like the child of recently divorced parents. I've been dividing my time between you. Today will be the first time we're all together in weeks."

"Trust me, not a comparable situation," Lisa says, holding up a finger. "But yes, I know things are weird right now. It's going to take time to get back to normal."

I nod like I understand, but I can't help the worry churning in my stomach. Senior year starts in a few days, and I don't want to begin my last year of high school without both my best friends at my side.

"But it'll get back to normal. Eventually," Lisa continues. "I know it. We were friends before we were anything else."

"You're really doing well, then?" I ask tentatively, twisting a strand of hair behind my ear. "With the breakup?"

I don't get to hear her response, because Andy slides into the seat next to me, his plate laden with samosas, pakoras, and other savory snacks. He looks handsome; the navy-gold kurta Nikhil lent him for the occasion suits his dark skin.

"Hey, Lisa. Arya." His voice is gentle. Lisa gives him a half wave that is so awkward, it makes me cringe.

"You're late," I say, desperate to move past any weirdness.

"Traffic was crazy," he says, shaking his head. "You wouldn't believe."

"You live two blocks away, Andy," I remind him. "So, no, I don't believe."

He grins brightly. "I promise I won't be late to the real wedding." He raises three fingers Scout's honor–style.

"Knowing you, you'd probably be late to your own wedding," I joke, and it's in that moment I become supremely aware that I am sandwiched between two recent exes. Lisa slurps her drink loudly in the pause that follows.

"Probably," Andy says lightly.

"Can you believe we're going to be seniors soon?" I say to change the subject. "I mean, summer's practically over." I pause for effect. "Winter is coming."

"Ugh," Andy says at the same time Lisa groans, "Worst joke ever."

They start to laugh, and even though it's at my expense, I can't help the feeling of warmth that settles over me because they are laughing together.

"I'm serious," I say, nudging them both. "It's kind of scary. Our last year of high school."

"It's going to be an exciting last year for me," Lisa says joyfully. "I've waited to captain since freshman year."

Lisa is the new captain of our girls' varsity basketball team. I'm not a big sports person, but I've never missed one of her home games. She is our school's starting point guard and pure magic on the court.

"Should be an exciting last year for you too," Lisa continues, tilting her near-empty glass of mango lassi toward me. "Vice President Khanna."

"Don't," I say, making a sour face at Lisa, because it's a John Adams–like vice presidency. I only became VP because I lost the presidential election. Dean Merriweather, a soccer player with charisma but zero work ethic, won by six votes. It's safe to say I am still bitter.

"Stop being negative," Lisa chastises.

"I am who I am," I quip, and then we all fall silent. Something like nervousness twists in my stomach. I don't know how to explain it to them, how much I need this night not to end. Tomorrow, I'll be worrying about senior year and student council, about my two best friends drifting apart, about Alina getting married and leaving again. Tonight, I can pretend none of that exists.

"Let's go dance," I say suddenly, tilting my head toward the makeshift dance floor Papa set up in the center of our backyard. Beneath the darkening sky, guests laugh and sway to the music. Alina's in the center, dancing with Nikhil, bright and happy.

"What?" Andy says, rightfully incredulous. Never do I volunteer to dance.

"I'm serious," I say, standing up and smoothing down the skirt of my lehenga.

"I don't know any of the Bollywood songs," Lisa points out.

"You'll learn," I decide. I slip off my heels and begin walking barefoot toward the dance floor. I glare at Lisa and Andy over my shoulder until they follow me, grumbling. Right then, "Desi Girl" starts to play on the speakers, and Lisa squeals excitedly.

"I do know a Bollywood song!" she exclaims, and I laugh, blowing her a kiss. She shouts the lyrics she knows, pretends to shout the ones she doesn't. Andy joins in a moment later, and I fill in the gaps in their memories. We shout and sing and dance until the sky turns to night and our feet are sore and aching.

Two
Senior Season,

On Monday morning, I have breakfast with Alina and Nikhil. Mamma's still asleep, and Papa's already left for work, so it's only the three of us. Our meal consists of leftovers from the Roka: a microwaved aloo tikki and two barfis each.

"You look nice," Nikhil tells me as I set my plate on the table. He's sipping coffee and working away on his laptop. He's got on a pair of thick, black-rimmed glasses today instead of his usual contacts. "Very first-day-of-school-ready."

"Thank you," I say, smiling at him. I've kept my makeup simple, and I'm wearing the outfit I picked out weeks ago: a flowy, floral top tucked into a pair of high-waisted shorts.

"Those are my earrings," Alina protests. She had been leaning against Nikhil's shoulder, but now she sits up straight, eyes narrowed at the small gold hoops glittering from my ears.

"What's the point of you being home," I say, unbothered, "if I can't steal your things?"

"I'm getting married; that's the point," she says with a

glare. "Anyway, don't forget we're going to the caterer's this afternoon. Drive straight over after class. I emailed you details last week."

"I wasn't going to forget," I say. I've been looking forward to the taste-testing session all weekend. "I'll be there."

"Good," she says. "It'll just be the two of us, since Papa's working, and Nikhil needs to drop his parents off at the airport."

Nikhil's parents flew to Boston from New Jersey just for the Roka. They'll be back a couple weeks before the wedding to help with any final preparations, but Nikhil is living with us for the next few months, working from home so he can be involved in each stage of the wedding planning.

I'm glad to have him around. I liked Nikhil the moment I met him, which had never happened with Alina's previous boyfriends. He and Alina started dating during her sophomore year at Columbia, a few months before she dropped out, and I met him for the first time that spring, on a weekend trip to visit Alina. He was kind, gentler than I expected for someone who loved my fiery sister, and he spoke to me like an equal even though I was an insecure thirteen-year-old. I've loved him like a brother ever since.

My brow furrows at Alina's math. "Just the two of us? What about Mamma?"

Alina picks at her barfi. "What about her?" Her voice is casual, but her mouth is tightening at the corners.

"Alina," I start. My voice is a warning.

"I don't see a need for her to be there," Alina says, voice rising preemptively. "I am totally capable of determining the menu by myself."

"What do you need me for, then?"

She sniffs. "Moral support."

11

"That is one of my skills," I agree. "And it'll be particularly useful to you if Mamma's there today."

Her nostrils flare. "I've made up my mind, Arya." She folds her hands on the table, her fading swirls of mehndi just visible in the kitchen light. "I'm not asking Mamma. And I'm the bride, so what I say goes."

Irritation is climbing up my throat, so I take a deep breath to push it down because I don't want to start senior year in a bad mood. But Mamma will consider it the greatest insult not to be invited, and the general unpleasantness guaranteed to follow will make home unbearable. Not the most promising start to shaadi season.

"She's your mother," I try. "You won't be able to sideline her at every stage of wedding planning."

"Don't underestimate me."

I groan and turn to Nikhil, hoping he'll be the voice of reason. "Talk to her, please."

He raises his hands. "I'm Switzerland," he says, but his eyes are apologetic.

An indignant sound escapes me. "Unbelievable!"

"Leave Nikhil out of this," Alina says. "Besides," she continues, pulling her long hair over one shoulder. "I really don't think Mamma's going to care. She hasn't even spoken to me since the Roka."

The words sound sticky on her tongue. She sips Nikhil's coffee in the pause that follows.

Some of the fight leaves my body since the source of Alina's insistence is clear. She and Mamma are terrible at reaching out to each other but very skilled at increasing the distance between them. This has been their way since Alina was in high school.

"I found a tikka online that I really like," I say finally. I know when to drop an argument. "Not too expensive, and it'll go great with the lehenga I have planned for the Haldi ceremony."

Alina leaps at the subject change. Jewelry discussion is something my sister can never turn down.

"Show," she orders, extending her hand.

I pull up the link on my phone before passing it to Alina. We spend the rest of breakfast brainstorming jewelry selections for the shaadi and asking a very reluctant Nikhil for advice.

I pull into the parking lot of Abigail Adams High School just after Dean Merriweather. As student council representatives, our assigned parking spots are right next to each other. His car windows are streaked blue and red, our school colors, and boyish lettering spells out SENIOR SEASON on the rear windshield. It's a loud, obnoxious paint job—very much Dean's style.

"Arya," Dean says cheerfully when I climb out of my car. He's standing at the parking curb, fingers curled around the loops of his backpack straps, waiting for me. He's dressed plainly, blue jeans and a T-shirt, but his dark hair is styled in a way that makes him look put together. "My second-in-command."

"Nice," I say. "How long have you been waiting to say that?"

Dimples cut into the sides of his cheeks. He has a handsome smile, even when he's making fun of me. "Thought of it over the summer."

"Clever, Dean."

"At first I thought I could call you Madam Vice President—"

"Certainly more respectful."

"—but then it's only fair if you call me Mr. President."

He raises his eyebrows, the corners of his mouth curving up. "What do you think?"

"I'd rather quit." I slip my keys into my pocket and walk past him, but he catches up to me with ease. He's taller, so his legs are longer; one stride of his equals two of mine.

"Don't get my hopes up," he says. "Every day I wish Josh Hartley had come in second instead of you."

"No, you don't." Josh Hartley had been the third and only other candidate in last spring's student body presidential race. He was a stoner who campaigned on the administration-rejected proposal of turning locker rooms co-ed, securing a clear majority of the male underclassmen vote.

"He's a Lakers fan," I say sweetly when Dean opens his mouth to respond. "I know the women's safety issue isn't a dealbreaker for you."

"Hey," he says, stung. "Women's safety concerns me plenty. The locker room policy would never have been a reality."

"Tell yourself that, Dean."

He rolls his eyes, clearly desiring a change of subject. "How was your summer?" Dean asks. There's sunlight in his eyes, so he's squinting at me through dark lashes. "I saw Alina got married. How was the wedding?"

"You can ask me again in four months." When he looks confused, I add, "Her wedding isn't until late December."

"Oh," he says, brow furrowed. "I just thought—on your Instagram story—there were lots of wedding-related videos."

"That was her engagement," I say. I tilt my head to meet his eyes, smiling a little. "Sweet that you watch all my Instagram stories, though."

He stops, momentarily flustered, but then his face slips back into an easy, unaffected smile. "Community service is really important to me."

14

"Right." We've stopped walking and are dawdling outside the library. We're both silent, studying each other, and his eyes are so blue and bright that I smile a little deeper in spite of myself. I blink, and the moment ends. "Happy first day, Dean. I'll see you in class."

Three
All of It Is Wrong

Andy and I have first period AP Literature together. We haven't shared a class for a couple years, and by sheer coincidence, we're back in the same classroom we were in for freshman English. Our teacher is new, a young woman named Ms. Bray with sunshine-colored hair and a personality to match, but everything else is familiar: royal blue wallpaper, splintery wooden desks, perpetually malfunctioning thermostat.

Andy nudges me, and I look up from my laptop. I just finished forwarding Alina's email with the information about today's catering session to Mamma, and I'm refusing to feel guilty. My sister needs a push in the right direction. Things with Mamma may be icy now, but the ice will melt with time and effort, and this is necessary effort. Alina can thank me later.

Conviction growing, I clear my throat and smooth a wrinkle in my blouse. "What's up?" I ask Andy.

His lips are pursed. "Have you spoken to Lisa today?"

I raise my eyebrows in surprise, because Andy has been so

intentional about not bringing up Lisa since their breakup. "Not in person. She sent me a good-morning text, but that's all."

To be precise, Lisa texted me: HAPPY FIRST DAY BESTIE JUST 180 MORE TILL GRAD at six a.m. and then left me on read when I asked her to bring me my coffee order before class. I figure the details don't matter much.

"Have you spoken to her?" I ask gently when Andy doesn't respond right away. I keep my voice low, not wanting to attract Ms. Bray's attention.

He shakes his head. "I haven't talked to her since Alina's engagement." He hesitates, then raises his dark eyes to meet mine. "I think she's avoiding me."

My brows draw together. "Why would you think that?" During the Roka, their initial interactions had been laced with some nervousness and discomfort, but the evening's end had left me hopeful that the three of us could eventually return to normalcy.

"I haven't seen her all morning."

"Oh," I say, and the worry in my stomach loosens a bit. "Is that it? We didn't meet every morning last year, either. She's late to school nearly as often as you are."

"Yes, but on the first day?" He gives me a meaningful look, and I don't know how to respond because he's right. My morning encounter with Dean had momentarily driven Lisa and Andy's breakup from my mind, but thinking about it now, I can't help but share Andy's concern.

"Let's be optimistic," I say, even as the tightness in my stomach returns. "Lisa's not a passive-aggressive person. She'll let us know if she needs distance."

He studies me, then straightens and nods. "I'm probably overthinking it. You're right."

"I always am," I say, and he shakes his head, lips pushing

into a small smile. We shift our attention back to the front of the classroom, where Ms. Bray is turning on the overhead projector, and don't return to the subject for the rest of the period.

The school day passes slowly. I don't share any other classes with Andy or Lisa, which isn't unusual considering our varying electives, but it's disappointing all the same. I walk to classes alone, wireless headphones stuffed in my ears, listening to Lizzo's latest album on full blast.

In Leadership, I depend on Emilia Lopez to make it through the hour without throttling Dean. Emilia is the school secretary and my closest friend on student council. She served as my campaign manager during election season in the spring, and I trust her judgment more than mine where Dean is concerned.

I keep my cool during announcements, when Dean begins polishing his name plate—a shiny gold block that reads STU-DENT BODY PRESIDENT in dark lettering—right beside me. But when he refers to me as his "assistant" while answering a junior representative's question, I can't keep myself from taking the bait.

"You're a child," I say, voice low to avoid the careful ear of our teacher, Mrs. Marina. "Somehow you win like a sore loser."

His smile deepens, and he sinks back in his chair, ridiculously amused. "Well, you would know."

"Easy," Emilia breathes next to me, squeezing my hand in warning before I can retort. "Ignore him," she advises, and I do my best.

When lunch rolls around, I wait for Lisa and Andy at our usual table in the cafeteria. Andy arrives first, balancing a hot tray and two bottles of cold brew in his hands. He has a free period before break this year, so he was able to get his meal before first-day-of-school traffic clogged up the lunch line.

"That for me?" I ask, reaching across the table to take one of the bottles before he even responds. The other is for Lisa. Andy doesn't drink anything caffeinated. But he's been bringing us cold brews since middle school, when Lisa and I first developed our coffee addiction.

"I feel like a waiter," he says, shrugging off his backpack and sliding into the seat next to me. "Without the compensation."

I laugh, about to reply when my phone buzzes next to me. It's a text from Lisa. Short and direct: going to sit with my basketball girls today. please don't be mad. love you, talk soon.

Something like bitterness pools in my stomach at the message. Andy looks at me questioningly, so I raise my phone to show him the text.

"So you were right," I say. He looks sorry, so I try to morph my face into a smile. "It's okay," I say. "I'm sure this is temporary."

"I'm sure," he says, too quickly to mean it.

I pick at the sandwich I packed from home just for something to do. It's only the first day and already all of it is wrong. Mamma and Alina not speaking. Dean in what should be my position. Lisa and Andy, my dearest friends, the one constant in my life the last few years, unable to be in each other's company.

Frustration at Lisa pushes against my lips. She could have made more of an effort, for my sake. Given advance notice, at the least. They are broken up and still I feel like a third wheel, an afterthought.

"Hey," Andy says, nudging me gently. He gives me a smile. "You're all I need."

I smile back in spite of myself. "You're all I need too," I say, leaning my head against his shoulder, trying to convince my-self the words are true.

I swirl a spoonful of sugar into my steaming cup of masala chai, waiting for the drink to cool. Next to me, Alina picks at her nail beds, ruining whatever is left of her perfect Roka man-icure. Mamma sits on my other side, hands resting elegantly on the table, the only one still and seemingly unbothered by the silence growing thick in the air between us.

We are waiting for Roshani Aunty, our caterer, to return to the dining room from the kitchen. Her home, simple as it is, serves as her place of business. Her services are in high demand; wealthy Desi families throughout New England book Roshani Aunty for every shaadi, holiday, birthday party. When plan-ning the Roka, Alina and Nikhil had found it difficult to even secure a consultation.

Alina hasn't spoken to me since I entered ten minutes ago, Mamma in tow. I sent her a warning text before our arrival, but it clearly wasn't sufficiently mollifying. Alina is radiating indignation.

As for Mamma, I know she's displeased to have received such late notice of the catering session. She must have guessed Alina's reluctance to have her here, but she's too dignified to comment on it in front of Roshani Aunty. In any case, Mam-ma's need to oversee shaadi planning supersedes all else.

I take a sip of chai for the sake of something to do. It burns my tongue. I swallow hard and try to convince myself I did right by inviting Mamma.

After what seems like an eternity, Roshani Aunty appears in the doorway, cradling a tray laden with finger foods and at least six different kinds of chutney. She's wearing jeans and a navy kameez with gold detailing that hugs her plump frame.

"First appetizers ready," she says, painted lips stretched into a smile. She rests the tray in the center of the table then takes the seat across from me. If she can sense the tension in the room, she doesn't comment.

"Ladke wale nahin aa rahe hain?" she asks, inquiring after Nikhil's absence.

Mamma clucks her tongue in disappointment. Her hair is up today, pulled into a neat bun with a banana clip. "Typical American boys. No interest in such things."

Alina glowers at me before replying, like I'm responsible for every misconduct of Mamma's because I brought her here. I sink lower in my seat and pretend I missed her glare.

"Nikhil is taking his parents to the airport," Alina corrects. She smiles an apology to our caterer. "Their flight is tonight. He really wishes he could have made it."

"So sweet of him," Roshani Aunty says. "Such family values are important in husbands. He will be very good to you, rani, I know it."

Beside me, Mamma sniffs at this assessment, disbelieving, but she doesn't dispute it. Nikhil Joshi is perfect husband material by every possible metric, but he was loved by Alina during the three years she wasn't speaking to Mamma, and that is a sin Mamma can never forgive.

"Thank you," Alina says, ignoring Mamma's reaction.

"Let's start, then?" Roshani Aunty says, and she launches into an explanation of the dishes before us. We are sampling aloo tikki, spicy deep-fried potato patties; and sabudana vada, crispy balls of tapioca pearls, golden potatoes, and crushed peanuts. An assortment of chutneys is laid out for us to dip our snacks in.

"Try with the cucumber chutney," Roshani Aunty advises as I help myself to one of the potato patties. "Shah Rukh's favorite," she adds as she spoons the thick green sauce onto my plate.

I take a sip of chai to hide my smile. Roshani Aunty catered an event attended by Shah Rukh Khan, one of Bollywood's most loved stars, a little over twenty years ago. She now speaks with authority on the actor's every preference.

Over the next couple of hours, Roshani Aunty brings out two more trays of appetizers: bhel puri, kadhi pakora, and dahi papdi chaat, among other savory treats. She intentionally included both Punjabi dishes for the Khannas and Marathi dishes for the Joshis. Everything is delicious, but we manage to narrow down our favorites, which Alina sends pictures of to Nikhil for approval. By evening, we have a working appetizer menu for each day of the shaadi.

"These three chutneys, na?" Roshani Aunty asks, confirming our selections, indicating the mint, cucumber, and coconut sauces before us.

"I think only the mint and cucumber," Alina says. "Neither Nikhil nor I are big fans of coconut."

"We will have the coconut," Mamma says, waving a hand dismissively. She directs her words to Roshani Aunty, not sparing a glance for Alina. "They may not want, but guests will want. You may excuse Alina. She thinks only for herself sometimes." She gives a gentle laugh to soften the words.

Alina bristles next to me. I squeeze her hand under the table, and she pulls it away. "Don't," I whisper, but it's too late.

"Isn't this the one point in my life I am allowed to think only for myself? It is my shaadi, after all, not yours."

Mamma's eyes flash. "Oh, yes," she says softly, matching Alina's even tone. There's a danger to her purr. "Koi ni, silly of me to forget. Your shaadi, your life. You make your decisions, Alina, like always." She dabs at the corner of her mouth with a cloth napkin, then pushes back suddenly from the table, standing up. "Please excuse me. I must visit the restroom."

Roshani Aunty watches Mamma go, brows raised slightly, but nothing else in her expression suggests anything out of the ordinary has occurred. She turns to me and Alina, smiling pleasantly. "I too will be right back. Let me put away the dishes."

She stands, stacking the trays and our dirty plates together, and returns to the kitchen. The door swings shut behind her.

Alina elbows me sharply the second we are alone. "You," she hisses. "Your fault. This is all your fault."

I rub my side, wincing. "I sent you a heads-up text!" I say, but the excuse is flimsy even to me.

"I *told* you I didn't want her here. This is exactly what I was trying to avoid."

"There would be nothing to avoid if you could just keep your mouth shut."

Alina glares at me. In anger, she looks more like Mamma than ever. Dark eyes, flushed cheeks, the same downward curve to her lips. "Why did she have to talk about me like that?"

I sigh, sympathy growing in my chest. "She's hurt," I say. "And proud, and she feels excluded from your life, which makes her lash out."

Alina opens her mouth to reply, probably to go on the offensive, so I add hastily, "I'm not saying her behavior is okay. I'm just explaining why she's like this. And she's not changing, so you have to change how you respond to her, otherwise it'll never end."

Alina glares harder, but there's less bite to the look now. "She makes me feel like a child," Alina says. It sounds like a confession. "I'm getting married, and somehow she makes me feel like I'm still a child. Still in high school, still her disappointment."

I squeeze her hand. "You're not her disappointment." *You're her sadness,* I want to say. Because that's the truth. Mamma's belly was already swollen with Alina when she and Papa arrived in Boston from Punjab. While Papa worked, Alina was Mamma's lifeline in a new country, in her new home. Twenty-three years later, Alina is as much her body and blood as she was then. Mamma has been missing a part of herself for three years, and that wound won't heal quickly.

"Mamma is how she is," I tell Alina instead. "But you can still make an effort. Don't rise to her bait." I tilt my head to meet her eyes. "Okay?"

She twists her engagement ring, a nervous habit. "Okay." Her eyes are wet, and she wipes at them before looking at me. "You sound so grown," she whispers. "When did you get so grown?"

Sometime in the last three years, I almost reply. Mamma's not the only one who felt Alina's absence. But it sounds bitter and combative and resentful, even in my head, everything I'm telling her not to be, so I just smile and shake my head and take the compliment.

When Mamma and Roshani Aunty return to the table, Alina clears her throat. She looks like she is chewing on her words. Her voice is forceful but somehow also bashful when she speaks. "Coconut chutney sounds nice."

Four
The Enchanted Bookshop

Your total is $17.86," I say in what I hope is a cheerful voice. It's Wednesday, early evening, and the day has worn me out. It doesn't help that working the register is my least favorite task, but Mindy's on a call in the back room working out details for an author reading we have coming up. Normally, she takes the register and lets me do inventory or organizing instead.

"Thank you for shopping at Belle's," I say after the customer swipes her card and takes her mystery novel from the counter. Her smile makes me hope my customer service skills are not as poor as I imagined.

Halfway to the door, she pauses. "I love that window," she says, staring at the painted woman on the textured glass pane. "She's beautiful."

I bite back a smile. "It's Mary Magdalene," I tell her, and the woman stops, puzzled, only to shake her head a moment later and click away.

Belle's Bookshop stands in what was once a very tiny

church, long inactive, on the edge of Chandler's downtown. Mindy, far less religious than her predecessors, repurposed the property into a cozy bookstore upon inheritance. All that remains of the shop's parochial origins are the bones of the architecture: stained glass windows, tall sloping ceilings, and the dark wooden chancel that now holds our register.

A longtime customer, I began working at Belle's my sophomore year of high school, after Mindy's only other employee left for college. With senior year starting, it's just a matter of time before I help Mindy hire my replacement, and I am dreading the task. Belle's Bookshop, with its floor-to-ceiling shelves and an aura that can only be described as enchanting, very much resembles the library its Disney namesake so adored. It has been my home for years, and I'm not ready to let go.

"Flyers, so many flyers!" Mindy exclaims, rounding the corner of the register. "Arya, my dear, you'll hang these up at school, yes?" She slides an elastic-bound stack of glossy orange flyers over to me.

"Of course," I say, looking them over, and Mindy beams. Each orange sheet contains details on the reading in a couple of weeks—a bestselling children's fantasy author is stopping by Belle's for the New England leg of her book tour. "I'll do it tomorrow."

"Perfect." She gives my arm a pat, then busies herself at the register, taking my place.

I always joke that Mindy Richey is like my fairy godmother, and in all honesty, she looks the part. Her short hair is a sparkling violet color, though it'll likely be hot pink or electric blue this time next month. She's nearing forty, but she's experienced a very Paul Rudd brand of aging. Between her heart-shaped face and colorful hair, she could pass as a college student any day.

"How's your sister?" Mindy asks. "Wedding planning going okay?"

I hear the question between the questions, and a smile tugs at my lips. "As okay as you might imagine," I say, and she laughs.

Mindy only knows of Alina through my stories; I started working for Mindy over a year into Alina's absence. Home was big and empty, and working at Belle's was comfort like nothing else. Mindy listened, just listened, with a kind of care and attention no one had ever shown me before. And when I didn't feel like talking, she pressed books into my hands like medicine. Somehow, she knew exactly which tales would bring healing.

Once, after I'd read Jane Austen's *Sense and Sensibility* at her recommendation, Mindy told me Alina and I reminded her of the Dashwood sisters.

"But inverted," she'd said, before I could reply that I was nothing like Marianne, the bold and passionate younger sister in *Sense and Sensibility*.

"You are an Elinor, so much," she had added warmly, and the words were so clearly meant as a powerful compliment that I could only take them as such. I had always envied Alina's spirit a little, the way she always did what she wanted, consequences be damned, but through Mindy's eyes I saw how my more logical, thoughtful nature could be a strength too.

"We went to the caterer's on Monday," I tell Mindy.

"Yeah?"

"Yeah," I say, leaning against the countertop. In between answering customer questions and helping Mindy at the register, I relay the whole tale to her. When I finish, she tilts her head, reflecting.

"Do you think," she starts, pushing the cashbox closed, "that you might be overinvolving yourself a little?"

I stop twisting my hair. "What do you mean?"

"I mean," she says, "maybe it's better to let Alina and your mom sort things out on their own. Instead of forcing them together."

"Oh," I say. "Maybe," I add, but I'm frowning. I know Alina and Mamma well enough to be certain nothing will mend between them without my mediating. They both have their grudges against the other, and they are each holding on too tightly.

Mindy must sense my disagreement, because she laughs and squeezes my hand. "Be mindful is all I'm saying. Even the best intentions can backfire."

I don't get to respond, because a customer arrives and Mindy turns to assist them. But I feel squirmy thinking about her advice. Mindy's logic is sound, but I don't think I can stay out of Alina and Mamma's affairs. There's an opportunity here, in a way there hasn't been for the last three years, to fix what's broken between them. As long as Alina is home, I can help her and Mamma back together.

Mindy calls my name, and I jump back to attention. I take over at the register as she needs and try to push the worry from my mind.

I'm late to student council in the morning. Outside of leadership class, Dean and I are meant to lead class officers during council meetings every Tuesday and Thursday before school. Tuesday was an informational meeting; Mrs. Marina spent most of the time reviewing protocol. Today is our first meeting of substance, and I'm nearly ten minutes late. I was up past midnight finishing homework after Belle's, then slept through my alarm.

Candace Lee, our school treasurer, is beginning a presentation on our events budget for the year when I walk in. I give Mrs. Marina an apologetic smile, which she ignores, before taking my seat next to Dean.

"You're late," he says. He's in a flannel, a hoodie, and jeans today, and his dark hair is unstyled, curling softly at the nape of his neck like he hasn't had a haircut in a while.

"Fashionably."

"You're in sweats."

"I make them fashionable."

He smiles at my answer and ducks his head to hide it. He turns his attention back to Candace, who is running through the funds we'll need for one of our biggest events of the year: autumn formal. It's not until November, but we haven't even procured a third of the needed cost yet, so panic is setting in.

"Thanks, Candace," Dean says when she concludes, scribbling a note on his agenda packet.

"That was a great presentation," I add even though I missed half of it. "I'm happy to brainstorm fundraising options and get my ideas to you all within the next couple weeks."

It's a strategic move; volunteering to take charge on our first big assignment will make it easier for me to lead our future ones. Unfortunately, this doesn't escape Dean. His eyes narrow in my periphery, and he straightens in his seat.

"*We* can get our ideas to you all within the next couple weeks," he says. My eyes snap to his, and the corner of his mouth quirks up. "Arya and I will work together on this one." He raises his eyebrows. "Unless that's a problem?"

I know what he's doing, and I hate him for it. In front of everyone, I can't refuse without coming off as difficult or uncooperative or, worst of all, still resentful over my election loss in spring.

"No problem," I finally grind out, but my resolve is tightening. Dean might have gotten his way this time, but I won't give him the opportunity to assume authority like that again.

Something like amusement glitters in his eyes. "Great," he says, and then he clicks his ballpoint pen and we continue to our next agenda items.

I try not to let my frustration with Dean distract me from the rest of the meeting, which moves as smoothly as it can. Our school spirit officers, Meena and Lacey, pass out a list of proposed spirit days for us to review. I give Mindy's reading flyers to Michael Wilson, our publicity officer, when he asks about community events to advertise. Emilia Lopez sends me a sympathetic glance after announcing the school's news show, which I'll have to anchor with Dean starting next week.

Despite the rocky start, it's an altogether productive meeting. By the time it ends, we've covered every item on our agenda and compiled topics for our next meeting.

"Arya," Dean says as I'm starting to pack my bag, and I look up, annoyed by the direct address. I was planning on giving him the cold shoulder for the rest of the day.

"What?"

He ignores the bite in my tone. "We'll need to present our fundraising plans," he says. "Does the September fifteenth meeting work for you?"

There's a draft in the room, so I cross my arms across my chest. "Yes, that's fine."

"Promise to be on time for that meeting?"

"Promise to be absent?"

He fights a smile. "I actually have a perfect attendance record," he tells me. "Come to think of it, that commitment level is likely why I won."

I roll my eyes. "Right. Jock solidarity had nothing to do with it." Dean has been known to caption his Instagram pictures with "#studentathlete" and "#riseandgrind," even though we left middle school four years ago. This social media branding resonates deeply with our school's athlete population.

Now he rolls his eyes. "We should probably meet outside of class to work together." He stands up straighter, fingers tugging at a hoodie string, and I'm reminded quickly of the steep height difference between us. "If you can find the time, I mean."

"I can find the time." My words come out more defensive than I intended, and his dimples deepen.

"Solid. I'll text you."

"Great." He's still looking at me, and something about the focus in his stare makes me nervous. I swallow quickly, glancing away. "See you around, Dean." The door slams shut on my way out.

Five
Food Coma Incoming

I loop my arm through Alina's, pulling her close as we walk down the veggies aisle of Bharat Bazaar. The air conditioning in the market is on full blast, and my thin cotton jacket is little protection against the cold.

"Let's get samosas after," Alina suggests as she adds a small bunch of cilantro to our cart. We're on a quick grocery run to get ingredients for dinner. Nikhil's making his mother's dadpe pohe tonight, a traditional Marathi dish consisting of flattened rice, garden vegetables, and a variety of herbs and spices.

"We still have leftover samosas from the Roka at home," I remind her.

Her lips stretch into a wicked smile. "Bharat Bazaar's are greasier. Fingers-dripping-with-oil-when-you-finish greasier."

"Not the selling point you think it is," I say, but she pouts, and I give in. "We can get one to split."

"Extra green chutney too."

"Not the coconut?" I ask innocently, and she elbows me

sharply. I giggle, and we continue down the aisle, adding to-matoes, carrots, and onions to the cart.

"So, the gallery's commissioning a piece of mine for the spring," Alina tells me a few moments later as she pulls a package of premade rotis from the store fridge.

I stop walking so fast, a shopper nearly bumps into me from behind. "Alina!" I gasp. "That's incredible." I pause, giving her an accusatory look. "You kept that quiet!"

She grins. "I heard this morning. Only Nikhil knows. I wanted to surprise you with the news."

I'm beaming so hard, my face feels like it might split in two. "I am so proud of you. You deserve this."

She smiles deeper. "I really do, don't I?"

I can only nod and squeeze her tight. I let go quickly because we're standing in the middle of the shopping aisle, but my smile stays wide. "So much."

Alina has been working as an assistant at a Brooklyn art gallery ever since she dropped out of Columbia. Her work has been featured in several showcases throughout the city over the years but never in the venue she helps run. It's an incredibly well-reputed place; artists from the gallery are routinely spot-lighted by the *Times,* among other publications. Alina applied for her job in the hope of one day having her pieces featured there too.

"Thanks, Arya," she says softly, eyes sparkling. "Don't tell everyone just yet, though, okay?"

From the way she's twisting her engagement ring ner-vously, "everyone" means Mamma. My stomach sinks at the request. But I don't want anything to overshadow my joy for Alina, so I don't fight her on it. "Okay," I tell her. "I won't say a word."

There is a beloved trope in my favorite Bollywood shaadi songs. In between dance sequences, the bride and her mother embrace each other tearfully, promising constancy and to-getherness even in such a season of change. In moments like these, it's hard not to think of how far removed Alina and Mamma are from that ideal.

Alina's decision to pursue art professionally has always been a source of conflict between them. In high school, while Alina won award after award for her pieces, Mamma was more than supportive. She saw it as a lucrative hobby; Alina's artistic résumé earned her thousands in scholarship money, as well as acceptance to Columbia University. But Mamma's support evaporated when Alina made it clear art was her chosen career path, not simply her step stool to a fancy college.

"She would be proud of you too, you know," I say gently. Alina pretends not to hear me, busying herself by searching for an unexpired package of ready-to-eat parathas. "Beneath it all, she would be proud."

Alina blinks twice, the only indication she's paying atten-tion, then clears her throat. Her voice is thick when she speaks. "I think we have everything we need."

Papa's home for dinner, the first time he's been so early all week. "My two ranis," he says, beaming, when Alina and I return from the market. "Rani" is Hindi for "queen," and with my sweatpants and unwashed hair, I feel like anything but. "Come give your papa a hug."

We give him a hug. He squeezes us tight, smelling faintly of soap and incense. He must have showered then prayed after coming home from work.

"Third rani's upstairs," he tells us when we pull away, still smiling. Alina got her dimples from him. "Our Sleeping Beauty."

It's comments like these that make me wonder if Papa is truly oblivious or making believe. He is such a terribly happy person that it's possible he simply cannot fathom his wife's sadness. But Mamma's evening naps make me worry she doesn't want to be awake.

"Will she be down for dinner?" I ask, but it's a useless question. Mamma only eats with us when we have company, and Nikhil no longer qualifies.

Papa is spared of having to answer by Nikhil's entrance. He's still in work clothes, a blue-checked button-down and black jeans. "Thought I heard you guys," he says, smiling. He kisses Alina's cheek, then takes a bag of groceries from her hands.

"Greasy fingers," he says, a frown wrinkling his brows. He gives her a look, equal parts amused and exasperated. "Samosas, really? You know I'm cooking tonight."

"Appetizers!" Alina insists. "In anticipation of your main course."

Nikhil gives a weary smile, and Papa chuckles. "My girls," he says fondly. "They can't keep away from samosas. Or any unhealthy foods."

It takes less than half an hour for Nikhil to make dadpe pohe, and even less time for us to devour the dish. Papa showers Nikhil with compliments until he is flushed with embarrassment, and Alina and I wash the dishes in appreciation of not having to eat microwaved meals for once. When we finish, I kiss Papa's cheek, wish Alina and Nikhil good night, then head upstairs to shower and finish my homework.

I stop by Mamma's room first. Her door is locked, and there is no light peeking out from under. I linger and consider knocking. I could wake her, ask her to try Nikhil's pohe. Then Papa laughs from downstairs, so loud and joyful that I falter. Throat tight, I turn to go, letting her sleep the night away.

Friday evening, I get ready like I'm going on a date. I've never been on a real date before, but I do my hair and makeup like I imagine I would if I had. Soft waves and silver hair pins, glowy skin and pink lips. I slip into a simple red sundress, pull on a pair of comfortable but cute sandals, and I'm ready.

Tonight, I am having dinner with Lisa, like I've done on the first Friday of every school year for all of high school. Our dinners are always lovely, but I've missed Lisa the past few days, so I'm especially looking forward to this year's. Sitting apart during lunch has just felt wrong. I have so many stories to tell, so many stories to hear. Mostly, I want to hear her tell me everything will be back to normal soon enough.

I answer texts from Andy while I wait outside the restaurant. Andy's at Kevin Chang's annual back-to-school party, but he tells me to send him any major Lisa updates through the night. Kevin captains our baseball team and is close friends with Dean, and his yearly parties are always the talk of campus. I agree, though I doubt he'll be on his phone much tonight.

Lisa hugs me tight when she arrives. She's wearing a strappy silver dress and her red hair is twisted back in an elegant bun.

"I've missed you, Greenfield," I say when we break apart, and her face pulls into a half smile, half pout.

"I've been here!" she exclaims, then releases a sigh when I give her a look. She twists at an earring. "Missed you too, Khanna."

My lips curve into a smile, and I scan our surroundings. The restaurant's OPEN sign is only half-lit, and there's a gas station and a twenty-four-hour pharmacy just across the street. "We are way too dressy for this place." As I speak, a family in matching Disney World shirts walks out of the restaurant.

"Ridiculously dressy. I love it."

I can't help the nervousness that's settling in my belly. This is Lisa, more familiar to me than almost anyone, but our relationship has changed since the breakup. I'm stuck playing mediator between my two best friends. It's like when Lisa and Andy were just starting to develop feelings for each other, and Lisa would send me to Andy to collect information. This time is worse, though, because it's the end of something, not the beginning.

"So," Lisa says once we've ordered and taken a seat. "Tell me everything. I've been dying to know." She pauses, the start of a smile playing on her lips. "How is the wedding planning going?"

I give her a look. "That is *so* not what you want to know." She giggles, confirmation, but doesn't prod, so I continue on my own after taking a deep breath. "He's okay. Feels sorry, I think. He worries that you're avoiding him. Which"—Lisa ducks her head, ignoring my gaze—"isn't that off base, is it?"

She glares. "We all deal in our own way."

"I know." I give her an apologetic smile, and we're both silent. "He hasn't said a word, you know," I begin. "About the breakup. He hasn't said a word about how or why." I haven't wanted to push Andy into talking before he's ready, and I don't want to push Lisa either, but I'm still hoping she takes the cue and tells me the story.

"I can't help you with the why," she begins dryly. Then she sighs, meeting my eyes. "He broke up with me. It was a total surprise. Arya, I didn't see it coming at all. He was kind about it, because he's Andy, and I guess it's kind of him still to keep it quiet after the fact." She twists at an earring again. "Doesn't mean it hurts any less."

I squeeze her hand from across the table. "I'm sorry." I'd guessed as much, given Lisa's desire for distance, but sympathy pools in my stomach at the verification. "He still cares about you. Lots. Misses you too."

"I know." She sniffs, picking at the hem of her dress. "I just need time. I thought I could force myself to pretend everything's fine, that I'm fine, but I'm not yet." She sniffs again, then gives me a tired, determined smile. "I just need time."

"Okay," I say. "That's fair." Lisa had called me, tearful, the evening of the breakup. She hadn't wanted to discuss specifics, but she'd told me it was over, and I drove to her place and held her while she cried. She loved Andy. So much, and it hits me now that I've been unreasonable, selfish, even, to expect a swift recovery. Especially since she's the one hurting most in the aftermath.

"Let me know if there's anything I can do," I say, meaning it. "I'm always here, okay?" Lisa nods, squeezing my hand tighter.

Our meals arrive. Penne pomodoro, chicken Parmesan, and margherita pizza. We divide everything in two and load our dishes with cheesy goodness.

"Is there a new boy in the picture?" I ask as I help myself to a slice of pizza. "Or girl?"

Lisa came out to me as bisexual in eighth grade, informing me immediately after, in no uncertain terms, that I was absolutely not her type. "No offense," she'd added, and I'd giggled, and we spent the next hour making a list of which qualities exactly fit her type.

She shakes her head fervently. "I am on a romance break," she declares dramatically. "Senior-year Lisa is focusing on herself and only herself."

I raise my brows, impressed. "Well, cheers, bestie," I say, raising my water cup to her. We clink glasses, and she grins.

"What about you, Arya?" She tilts her head at me, playful. "Are you interested in anyone?"

I pierce a piece of penne with my fork. "No, but I promise you'll be the first to know if that changes."

"Hm." She takes a bite of pasta and chews thoughtfully. "Dean Merriweather is cute," she says conversationally. "Don't you think?"

I give her a look, but she just sits there, waiting for my response. I know where she's going. We've had a similar conversation pretty much every year since Dean and I joined Leadership together in the fall of ninth grade.

"Yes," I admit finally. Her words are so unquestionably true, it would read more suspicious if I tried to issue a denial. "Yes, but I would never."

She ignores this. "I feel like there's definite potential there," she says. "I would even venture far enough to give him my personal endorsement, which I feel fully qualified to do, since we've been going to the same temple forever."

"Lisa, you haven't been to temple since middle school."

She ignores this too. "Why aren't you nicer to him?" she asks, her voice curious.

"I'm nice!" I exclaim. She raises her eyebrows. "I'm neutral," I correct. Her brows rise higher, and I glare. "I am as nice to him as he is to me."

She groans. I tuck a lock of hair behind my ear and sit up straighter. I feel like I owe Lisa an honest answer, since it's so rare for her to ask after me. I always try not to take that personally. Lisa's life has always been more exciting than mine, and I'm hardly the most forthcoming person either.

"I hate that he won," I say at last. "Maybe it's annoying or bitter of me, but I hate that he won, and the hate is so deep, I don't know how to move past it."

Her eyes are sympathetic, but there's a trace of exasperation there too. "It was just an election, Arya."

"I know that." It's hard for me to explain why the position matters so much to me. "It's just," I start, "I've always felt like Leadership was the one thing that was mine. The one thing that was mine and that I was good at." I stop twirling my fork around in my pasta and raise it for emphasis. "That, and I worked harder than him."

Throughout high school, Mamma complained every so often that I lacked ambition and a strong work ethic, and my commitment to Leadership was always my evidence she was wrong. I never want to fixate on her criticism, but losing the election made me feel insignificant, like I'd proved her right.

"Okay," she says. "I guess I get that. But this is recent. You and Dean have never gotten along. Far before junior-year election season."

I return to my pasta, shaking my head. "That's on him," I say. "I'm blameless. He's always picked on me. I meant it when I said I'm as good to him as he is to me."

"Right." Lisa rolls her eyes. "I forgot. Saint Arya."

I blow her a kiss. "That's me."

"Well, it won't kill you to be nicer, that's all I'm saying," she replies, and I shoot her a look because I think I would quite possibly drop dead if I were to start being nice to Dean Merriweather.

"Perhaps you should give him that advice, Lisa," I quip, and she groans, finally quitting the subject.

We stuff ourselves with as much pasta and pizza as our stomachs can hold, then request the dessert menu. Lisa tells me the newest drama from her basketball team as we dig into plates of tiramisu, strawberry cheesecake, and rich chocolate cake.

"Food coma incoming," she moans to me as we hug goodbye outside the restaurant, and I laugh. Her lanyard is in her hands, and the metal of her car keys is cool and sharp against my back.

"I love you," I say when she releases me. I try not to think about how long it'll be before we hang out like this again. We don't share any classes this year, she's not ready to start sitting with us, and preseason for basketball starts Monday, so she'll be even busier outside of class. "Dinner again soon, okay?"

"Yes." She smiles bright. "I love you more."

She waves to me from her window as she drives away.

Six
Christmas Is Canceled

On Monday evening, I wait for Dean outside of Belle's. Mindy agreed to let me leave my shift early for our meeting since I'll be working double this Sunday for our author reading. Balancing a new romance novel (Mindy supplements my minimum-wage salary with a weekly book allowance) and my purse in my hands, I scan the street for a familiar brown-haired boy.

He arrives after I've been waiting for a few minutes, backpack slung over one shoulder and a small pink box in his hand. He's dressed in joggers and an Abigail Adams High sweatshirt, and his dark hair is wet like he just got out of the shower. "Arya," he says pleasantly when he spots me.

"Hi, Dean."

"I packed us some brownies," he says, tapping the pink box. "That's why I'm a bit late."

"Brownies?" I repeat, and he lifts the lid to show me a half dozen squares of chocolaty goodness. Ms. Merriweather owns a local bakery, so the treats probably didn't cost Dean anything, but it's a thoughtful gesture all the same. "Tell your mom thank you from me."

"They're two days old. Only reason she let me take them." He tugs at a backpack strap. "Still, you should probably get me a World's Best Boss mug."

I ignore the dig. "We can work at Mellie's?" I suggest, naming a coffee shop a block away from the bookstore. Dean nods, and we head in that direction.

"What are you reading?" he asks as we walk, pointing to the book I'm carrying.

"Oh," I say, shifting it away from him, suddenly very aware that the cover art consists of a half-naked couple posing seductively under a sunset. "Um, just a novel."

He makes a face at my answer and snatches the book out from under my arm before I can stop him. He skims the cover then turns to me, raising an eyebrow. "*Unquenched Desire?*" he says, voice laced with amusement.

"Give me that." I grab the novel back, face warm. I clear my throat and straighten my shoulders, because what do I have to be embarrassed of? "I don't need your judgment. Romance is a perfectly valid genre."

"No judgment," he says, palms up. "Read what you want."

"Yes," I say. "I will."

"Just," he says, trying and failing to fight a smile, "I hope you find someone to—what was it?" He leans over my shoulder to catch a glimpse of the cover as I unsuccessfully try to tug it out of sight. "Right, quench your desire or whatever."

I groan, smacking him once with the book before stuffing it in my purse. He laughs in response, and I let him have his moment before giving his arm a not-so-gentle squeeze. "From now on, let's do these meetings on FaceTime."

At Mellie's, I munch on brownie pieces dipped in my mocha's whipped cream. I probably shouldn't be having coffee this late, but I can't practice restraint at Mellie's. Lisa likes to say they serve orgasms in drink form.

I pull out my binder and laptop a few minutes after our orders arrive. I asked Candace, our treasurer, for donor lists and financial records at lunch yesterday, and I spent all last night logging information into a Google Drive document. "I wrote out a timeline for us to reach funding goals by," I say, nodding to the open planner. "We should work on the Google Doc today too."

Dean shudders as he looks through my materials, like he can't imagine anything worse than clear penmanship and color-coded spreadsheets. "I forgot how type A you are."

"What's your plan, Sharpie info on your palm and hope the words don't sweat off?"

He waves his phone at me. It's open to the Notes app. "Give me a little credit."

"I swear to God. One of these days, Twenty-Fifth Amendment."

He ignores this, though it's certainly possible given his inattention during civics class that he doesn't recognize I just questioned his fitness for the office.

Dean learns soon enough why my organization might just be a blessing. We're swimming in numbers, none of them pretty. The cost of autumn formal is about $15,000, and we have under four grand in our account. Last year's student council, developing a severe case of senioritis, dropped the ball on the end-of-the-year fundraisers we normally hold to balance the budget.

"So," Dean says, resting his cheek in his palm. His fingernails look newly trimmed. "I'm thinking we have a bake sale, yeah?"

I make a noise in the back of my throat. "You want to raise over ten thousand dollars by selling cupcakes?"

"And cookies." He frowns when he sees my expression, voice turning defensive. "Americans love processed sugar, Arya."

"Not *that* much."

He gives me a dark look. "What's your master plan, then? Let's hear it."

I'd been waiting for him to ask. I straighten in my seat. "I think we should host a pumpkin patch at AAHS." He raises his eyebrows, and I continue, words rushed. "There's a small New England business that does portable pumpkin patches. You book them for a day, and they bring the pumpkin patch to you."

From my binder, I pull out a flyer I printed off the company's website and slide it to him. He takes it wordlessly.

"I know it looks a bit pricey," I say quickly, "but I called yesterday, and they said they'd be glad to give us a school discount. The owners are this sweet elderly couple, and they usually do farmer's markets and corporate retreats, so this is a nice change of pace for them."

Dean still doesn't look wild about the idea, so I push on. "I really think we'll earn a steep profit. There's general community interest for these kinds of events, so attendance won't just be students and their families. Plus, we can hike up admissions prices as the event date draws closer."

I sink back down when I've made my case. It took hours of late-night Googling, but it's a solid fundraiser. Chandler is a predominantly white town, and white people *love* their pumpkin patches. The nearest one is a half-hour drive away, so by hosting, Abigail Adams High is guaranteed large local turnout.

Dean runs a rough hand over his neck as he studies the flyer. "Wow," he says finally. "You've really got it all sorted out."

A smile spreads on my lips. "Thanks." The smile falters. "Well, mostly. There is another thing."

He looks up from the flyer, eyes impassive. "And what's that?"

I take a deep breath. "We're really short on money," I say. "Like really, really short. Fundraising is necessary if we want to have a dance at all. But we still might not raise enough to hold, um, the most traditional formal."

Dean furrows his brow. "Meaning?"

"We need to substantially reduce costs," I say. He doesn't seem to understand. I pick at my nail beds as I continue. "We have to change the venue." Dean's face starts to twist in horror, but I press on. "We'll need to have formal on campus."

"No," he says automatically. He sits up straighter, shaking his head vehemently. "No, we'll find another way."

My stomach squeezes. I don't like this any more than he does. Autumn formal is AAHS's boasting point, a classy alternative to school-gym homecoming dances. The school has held formal every year since its founding, and we've hardly ever had to host the event on campus. I don't want to be responsible for breaking the streak. Everyone in school would hate us.

"There isn't another way, Dean. We just don't have the money. Venue alone costs five grand." He's still shaking his head, eyes hard, jaw set. I feel a flicker of annoyance at his surprise and denial. He'd know all this already if he'd researched our financials beforehand.

"Can you not look at me like I just canceled Christmas? I'm not a fan of this either."

"I'm Jewish," he says hoarsely.

"We'll make the most of it. Create a cute theme. Decorate. It doesn't have to be a bad formal."

"Didn't we have to place a deposit?" he asks, and I nod. It was about the only thing last year's council took care of for us. "We'll lose money if we change venues now."

"It's refundable if we cancel by the end of next week." I'd checked the terms during my shift at Belle's.

"Give me till the end of next week, then."

I tilt my head at him. "Dean," I sigh.

"You don't get to make these decisions unilaterally. We're working together, remember?" His tone is mild, but the words make me sit back, stung.

"Yeah, I remember. Do you remember that we're supposed to be *working*?"

He glares. "What's that supposed to mean?"

"I wouldn't be making any decisions on my own if you'd decided to do the homework."

He leans back, expression cool. "This was meant to be a brainstorming meeting, Arya. I showed up, ready to *brainstorm*. It's not my fault you took it upon yourself to do all the work ahead of time."

My cheeks flush. He's not entirely wrong; it's always been my nature to work harder than needed. But I'm not the demanding, workaholic type he's framing me as either.

"I didn't ask you for planners or spreadsheets. That's my thing, I get it. But I don't think it's too much to expect that you skim through our financial records ahead of time."

He glares again. "I skimmed."

"Then you know a bake sale won't cut it. And you know we can't afford the venue. Not without some miracle cost-reduction plan."

"Let's create that miracle, then." His voice comes out calm, but his expression is still tense. He clicks his ballpoint pen impatiently. "Don't cancel the venue yet. I'll figure something out by the refund date."

"Fine," I say, even though I couldn't have canceled our reservation regardless. Student council would need to vote before I could take that action.

"Fine," he says. He seems to realize how childish his repetition sounds because a ghost of a smile curves on his lips. He dips his head down to hide it because we are still upset with each other.

We work in silence. I sip at what's left of my lukewarm mocha as I add bullet points to our shared document. His cursor hovers above mine as he reads each addition to the list.

Dean breaks the quiet when we're getting ready to leave. It's almost dark out, and the shop is closing soon. We managed to pack up without exchanging a word.

"Arya," he says gently. His Adam's apple bobs in his throat. "We're on the same side again." His eyebrows lift slightly. "Okay?"

I know what he means. Dean and I have always clashed, but as class officers, we were on the same team by default. We didn't become true opponents until election season, spring semester junior year. I haven't totally been able to shake that mindset.

I swallow. "Okay." And because I can't stand the awful tension in the air, I add, "As long as you keep bringing me brownies. Even if they're two days old."

He gives a small smile. "They weren't two days old." His mouth opens like there's more to the admission, then closes as he seems to think better of it. He opens it again. "I had to pay for them." The words are rushed, and his smile deepens bashfully at my bemused expression. "See you in class, Arya."

Seven
You Are My Soniya

Wednesday night, Sheila Jawani comes over for dinner. She's Alina's best friend from grade school and a law student in New York City. She had to FaceTime in to the Roka because she was abroad for the summer, interning at the American embassy in Edinburgh. But she's back in the Boston area now, home for a week before her fall term begins.

Sheila shares the title of Alina's maid of honor with me. I tried explaining to Alina when she told me the news that there could only be one maid of honor, but she wouldn't listen.

"Desi weddings don't even have maids of honor," she said. "I've already broken one rule; why not break another?"

I got over my frustration quickly because I love Sheila so dearly. She introduced me to the magic of Percy Jackson books and taught me how to put in my first tampon. She is vibrant, kind, and silly, and she's been a part of my life for as long as I can remember.

Sheila also serves a crucial purpose to the bridal party. Part of every Punjabi wedding is the Sangeet, which takes place prior to the marriage ceremony. It's a song- and dance-filled celebration of love, and the highlights of the event are always when the bride's side and the groom's side perform their respective routines. Alina's deepest desire is to outperform Nikhil and his friends at the Sangeet.

Which would be difficult without Sheila's help, since Alina and I both inherited Papa's two left feet. But lucky for us, Sheila captained a Bollywood dance troupe in high school and worked at a children's dance studio during undergrad. She'll choreograph a spectacular number for us.

We brainstorm song titles for the Sangeet while stuffing ourselves with cheap Thai takeout. Sheila and I are sprawled out on opposite couches, while Alina sits at the kitchen island, chair swiveled out to face us.

"'Bole Chudiyan' is my first choice," I say, naming a bouncy Punjabi tune from one of my favorite childhood films.

Alina lets out a very unladylike snort. "When's my shaadi, 2005?"

"Alina!" I say, outraged. "It's a fucking classic. One you love. Put it on the list or I'm not coming."

She waves a dismissive hand. "Great, one less mouth to feed."

I glower. "Mamma and Papa are paying for the shaadi, Ms. I Can Barely Afford Rent. That line doesn't work."

Sheila, ever the mediator, interjects before Alina can snap back. "It's on the list, Arya. Don't worry. We'll give it serious consideration." I pretend not to notice her mouth *No, we won't* to Alina when she thinks I'm not looking.

"What are you searching for, then?" I ask Alina, exasperated but still wanting to be helpful.

Alina munches thoughtfully on a bite of pad kee mao. "Something fun," she says after swallowing. "Something fun, something sexy."

"Hrithik is in 'Bole Chudiyan,'" I try again. Hrithik Roshan, one of Bollywood's golden boys, is Alina's forever crush. She'd once described his appearance in *Dhoom 2* to me as her sexual awakening.

"Yeah, clothed. Next."

"'Badtameez Dil' is my preference," Sheila says dreamily. She sits up straighter, tucking a lock of glossy hair behind her ear. "Nothing sexier than Ranbir Kapoor in that music video."

Alina scrunches her nose in disgust. "Hard disagree," she says. "Ranbir Kapoor's a five on a good day. He's also only in movies because his parents were hotshot actors."

Sheila rolls her eyes. "Like everyone else in the business."

Bollywood is infamous for its nepotism problem. A handful of families have long dominated the Hindi film industry. Papa likes to joke that Bollywood has just enough diversity of surnames that direct relatives have not yet been required to romance each other onscreen.

We've been going back and forth for another twenty minutes, debating and adding song titles to an ever-growing list, when an idea starts to take root in my head.

"Hey," I say. I look at Alina. "What about 'You Are My Soniya'?"

I'm proposing a song Alina and I used to adore as children; I memorized the lyrics when I was still learning to read. It's nostalgic, romantic, and an absolute staple of early 2000s Bollywood scores.

"'You Are My Soniya,'" Sheila repeats, musing. "Definitely a solid option. More Hrithik, too, and in less clothing this time." She turns to the bride. "I really like it. But totally your call."

Alina considers. "It's kind of perfect," she says. She smiles warmly at me, and I know she's remembering the hours we spent shouting along to the song on car rides throughout our childhood too.

We are prevented from deliberating further when Nikhil appears in the doorway, back from his evening run.

"You're banned," Alina says immediately, but he sinks down into the seat beside her anyway.

"Hello to you too," he says, kissing her gently on the cheek. Before he can pull away, she kisses him on the mouth.

Sheila laughs. "I take it our planning session is over?"

"Sorry," Nikhil says, not looking sorry at all. He grins. "We can watch a movie?"

We settle on a Mission Impossible film, one of the early ones where Tom Cruise still has a love life. I watch all two and a half hours with the three of them, even though it's a school night and I still have homework and college app essays left to begin upstairs.

"**Did** you ever buy Lisa dessert?" I ask Andy. It's first period, literature class, and we have the hour to ourselves. Our teacher left our substitute with detailed lesson plans and a packet of assigned readings, but not a soul (sub included) is following through on her instructions. For our part, Andy and I have been watching an old episode of *The Office* through shared headphones for the last twenty minutes.

He hits pause, the screen freezing on a particularly wild shot of Dwight's face. "You mean, like, at a restaurant?"

I shake my head. "No, um, just buy and bring her dessert. Like brownies or something."

He looks confused at the question. "On holidays or birthdays, maybe. I don't remember. Why?"

I pick at my fingernails, feeling a little foolish. "Never mind. No reason." I go to hit play, but he stops me.

"Wait a minute." He nudges my shoulder, grinning slyly. "Who's been buying you brownies, Ms. Khanna?"

I groan, elbowing him back. "Drop it, Andy," I say, and to his credit, after giving me an amused, questioning look, he does.

I haven't spoken to Dean outside of class since our evening at Mellie's. Not much in class, either. He asked to borrow my notes during Civics yesterday, and we spoke briefly about autumn formal during Leadership, but nothing more. We have been tiptoeing around each other since our argument at the coffee shop.

Dean and I have fought a million times over the years, and I am used to our post-fight routine by now: frosty glares, passive-aggressive quips that read benign to any listeners, interrupting each other's suggestions with "Just to play devil's advocate . . ." But politeness like this has never been part of the routine.

It hits me that maybe he doesn't feel allowed to be too rude to me anymore. That the dynamic has shifted now that he's president. Now that he's already beat me.

Does he feel bad for me? My stomach twists. I can't stand the thought of Dean believing himself so superior.

The episode ends, and Andy tilts his head at me. "Another?" he asks.

I nod and smile, trying to push the worry from my mind. Andy clicks play.

Eight
The Aunties

"Let's go over the plan again," I say encouragingly, meeting Alina's eyes in the mirror. She's twisting a pair of dangly gold jhumke into her ears. They add character to an otherwise simple look: plain pink salwar kameez, chunni resting elegantly over a shoulder, and dark hair swept back into a half pony.

She pouts at my reflection. "It's hopeless," she says. "There are too many of them. We'll never keep track of them all." Done with the earrings, she reaches across the counter for her sparkly bangles.

We're getting ready for Ganesh Chaturthi. Like every year, the Sinhas are hosting celebrations at their seaside estate. It will be a day filled with food, prayer, and importantly, more than fifty guests. It's our final opportunity to interact with the Desi aunties and uncles in our community before shaadi invites are sent out in two weeks.

Mamma already filled a few dozen wedding spots with the names of those she is unwilling to slight by not inviting. But we have free rein on the rest of the invite list.

"We'll keep track if you stick to the plan," I say patiently. "You only have three families to speak to. Nikhil and I each have five. Live-text your thoughts after each conversation, and I'll update the list accordingly." I lift up the clipboard in my hands, where I've written down names with a corresponding section for comments.

Alina rolls her eyes at the clipboard, but she holds her hand out anyway. "Let's see."

I pass it over, and she skims through, eyes narrowed. She lets out a snort halfway down. "I don't need to speak with Deepti Aunty to know I don't want her at my shaadi."

Deepti Aunty is the biggest gossip in our family friend circle. Her daughter, Shruti, was in Alina's class at Columbia. It took all of two hours after Shruti told her mother that Alina dropped out of school for the information to reach most every person in our mutual acquaintance. Ultimately, Mamma heard Alina's news through the aunty grapevine before she heard it from Alina herself.

"There's bitter history, I know," I say. "But she's so rich. Don't you want a lifetime membership to a country spa? That's what she got Maya Kapoor for her wedding last year."

"Hm," Alina muses. She bites her lip, weighing cost and benefits. "Okay, keep her on for now." She hands back the clipboard, her gaze warm. "I'm grateful, so you know. You are a big help, Arya. I couldn't do this without you."

I lean into her, and she wraps an arm around my waist. I smile at our reflection, squeezing her back. Out of everything, moments like these are what I missed the most. "I know."

By the time Nikhil, Alina, and I arrive at the Sinha residence, most everyone is already here. Mamma and Papa left before us, bringing with them modaks and fresh fruit for our hosts.

We slip off our shoes on the porch before entering and helping ourselves to rose chai as we wait for Pooja to begin.

Rakhi Aunty is the first person on our list that we encounter. I know nothing about her except that she and Mamma hosted rival dinner parties for Diwali one year. Mamma kept a close tab on which mutual acquaintances chose Rakhi Aunty's event over her own.

She embraces us all, then congratulates Alina and Nikhil on their Roka.

"I clicked through pictures online. It looked beautiful. Of course, it was very hard to tell only through Facebook posts." She pauses here, smiling widely. There's a smudge of red lipstick on an incisor.

We've prepared for this angle of conversation. Alina responds smoothly, eyes apologetic. "It was a small event. Just family. We so wish our home could have accommodated more guests."

"Oh," Rakhi Aunty says with a gentle laugh. "I didn't know Arya's pale friend had joined the family."

Alina opens then closes her mouth. I try not to choke on my chai at Lisa being referred to as my "pale friend."

Within seconds of getting away from Rakhi Aunty, we run straight into Deepti Aunty. Alina groans beside me, and I kick her ankle to make her stop.

"My dear girls," she says, beaming, squeezing us tight. The folds of her emerald sari rustle together with each movement. "So long since we met last, no?" She pulls back to give Alina a once-over. "You are the same," she announces, smiling deeper. It is not a compliment.

Before Alina can respond, Deepti Aunty turns to Nikhil. "This must be the groom! You know what you are getting into, beta?"

Alina bristles, and Nikhil squeezes her hand. "I—"

"Better that you don't," Deepti Aunty interjects. She laughs at her own joke. "I am only teasing."

Alina attempts a smile, but it comes out as a grimace. "How are—"

"Tell me, rani," Deepti Aunty says, cutting in again. "Have you thought about how many kids you want? Please know you may stop by the office anytime. I will advise. Just be sure to call first."

Deepti Aunty runs a fertility clinic in Boston. She advertises her business to every new bride in our social circle.

"Nikhil and I don't want kids for a while. Our careers are most important to us right now."

"Hm," Deepti Aunty says, disapproval clear. "You must not wait too long. Soon you will lose your prime years."

"But," Alina starts, her smile true this time, "think how much more need I'll have of your services then."

"Tell more about this career of yours," Deepti Aunty says after a long pause. She raises a penciled brow. "You are still making your drawings?"

"She paints, actually," Nikhil says. Both women ignore him.

"I just sold a piece for an upcoming showcase," Alina says. She straightens. *The New York Times* will be covering the event."

"How exciting," Deepti Aunty says. "My Shruti wrote an article for that paper not too long ago." She beams at us. "So nice catching up. We will talk soon?" She touches my cheek as she passes.

"I hate her," Alina growls the moment Deepti Aunty is out of earshot.

"Yes," I say, almost offended she didn't have any veiled insults to toss my way. I normally get at least a few obnoxious questions about my SAT scores or professional aspirations. "The worst."

My phone buzzes right as Pooja begins. The silk trousers of my salwar kameez cling tight to my skin, and I have to half stand to fish my phone out of my pocket. Several nearby guests shoot dirty looks my way, but I ignore them.

There's a message from Lisa that makes my stomach drop a bit: probably doing pictures w/ the team but I'll lyk. I'd texted last night to ask where we wanted to take our formal pictures this year; the best part of school dances are always photo shoots before, and it's tradition for Lisa and I to take our pictures together. A tradition that might be over, apparently.

But I refuse to worry about that when I have a mission to accomplish, so I click on Alina's latest text instead:

> Seema Aunty is a NO
> She asked me why I'm not marrying a Punjabi boy

I'm writing a reply when my phone buzzes with: also she could do with some deodorant.

I bite my lip to keep from smiling and text back telling her to hurry to the Pooja. The Sinhas and the priest are toward the front of the room, already leading us in song and prayer. I know maybe three of the words, so I clasp my hands together and hum along softly instead.

Moments later, Nikhil and Alina join me on the plush white rug the Sinhas have spread over their marble floor to make seating more comfortable for guests. "Where are Mamma and Papa?" Alina whispers to me.

"They're ahead," I say, nodding toward the front. Elders tend to clump together by the worship area at these functions, while younger people hang back.

"Thank God," Alina says. "Because Mamma's going to kill me when she finds out I'm not inviting Preeti Aunty to my shaadi."

"She's not on the list," I say, brow furrowed. "Mamma already reserved her an invite." Preeti Aunty and Mamma share a unique kind of friendship. Every Thursday evening, they have a standing appointment for gossip and tea over FaceTime. Even on her worst days, Mamma never misses these calls.

"Well, consider it unreserved. She spent twenty minutes giving me very unsolicited advice on how to lose weight before the wedding."

"Unnecessary, too," Nikhil adds, and Alina grins.

She leans into him, one hand tangled in his. "This is why I'm marrying you."

My chest tightens a little as I watch Alina with Nikhil. This is the first time in years that she's attended a Pooja with the family. I try to remember what she did for Ganesh Chaturthi or other holidays when she was in Paris or New York, then realize I don't know the answer.

"Let's sleep on it," I suggest, knowing Alina will have forgotten the interaction by morning and upsetting Mamma with the news will have been pointless. I nudge her shoulder. "Now hush and pray."

She nudges me back, and we giggle, quieting only when glares are sent our way.

The evening progresses slowly. During dinner, we make progress on our list, crossing off names and adding comments after every conversation.

"Stat test Monday," I tell an uncle after he sees me hunched over the clipboard and looks at me questioningly. It's not a lie, though the suggestion that I would ever study for it certainly is. He gives an approving smile before turning away.

"You are so *obvious,*" Alina hisses. I elbow her in response.

We hug and speak with a few more families, and finally, we are finished, only a few maybes still lingering. We plop down on floor cushions, leaning against a wall, and Nikhil brings us bowls of cold, sweet rasmalai from the kitchen in celebration.

"We earned this," he says, holding out the dishes, and Alina reaches hungrily for hers.

I take slow, small bites of the creamy dessert, savoring every spoonful. Alina wolfs hers down in minutes.

After an hour or so of lounging, lazy from conversation and overeating, Mamma and Papa appear to say it's time to leave. They've been apart from us for most of the evening, chatting with other guests.

As we wish everyone goodbye, Deepti Aunty clasps Mamma's hand at the door. "Our dearest congratulations, Nandani. You must be so proud, not only of Alina's engagement, but her blossoming art career. Who expected that when she dropped out of school?"

There's a delicate pause, and that's when I know Alina never got around to telling Mamma about her commission. Alina stills next to me, and my stomach sinks at the confirmation.

"Yes," Mamma says. Her painted lips pull into a believable smile. "We are so proud."

"I will ask my Shruti to take pictures of the showcase. Of course, she is so busy these days, such a hard worker, so she may not be able to attend. Lucky that we may read in the news instead."

"Yes," Mamma repeats. She pulls her chunni tighter around her. "Very lucky."

When the door closes, Papa looks to Mamma. "I will go

bring the car," he says, either oblivious or pretending to be. He leaves, and then the four of us are alone. Nikhil hangs back uncomfortably, like he's unsure if he should leave too.

Silence swells in the cool air of the long, winding driveway.

"I meant to tell you myself," Alina says finally. Her voice is more defensive than apologetic. "Eventually."

"Please," Mamma says. She adjusts her chunni again. "I know you must always embarrass me in front of friends. Everyone but your Mamma must always know your life."

"Deepti Aunty is not your friend," Alina says, and my stomach sinks lower. She is all grown up but still doesn't know how to respond to Mamma's hurt.

Mamma's eyes flash in the lamplight. "Are you sure? I learn much more about my daughter from her than I do from you."

"Maybe if you left your room every once in a while I could tell you things."

Silence again. I squeeze my eyes shut, wishing the night over. Mamma's voice is soft when she speaks next. "Thank you, Alina. Very nice."

Papa brings the car around, and Mamma enters wordlessly. They drive off, and the three of us make our way to Nikhil's car.

"Did you have to say that?" My voice is half exasperation, half anger. I look at Alina, but she doesn't meet my eyes.

"Leave it, Arya."

"Why couldn't you just tell her about the commission?"

"Because I was happy," she says hotly. "I was happy and excited, and I didn't need her to ruin it."

"Look how well that worked out."

She glares at me. "Why can't you stay out of it? When did you get so interfering?" She glares again then storms ahead of both me and Nikhil, arms crossed tight against the cold.

I clamp my mouth shut to keep from saying something I'll regret. Because this is nothing new, Alina behaving as though her actions don't have consequences for me. Her fights with Mamma affect my relationship with her too. I'm always the one who has to deal with her sadness. Alina just leaves.

As soon as we arrive home, Alina rushes to her room. Mamma's door is already locked, and Papa is nowhere to be seen. He must have gone on one of his evening walks.

"Do you want to watch something?" Nikhil asks tentatively when I sink down onto the living room sofa. He'd knocked on Alina's door a while back, but she asked him to go. I wonder at how quickly the night turned to shit. "Maybe Bollywood?"

I'm still wearing my salwar kameez, but I'm too tired to go upstairs and change. "Only if I get to pick," I say, and he smiles in agreement.

I decide on *Mujhse Dosti Karoge,* a movie title that directly translates to: Will you be my friend? It is the ultimate movie about escaping the friend zone, and I've seen it so many times, I can mouth lines along with the actors as we watch.

Nikhil makes microwave popcorn, and we eat straight from the bag, passing it between us until only kernels remain and the credits roll.

Act II
The Friend Zone

Nine
Magic Awaits

"Pass me another case," I say to Andy. My box is empty, and there are a few girls approaching the checkout line who look like they're here for the reading. They're all wearing dragon-themed tops and blue pearl necklaces, characteristic of the Dragon Witch series, the young adult fantasy novels our author of the day, Vicky Lane, has been writing for the better part of a decade.

"You mean do your job for you?" he says lazily, reaching for the case beside him nonetheless.

"I let you behind the register. It's your job now too."

He grins, sliding the case over to me. I pull out four signed copies of the newest installment as the girls scramble to show me their receipts.

"The reading will begin in twenty minutes. You can seat yourself in the back room." And then, only because Mindy has specifically required it, I add, feeling foolish, "Magic awaits you."

The girls giggle at this quote from a famous Dragon Witch scene. Andy takes a long sip of tea to hide his amusement. I let it pass because I'm grateful for his company. His little sister is a big Dragon Witch fan, and he tagged along with her for my benefit. Reading days are the most grueling part of my work schedule.

Belle's is a two-employee business, a truth that becomes exhaustingly obvious when authors visit. Thankfully, Cleo, Mindy's wife, is home to help out today. She's a reporter for *The Boston Globe*, constantly traveling on assignment, but this weekend is a lucky exception. Cleo and Mindy are directing customers in the back room while I run the register.

I'm grateful to be out of the house though, even if it means I'll be surrounded by middle schoolers all day. Mamma and Alina haven't spoken since Friday night, and I haven't had the will to mediate. Home is tension-filled, especially since Nikhil left early this morning on a business trip to San Francisco. He'll be back in two weeks, and I am counting the days. His presence is a comfort.

Ten minutes later, the door jingles as I'm slicing open yet another cardboard case of Dragon Witch books. I straighten at the noise, then startle. Dean Merriweather and the twelve-year-old-girl version of him are standing at the register.

"Dean," I blurt. He's wearing a turtleneck, and I don't know how to feel about it. I realize I'm gawking, and my eyes flit to his sister—Dakota? Virginia?—who I've met only in passing. "Um, welcome."

"Hi," he says. He stares for a second, like he's struck by the sight of me too. He rushes to explain. "Georgia's a big Dragon Witch fan. She dragged me over."

Georgia. I knew the name was an American state. I manage a smile at the rosy-cheeked girl. Her dark curls are long and tangled, framed with uneven curtain bangs that are very likely self-cut.

"I didn't know you were going to be here," he adds quickly.

Georgia frowns at her brother. "But you did," she says. Her voice is as clear and sweet as Dean's is on presentation days. "He said so in the car," she tells me.

I look to Dean. He throws a dark glance at Georgia. She examines the chipped gold polish on her fingernails, lips turning up.

"I know you work here, that is," he amends. His words are easy, but his ears are unmistakably pink. He clears his throat. "I meant I didn't know if you'd be working today."

"Sundays aren't my usual," I say. "But we need all hands on deck for big events."

"And this is a big event?"

I blink. "It's Vicky Lane." She's one of the most celebrated names in publishing.

"Dean doesn't know how to read," Georgia explains.

Mindy's office door opens before Dean can retort, and Andy exits, cradling a reheated cup of tea. I've allowed Andy wide access to Belle's amenities today, and he's been taking full advantage.

"Hey, man," Andy says, sounding surprised. He rests his mug on the countertop, and the boys do a bro-five. "Georgia, hi," he says next. "Mia's already in the reading room."

Andy's little sister, Mia, is in the same Girl Scout troop as Georgia. I've bought my Samoas from Mia ever since my troop disbanded at the start of high school. She runs a popular Dragon Witch fan page on Instagram, so today is pretty much Christmas come early for her.

Georgia perks at the information. "I hope she saved me a seat," she says. She hurries to show me her receipt, and I pass back an autographed copy.

"Magic awaits you," I remember to add as she slips into the back room. Georgia beams, Dean raises an eyebrow, and this time, Andy doesn't bother to hide his laughter.

"On that note," he says, scooping up his tea, "I'm going to join them." He disappears even as I urge him to stay with my eyes, and then Dean and I are alone.

I wonder if Dean will follow, but he moves to the display table, studying the new releases. I drum my fingers nervously on the counter. There are only a couple of browsers in the shop, but Mindy's assigned me to the register until the reading officially begins, which is still a few minutes away.

"I like your sister," I say finally.

He doesn't turn to face me, but I see the corner of his mouth quirk. "Because she makes fun of me for you?"

"Because she's got spunk."

"You mean nerve."

"Is there a difference?"

He turns to me now. The dark blue of his sweater matches his eyes. "Georgia is great," he agrees. "Exasperating and great." He rests against the counter. "Are you ready for Tuesday's council meeting?"

Tuesday's meeting is when Dean and I will share our fund-raising ideas for formal. We've divided the speaking time so that I present first, and Dean will go after.

"Yes," I say. I frown. Something about the animation in his voice is unsettling. "What about you?"

His smile stretches wide. "Very much."

I try not to take the statement as cause for concern, but with Dean, it's hard not to. His idea of a successful meeting often comes at my expense. In the spring, when we were in the thick of campaigning, Dean closed his speech to the student council with a PowerPoint slide that read: ARYA ready to vote Merriweather for president?

It was a play on my slogan: ARYA ready for a president who works for you? (This phrase was often accompanied by a picture of me as Rosie the Riveter, with the speech bubble: She KHANNA do it!)

I had been furious watching Dean's speech. He had been calm and pleased and maddening when I yelled at him in the courtyard right after.

But it's been months, and I don't plan to let Dean embarrass me like that ever again. I clear my throat loudly and attempt to return his smile. "That's wonderful."

From the back room, I hear a smattering of applause. The reading must be starting.

"We should go?" I say, and I don't wait for his response. I turn to leave, and Dean follows behind.

When the reading ends, I approach Andy as he's packing up. Dean and Georgia have left, and Mia is waiting for him outside.

"Did you know Dean was going to come today?" I ask. I've been wondering since he showed up, and I will be so angry to be proven right.

He fights a smile. "I knew Georgia was coming," he clarifies. "Mia told me they had plans."

I give him a look, and he rushes to add, "I didn't know Dean would accompany her. I still can't say why he did." He slings his book bag over his shoulder. "But," he says, and the smile is unrestrained now, "the brownies were from him, right?"

I draw back, startled, and Andy laughs at the confirmation. His eyes are dark with mirth. "One mystery solved."

The first thing I notice when I return home is that someone is using the kitchen. The lights are on, and the faint smell of spices hits my nose as I close the front door behind me. Papa is never this early, Nikhil is on a plane, and Alina's out shopping (something I only know because I checked her Instagram story), not that she would cook, anyway. Which means—

Mamma is at the kitchen island when I walk in, hands deep in a wide steel bowl filled with floury dough.

"Hi," I say, trying to mask my surprise. I set my keys and purse down on the breakfast table. "What are you making?"

"Gobi ki paronthi. Early dinner," she says. There's a lock of hair in her eyes, but her hands are doughy, so she uses a forearm to sweep it away. It kind of works. She looks to me. "You will have?"

I nod. It's been a while since I've tasted Mamma's cooking, and I'm not dumb enough to turn down the opportunity. Aside from the occasional sabzi to go along with prepackaged roti, Mamma doesn't cook much now unless we have guests over. Homemade parathas are a delicacy I haven't had in months.

"Do you want help?" I ask, tentative. My cooking experience is minimal, to say the least, but I want to stay inside this rare moment with Mamma however I can.

She looks at me appraisingly, then shifts to make space for me at the counter.

I wash my hands, then roll spiced dough into smooth balls for Mamma to flatten, shape, and flip onto the stove. We work in a comfortable silence.

When Alina and I were younger, Mamma played slow, sweet Hindi ballads from her childhood each evening as she cooked, and we sat at the countertop and watched. Mamma wasn't a joyful woman then either; she's never been like Papa. But her loneliness is new. We don't spend time with each other anymore. Cooking with Mamma now is the first I have purposely been in her company in ages.

We spoon ghee onto our parathas then carry our plates to the table. Mamma sits on a chair and I sit on the nook across from her.

"My mamma loved gobi paratha," she tells me. She tears a piece of paratha and dips it in ghee. "Her favorite food."

My naniji passed away years ago. I was barely six, and she lived an ocean away, so I have no memory of her other than the gift packages she mailed for birthdays and Diwali. Filled with more sweets than a town could eat, always. I wonder if making Naniji's most loved meal helps Mamma miss her a little less.

"One of my favorites too," I say, and after a moment, Mamma smiles.

"School is going well?" Mamma asks next. "Lisa is good?"

I blink at the questions. It's been ages since Mamma has asked after me. Ages since she's had the opportunity. "Yes," I say. "School is good, and so is Lisa."

In all honesty, I haven't spoken to Lisa since that message on Ganesh Chaturthi. I texted asking to plan a study date yesterday, but she left me on read. Lisa has never been good at responding, and with basketball starting, I know she's busier than ever, but it's hard not to be bitter. I've often felt like a side character in Lisa's story, the friend she goes to for boy advice and reassurance without always returning the favor, and her breakup aftermath has only exacerbated the feeling. Perhaps Mamma has noticed a difference too.

"Student council is taking up most of my time," I continue, and Mamma listens, attentive.

Our plates are clean in a matter of minutes. We both go back for seconds. This time I savor each bite.

Ten
Breakups and Make Ups

On Monday morning, Andy and I work on college essays in the Leadership room before school starts.

At least, we give it a valiant effort. I sign into my Common Application and decide to reward myself for taking that initiative with some online shopping. I've added four hair scarves I'll likely never wear into my cart when Andy nudges me.

"Arya?"

"Hm?"

"I just realized," he says, "I won't be going to autumn formal with Lisa this year. I've never not gone with Lisa."

My eyes snap up. His voice is blue, but he smiles in spite of it. I tilt my head in sympathy.

"It is kind of your fault," I say. I lower my laptop screen, giving him my attention. "You broke up with her."

"I know. I don't regret it. I'm still allowed to feel some nostalgia, though. We were best friends once."

I nod, even though it was always more than that for Lisa. She'd had a crush on him since middle school. She told me she

72

was over it when she asked him to formal freshman year, that they would go "just as friends," but they paired up again as sophomores. By junior-year formal, they were officially dating.

"Why did you break up with her?" My voice is gentle. I've never asked him outright, but he's the one who brought up Lisa, so I feel more comfortable approaching the subject.

He picks at a loose thread on his hoodie. "It had been coming on for a while. But one day she asked me what my plans were for after graduation, and I sort of panicked. The thought of staying with my high school girlfriend through college . . . it just felt so intense."

Out of care for Lisa, I don't voice my understanding, but I get where Andy's coming from. It's not as though Lisa heard wedding bells, but she always saw Andy as a long-term partner. And I get the impression that Andy just saw her as a good first relationship.

"When we started dating," he continues, "I thought it made so much sense. I was into her, we were already so close, it felt like a natural next step. But that initial excitement faded . . . and now I wonder if it would have been best to just stay friends. I miss having her as my friend more than I think I ever really wanted to be her boyfriend."

I squeeze his hand on the table. It's not the same, but in some ways, I feel like I'm losing a friend too. Lisa and I go days without speaking now, and I'm the initiator when we do. Andy squeezes my hand back.

"And now," he adds dramatically, "I'm forced to go to my final formal stag."

I crack a smile at this. There's a pause. "Actually," I say, thoughtful. I look up to meet his eyes. "Maybe not. We could go to formal together."

He raises his eyebrows. "Yeah?"

"Yeah," I say. The idea is just now forming in my mind, but I can't think of a better way to spend our last autumn formal under the circumstances. If my dynamic with Lisa has to change, I'm glad to have a constant in Andy. "It'll be like the old days. Our middle-school-dances era. Except we're way more attractive now."

And except Lisa is unlikely to join us this time. But I feel a desperation to return to a moment when everything was so much simpler, when all my relationships were still intact, so I shove the thought away.

Besides, maybe Lisa *will* come around. Maybe the distance she's created has served its purpose. Maybe, by formal, she will be all moved on. Maybe she will even start responding to my texts.

Andy's lips quirk. "No more neon braces?"

"Or side bangs. Or crimped hair."

He pretends to think about it. "Do I have to get you a corsage?"

"Of course," I say. "Match your tie to my dress color and everything."

He makes a face. "Gross." He grins. "Let's do it."

For the rest of the morning, we plan for formal, college apps forgotten. I show Andy outfit choices, and he gives me good-natured advice on each pick. Emilia joins us a few minutes before the bell rings, and she adds her feedback to the mix. By the time class starts, I've got options narrowed and new optimism in my heart for a memorable final formal.

In the evening, Alina asks me to help her with wedding invites. Our shipment arrived last week: 250 sheets of thick navy cardstock with elegant gold lettering, RSVP forms and address labels to match. We'll send each invite with a small box of nuts and sweets. Alina and I haven't spoken much since Friday night, so she and Nikhil must have finalized the guest list on their own.

Ceremony invitations are scattered across the dining table. I pick one up, being careful not to crease the paper.

NANDANI & RAJESH KHANNA
JOYFULLY REQUEST THE PLEASURE OF YOUR ATTENDANCE
AT THE MARRIAGE OF THEIR DAUGHTER
ALINA KHANNA
TO
NIKHIL JOSHI,
SON OF *RUPA & YASH JOSHI*

Something warm twists in my stomach at the words. Gently, I trace over the cursive with an index finger.

"Will you write the addresses?" Alina asks. "You have the best penmanship." Her voice is gentle.

The claim is a stretch; my handwriting is not superior to Alina's. She's the artist in the family, after all. But she's trying to smooth the tension between us, so I don't press. "Sure."

She smiles, hesitant, then slides a printed list of guest mailing addresses to me across the table. "We can start with these."

Alina plays '90s Bollywood music while we work. She tucks an invitation, events information page, and response form into each envelope, and I stick a white-and-gold label on the front before neatly printing the address in black ink.

"I'm sorry," Alina blurts out about twenty minutes in. It's poor timing; the Hindi ballad playing in the background is swelling to a climax. Lata Mangeshkar's thick, sweet voice floats through the speakers, and Alina fumbles for the volume button.

"I'm sorry," she repeats after lowering the music. Her words come out rushed, squished together. "I was upset with Mamma and took it out on you. I was wrong to snap at you after the Pooja."

I'm too surprised to respond right away. I can't remember the last time Alina apologized to me.

She continues. "Especially because you've been so good throughout this process. Not just with wedding stuff"—she stumbles, gesturing at the invitations—"but also with me being home again. I know I haven't always made things easy for you on that front."

It's the closest she's ever come to discussing how her absence has affected me these past several years. I missed her too much to resent her at first, but she's back now and some bitterness is starting to sink in.

For now, this is enough. "Okay," I say. "Thank you."

She nods, and then there's a pause. "Have you spoken to Mamma?" I ask. *Apologized to Mamma* is what I mean, and I can tell by the way her cheeks flush that she knows it.

She peels off a stamp. "Not really," she says. She doesn't meet my eyes. "I told her we were going to start preparing invites, but that's all."

Her answer isn't a surprise, but disappointment twists in my belly still. For all their differences, Mamma and Alina are more alike in manner than any two people I know, good at hurting each other without ever attempting to repair the hurt.

When Mamma learned Alina dropped out of Columbia, she told Alina she wasn't welcome home until she decided to go back. Mamma thought it would pressure Alina into getting her college degree, but Alina took Mamma's words to heart. She went to Paris for her art fellowship, the initial reason she had decided to leave in the middle of spring term, and moved in with Nikhil after the fellowship's conclusion.

Mamma was too proud to retract her words, and Alina stayed away. She spoke with Papa on the phone every so often, and I went to New York to visit her a couple of times, but Mamma and Alina didn't speak again until her engagement last winter. Mamma could never let her daughter get married without close involvement in the planning, if only for appearances. Shaadi cost is likely what persuaded Alina to allow the interference.

"You should apologize to her," I say. Alina's eyes narrow, but I press on. I have the smallest bit of leverage right now, and I plan to use it. "For my sake, if nothing else."

I keep my gaze level with hers. It's a challenge—how much is her apology really worth if she can't do this one thing for me? I notice the reluctance in her eyes, and I see the moment she finally relents.

"Fine," she says on an exhale. She winds a lock of hair behind her ear and sniffs. "Later. Now lick some envelopes."

I look down at my stack of invites, trying to hide the smile tugging at my lips. These are small victories, but I'll take them all.

Eleven
The Superiority Complex Is Getting Old

I highlight and delete my introduction sentence for what must be the tenth time in the last half hour. Emilia and Candace are loudly discussing how Candace plans to ask her boyfriend to formal over cups of now-lukewarm cafeteria coffee. Certain I won't be accomplishing anything before the morning bell rings, I close my laptop screen to join the conversation.

Ever since Lisa began sitting with her basketball team, I have been spending a lot more time with Emilia Lopez. I don't know Lisa's friends well enough to fit in there, not that she's asked me, and I would feel bad leaving Andy behind. Since Andy and I already have so many mutual friends with Emilia's group, it's felt like a natural, if bittersweet, shift.

Today we're in the back corner of the school library. Class isn't for a while, and I had planned to make some progress on a college essay in the interim. But I sit straighter in my seat and try to convince myself girl talk is just as productive a use of my time. My earliest deadline is weeks away, after all.

"Do not," Emilia says, shaking her head fervently at Candace's idea for a scavenger hunt formal ask. "You're not fourteen."

Candace gives her an injured look. "It's romantic!"

"It's obnoxious," Emilia corrects.

"I'm with Emilia," I say apologetically when Candace looks to me for support, and she groans.

"Nick won't care how you ask him," Emilia says. "He's probably not even expecting anything. Isn't it guaranteed that you'll go together?"

Candace has been dating Nick Casey, a lanky boy with red hair and an affinity for plaid flannels, since freshman year. He's part of Emilia's friend group, and he and Andy are close through their various science-related extracurriculars. Nick is the main reason Andy was so willing to begin sitting at Emilia and Candace's table in the first place.

"I know," Candace says. "I just want to do something nice, is all."

"Flowers are nice," I say. "Much nicer than what would basically be a game of hide-and-seek across campus."

She slumps in her chair. "Help me come up with a poster to go along with the flowers, then."

"Roses and a *Bachelor* reference?" Emilia offers.

Candace gapes. "I can't believe I let you make me feel bad about the scavenger hunt idea."

I bite back a smile as Emilia argues why a *Bachelor*-themed formal ask is actually a terrific plan. Part of me agrees, but I keep quiet because I don't feel like being made fun of.

Moments later, I notice Lisa standing with a couple basketball teammates by a neighboring bookshelf. Her hair is wet like she just showered, and I remember hearing that morning practices began this week for the basketball preseason. I haven't spoken to Lisa in a few days, and Emilia and Candace are still absorbed in their *Bachelor* debate, so I slip away quickly to say hello.

"Hey, Greenfield," I say brightly when I reach her. She looks up at the interruption.

"Hi, Arya." She's unsmiling; Lisa hates mornings, and grueling six a.m. practices are hardly a mood improvement.

"How was basketball?" I ask. The question applies to the two girls by her side as well, so I give them a small smile. I get disinterested stares in return and try not to take it personally. I've never really been close with Lisa's team.

"Fine," she says. "Not too bad."

I nod, surprised by the short reply. "Okay," I say. I pause, waiting for her to add something more, but she's silent. I push a strand of hair behind my ear. "Are you doing anything this evening?" I ask spontaneously. We haven't hung out since dinner our first week back at school, and that feels like ages ago. "We could head to Mellie's and catch up."

I want to show Lisa my dress options for formal, debate each contender like we've done every past year of high school. Maybe use that topic as a segue for her general formal plans and test the waters on that front. But she lets out a slow breath and twists at her lanyard. "I'm taking a break from coffee."

I'm about to ask when she decided that—Lisa's bloodstream has been more cold brew than water for as long as I can remember—or at least remind her Mellie's serves other drinks too, but she cuts in before I can get the words out. "Hey, I'm running late for first period. We'll talk soon?"

She turns away before I can say anything. Her teammates follow, and then I'm alone.

I blink twice, thrown by the interaction. Stilted conversation is one thing, but that was a total brush-off—first period doesn't start for another ten minutes. I can't make sense of it, especially from Lisa, who's never been afraid to tell me what she thinks. My stomach feels tight as I walk back to Emilia and Candace.

"She's decided on roses," Emilia informs me when I take my seat. "*Bachelor* poster's being taken under consideration."

"It most certainly is not," Candace says fiercely. Emilia giggles, and I try to laugh along with her.

I'm still thinking about my conversation with Lisa during the student council meeting. Twice, Dean has to nudge me beneath the table to get my attention because I'm too distracted to notice a question directed at me. Conflict with Lisa always makes me anxious, especially when I don't know the source of it.

The third time I don't respond right away, Mrs. Marina narrows her eyes. "What's going on with you today, Arya?" she says, purple frames low on her nose.

Embarrassment rises in my cheeks. Mrs. Marina rarely does more than distantly observe our meetings; public reprimands are practically unheard of. "I'm sorry," I say. I clear my throat and flutter through the papers in front of me. "Um, where were we?"

"Dance theme," Dean says softly beside me. I feel a flicker of irrational annoyance that he's on top of everything while I'm not and try to remind myself he's just being helpful.

"Right," I say. I lick my lips. "Dance theme. I was thinking that we could create an idea form to email out to the student body this week. People can send their suggestions, and we can choose from the most popular ones. How does that sound?"

There are murmurs of assent around the table. Lacey volunteers to create and send the form, and then we move on to related topics. Wary of another comment from Mrs. Marina, I force myself to focus and contribute. After a brief discussion on dance royalty nominations, it's time for me and Dean to present our fundraising ideas.

I pass flyers for the portable pumpkin patch around the table before taking my position at the front of the room and donning my best salesperson voice. "For most New Englanders, fall is incomplete without a trip to the pumpkin patch," I begin.

The corner of Dean's mouth twitches at the opener. Emilia leans forward to listen better, ever the supportive friend. I venture on.

When I've talked through the logistics of the event, Candace nods in approval. "This is good," she muses. "White people love their pumpkin patches. We would have a terrific turnout."

I nod enthusiastically. "Exactly my line of thinking."

"But will it be enough?" Michael Wilson asks.

I twist my pinky nervously. I hate being the bearer of bad news. "Most likely not for our typical formal," I say. "But, um, if we make some adjustments, I think so."

Brows furrow in confusion around the table. I take a deep breath and decide to rip off the Band-Aid.

"Venue is by far the biggest expense: five thousand dollars. Even with the pumpkin patch, given our financials, it makes the most sense to host formal on campus."

The effect is immediate. One junior officer lets out an audible gasp. Emilia's coffee cup freezes on the way to her mouth. Michael Wilson's eyes look like they're about to pop out of his head.

"Like, in the school gym?" Lacey, one of our spirit officers, asks after a moment of horrified silence.

Her partner, Meena, practically convulses at the thought. "My Instagram aesthetic would never recover."

"Maybe," I say to Lacey, trying to keep my voice light. I swallow. "Or the courtyard, if the weather's nice."

Michael snorts. "Nice weather? On a November night in Massachusetts?"

The room breaks out in titters and criticism. I lift a hand to massage the back of my head.

"Actually," Dean says, interrupting what sounds like Meena's panicked eulogy to her social media presence. He turns to me, expression unreadable, and something about the look makes my stomach drop. "This discussion might be a little premature. I called the manager of the community center. They'll allow us to rent the venue for just three grand."

There are squeals of relief around the table. Emilia sighs into her coffee mug.

"You scared me, Arya," Meena says.

"How?" I ask Dean, astonished, even though I know I should probably be thanking him for getting us a 40 percent price cut.

He answers my question to the rest of the room. "Turns out venue cost includes setup, cleanup, and decor. I told them we'd do that labor ourselves. I also promised we'd host formal at their center next year too." His smile is quicksilver. "The manager agreed. Guess I can be pretty charming."

"That was, um, smart." I clear my throat. "Thank you."

He tilts his head and gives me that same unreadable expression. His eyes glint, and then he looks away.

"Good work, Dean," Mrs. Marina says approvingly, and he gives as obnoxious a bow as is possible while remaining seated.

Candace glances at Dean. "So this means we don't need to host autumn formal on campus?"

He leans back in his seat lazily, long fingers pulling at a hoodie string. "Ask Arya," he says. "She seems to have everything figured out."

Heads swivel to face me. I step back, suddenly feeling terribly uncomfortable to still be standing at the front of the room.

"I'll need to look through the numbers again," I say after a beat. "But the discount does seem really hopeful." I start to collect my pitch materials, cheeks warm. "Maybe we can move on to the other agenda items for now and circle back to formal prep at our next meeting."

There are only a couple minutes left in the period, so the suggestion is met with little resistance. I return to my seat, and Dean makes sure to avoid eye contact. I remember our argument at Mellie's, and I was probably wrong to underestimate his ability to come through with the venue, but it was still unfair of him to put me on the spot in front of the entire group.

The lunch bell rings as Emilia is explaining to a sullen junior officer why a kissing booth fundraiser violates basically every rule in the student conduct handbook. I hang back as everyone files out the door.

"Hey," I say to Dean when we're two of the last people remaining. He's zipping up his backpack, and I stand to the side. "What was that?"

He raises his eyebrows, finally meeting my gaze, and I cross my arms across my chest. "*Ask Arya?*" I repeat.

"I thought you'd appreciate the authority."

"You can't be serious," I say. "You embarrassed me in front of the council."

He makes a sound in the back of his throat. "*You* can't be serious." His voice is low to avoid attention, but his eyes are dark, angry. I realize I've never seen Dean angry before. Frustrated, *frustrating,* but never angry. "You're not allowed to be upset with me. I told you I would handle the venue. Why didn't you listen?"

I am so used to the untroubled, perpetually amused version of Dean that it takes me a moment to respond to the boy before me.

"I guess I forgot," I say, but we both hear the lie. I assumed Dean would fall flat on this task.

"Just how incompetent do you think I am?"

I shift my stance, wondering if some humor will help his mood. "No more so than Josh Hartley."

It's the wrong thing to say. His mouth tightens at the corners. "You need to stop acting like you're better than me, Arya. The superiority complex is getting old."

I don't expect the words to hurt. I take a step back. "That's a mischaracterization."

He rolls his eyes. "It's unbelievable that you can be so arrogant even after making a mess of the meeting earlier."

Heat rushes to my face. "Are you calling *me* incompetent?"

He doesn't back down. "I'm saying you were today."

Now *I'm* angry. "Dean, you did one thing right and surprised the room. You're hardly qualified to lecture me on responsibility."

His eyes harden, but his tone is even when he speaks next. "You lost to me, Arya. I think you forget that sometimes."

He is careful not to brush against me as he walks to the door.

Twelve
Bollywood Beauties

Well, you're not going to like my advice," Mindy says. "But you should apologize."

"Mindy." I blanch. I whip my head around to face her. She's on the floor behind the register, unboxing a new shipment of the Dragon Witch books. They've been practically flying off the shelves. "You've got to be joking."

She covers her smile. "I said you wouldn't like my advice. Here, put these on the display."

I take the copies from her hands, avoiding reading the back covers, and head toward the window display case. I began the series a few days ago and am halfway through the second book; I don't want the story spoiled from the summary of the third.

It's Friday evening, and I related Tuesday's argument with Dean to Mindy during a lull in business. Dean and I barely spoke to each other the rest of this week, making for terribly unproductive Civics periods. We were placed in the same discussion group on the Supreme Court case *Brandenburg v. Ohio,* 1969, and communicated exclusively through passive-aggressive Google Doc comments.

Beyond Civics, not talking with Dean means we haven't made any progress on formal prep. Even with the discount, the venue is costly, and there's no guarantee the pumpkin patch will raise the needed cost. I'm meant to present ideas to everyone in a few days, and I have zero material prepared.

It's safe to say that between council tasks, tension with Lisa, and shaadi stress, I've been needing my migraine medication every day this week.

"He called me arrogant," I remind Mindy when I return to the register. "And incompetent."

"That was unkind," Mindy agrees. "And untrue," she adds solemnly when I give her a pointed look. "I'm not saying he's faultless," Mindy clarifies. "But neither are you, and you can own up to the mistakes you've made. Handling him, for example."

"I don't *handle* him," I say, but there's some truth to her words. It didn't even occur to me that Dean might come through with the venue.

"Maybe it's because you want to prove that you can do the job better? In any case, he clearly thinks that you think he's stupid."

"I don't think he's stupid," I say sincerely. "Irritating, maybe."

She ignores the last part. "Sometimes I think you take this rivalry a lot more seriously than he does," she says. She's finished unboxing and is scooping her newly dyed turquoise hair into a bun. Baby hairs curl at the nape of her neck. "Like it's sport for him, war for you."

I huff in a breath. "Because I lost." The words tumble out, heavier than I intended. I don't know if anything has made me feel quite as unremarkable as placing second in an essentially two-person contest. Placing second to Dean of all people, given our years of conflict, is not a bruise that will heal quickly.

She gives me a warm look. "You're going to have to get over that," she says simply.

I know she's right. "I will," I say, and she squeezes my hand. "Let's not give Dean too much sympathy, though," I say. "He's no hero. He made fun of my haircut for weeks last year, remember? Told me I looked like Dora the Explorer?" The comparison had been particularly hurtful because it was my first time cutting my hair myself. I haven't attempted even a trim since.

Mindy busies herself at the register. "Well, where was the lie, honey?" she says airily. The phone rings before I can reply. "Belle's Bookshop," Mindy sings into the phone in lieu of hello, and I settle for glowering at her. She blows me a kiss.

On Saturday morning, Alina is in a frenzy. We're at the Boston location of Maharani Bridal, a Desi wedding dress chain. Alina's custom shaadi lehengas arrived today from Jaipur, and she brought Mamma and me along to watch her try them on. Mamma left with the tailor to bring the pieces a few moments ago, and Alina's been wringing her hands ever since.

"I'm nervous, I'm so nervous," she says. I'm sitting cross-legged on the plush white love seat by the window, exasperated as she paces around the dressing room. She shoots me a desperate look. "What if it's all wrong? We don't have enough time to do a reorder."

I shrug. "Then you'll look terrible on your wedding day." She scowls, so I backtrack, concealing a smile. "It's going to be perfect. You chose perfectly."

She truly did. Over the summer, the two of us went on a

dozen day trips to Maharani Bridal. We analyzed color patterns and fabric swatches, and Alina modeled lehengas they had in store to determine which styles best suited her. Our final selections were forwarded to a Jaipur seamstress whose previous work had earned even Alina's reverence.

"We can always get alterations done," I remind her when she doesn't say anything. "And remember, the mock-ups were beautiful."

This makes her smile. "They were, weren't they?" she says. She seems to loosen. "I don't know why I'm making such a fuss. I spent weeks finalizing designs."

Alina is composed when the tailor, a middle-aged woman named Veena Taparia, wheels a clothing rack into the room. Several white garment bags hang from the steel bars. Mamma follows behind, a manicured hand resting on the rack.

"Have all dresses been pressed?" Mamma asks our tailor.

"Yes, Nandani, of course." Veena almost looks insulted by the question. "We always prepare for such sessions," she says, and Mamma gives a nod of approval. I can tell she's impressed by Maharani Bridal, though she would never say so aloud.

It had been the best kind of relief to learn that Alina had asked Mamma along to today's fitting. I'd anticipated an unfortunate repeat of our taste-testing session and had been brainstorming clandestine ways to ask Mamma myself, treading the delicate balance between not angering Alina and not making Mamma feel unwanted, when I got a reminder email from Veena about today's appointment—stating we had a room booked for three.

Color flushed Alina's cheeks when I asked her about the fitting. "I thought she might want to see what her money's buying, that's all." She shot me a dark look. "Don't read too much into it."

I had nodded, but how could I not? Alina hadn't needed my

meddling to reach out to Mamma. Maybe things were finally changing. Maybe Alina and Mamma weren't so far away from the Bollywood bride and mother ideal after all. Hope bloomed in my chest, warm and flimsy.

"Please know I am here to help with fittings," Veena says. She speaks with a barely there accent. "We can take note of anything that needs to be altered as you try on." She pauses to smile at Alina. "I hope the pieces match your vision."

"I'm sure they'll be just right," Alina simpers, and I try not to laugh.

The first lehenga Veena unveils is made of blush- and champagne-colored silk. The blouse is lovely, open-backed and set with jewels. But my breath catches as Alina slips into the skirt. Yards of shimmery fabric swoosh and fold with her every movement. Floral embroidery spirals up the train. Veena drapes an elegant gold-trimmed chunni over Alina's shoulder to complete the look.

"Oh," Alina breathes, turning this way and that to watch how the material catches light. She meets my eyes in the mirror and beams. "It's everything I wanted. More."

The next lehenga is a gorgeous periwinkle that Alina intends for her Sangeet. The skirt is light and limber to allow for dancing.

Her ceremony gown is a traditional red and gold, and she's chosen a Marathi-inspired emerald ensemble for the reception, in honor of Nikhil's family.

One garment bag remains, though Alina is done trying on her lehengas. I look at her questioningly.

"I had one made for you," she says. "A gift for my maid of honor."

My heart squeezes at the gesture. I'd planned on purchasing

something off the rack. "You're not going to make me and Sheila twins, are you?"

"Wish I thought of that sooner," she muses, and I giggle at the image.

Mamma helps me dress. The blouse is midnight blue with an open back, and glass beads trim the sleeves. The skirt is flowy and delicate. Pink-and-gold handwoven peacocks spiral up the dark silk. I rest a simple pink chunni over my shoulder, and then I am finished.

I have never felt so beautiful. Alina joins me in the mirror, and I wrap an arm around her waist. "Thank you," I whisper. "It's stunning."

She kisses my cheek. "You're stunning."

"Both of you are looking like Bollywood beauties," Veena says. She lifts a penciled eyebrow. "There are no sizing issues?"

"Better try each piece again to be sure," Alina says, shooting a sly look my way. "I'll start with the champagne one."

I take pictures of Alina as she models lehenga after lehenga for the next hour. Mamma watches in silence from her spot on the love seat.

Thirteen
Forgive Me, Forgive Me Not

I turn off my phone and slip it into my back pocket. I've been checking it every few minutes for the last two hours, but Lisa still hasn't texted me back. I sent her pictures of my new lehenga this morning, along with some options for her that I pulled from my closet—Lisa's favorite part of attending Desi events with me has always been the clothes. But no response.

I wipe my hands on my jeans and convince myself she is simply injured to the point where a full recovery is guaranteed but checking her phone is inadvisable at the moment. Then I put the subject out of my mind. I need my focus.

Dean walks into the classroom a few seconds later. His eyes narrow when he sees me in the desk next to his.

He glances away. "Your seat is on the other side of the room," he says as he slides into his chair.

Off to a spectacular start. "We're still in passing period," I remind him a little tersely. I arrived early to Civics with the intention of apologizing like Mindy had recommended. My plan depends on Dean allowing me to.

I clear my throat. He stretches a long leg out under his desk.

I resolve to get it over with. "I wanted to say I'm sorry." My words are rushed. I lick my lips. "For the meeting and also for, um, not handling the election as gracefully as I could have. I haven't been very kind to you. So. I'm sorry."

He sits up straight and knocks a knee against the metal chair leg in his surprise. A faint blush rises to his cheeks at the gaffe.

I continue. "I don't think you're incompetent."

He nods once. "Okay."

I wait. "This is the part where you tell me how you don't think I'm incompetent either. Or arrogant. Or any of the other things you've said about me."

He ducks his head to hide a smile. "You're not incompetent." He doesn't deny the rest. I don't press him.

"Good."

"Good."

I feel the need to keep talking. "I mean, to be clear, it's not like you're an easy person to be kind to. You pick on me constantly. You can be incredibly frustrating."

"Really crushing the apology, Khanna."

I stop. I pick at the belt loop of my jeans. "We're all right, then?"

"We're all right."

"Perfect," I say. "From here on out, I hope we can be better, um, colleagues."

He doesn't bother to cover his smile this time. "Colleagues?" he repeats, looking at me sideways.

Embarrassed, I correct myself. "Partners, I mean."

"Partners," he agrees. "Though, not really, since I'm still your superior." He catches my expression and laughs. "I like the sentiment, though."

93

"Go on," I say. "Ruin the moment."

His eyes are dark with amusement. "I didn't know we were having a moment."

My cheeks flush. I decide it's time for a subject change. "We still need to figure out a plan for the fundraiser," I say. "I don't know if the discount is enough to keep the venue. Though it helps, certainly."

"I might have an idea," he says. He gives me a look. "Try not to shit all over it, okay?"

I refuse to dignify that with a response.

We spend our passing periods revising Dean's proposal, and by Leadership, we have a pitch ready for the council.

"Arya and I believe we may have found a way to host formal at our desired venue after all," Dean says at the start of the meeting. His voice is all pleasant authority, very presidential. "We are excited to introduce you to the first annual AAHS Fall Festival."

"First and only," I correct. "The goal is kind of to never need a fundraiser like this again."

He ignores me. Meena stops doodling to pay attention, and Mrs. Marina sips her iced coffee in the background, looking thoroughly bored.

We get on with the details. We're planning an event for the Saturday before Halloween, the day I'd originally intended for the pumpkin patch fundraiser. Dean thought of elevating the pumpkin patch plan to something that would be even more of a moneymaker but also be relatively easy to pull off within the tight time frame. And so Fall Festival was born.

Most of the details are TBD, but the general idea is to charge for general admission as well as each of the additional activities we want to add to the event. With Dean's discount, we only need to make a three thousand dollar profit to keep the venue, which is achievable if we manage to get a couple hundred guests to attend the festival. Not an impossible goal, in theory.

"I would like us to revisit my original idea for a bake sale fundraiser," Dean says after we walk the council through the gist of our plan.

Maybe impossible, after all. I massage the back of my neck. Dean must notice my reaction, because he fights a smile and says, "A variation of it, that is. Let's add a cakewalk to the festival."

This has my attention. "A cakewalk," I muse.

"It's kind of like musical chairs," Dean explains. "But with pastry prizes."

I give him a dark look. "I know what a cakewalk is," I say. "I was going to say I think it's a good idea."

"I have a lot of those," he says. "It would be a popular event, and free on our end, too, if we get my mom's bakery to donate the prizes."

Lacey furrows her brow. "Would your mom do that?" she asks, voicing my thoughts. I remember Dean telling me how he had to purchase the brownies he brought me and find it unlikely.

"Since it's a school cause, I'm sure she would," he says. "In exchange for me working extra hours," he amends. He glances around the table and adds quickly, "Which I would be glad to do, of course."

The corner of my mouth tilts up. Dean's cakewalk is added to our working festival itinerary, and over the next twenty minutes, other council members toss out their ideas too. Meena, who runs the Art Club, offers to set up a face painting booth, and Michael proposes a costume contest, much to Emilia's delight. She adores dressing up for Halloween and always throws together the most ludicrous costumes, very Mindy Richey–style.

We have to say no to the suggestions that aren't cost efficient and are unlikely to turn a steep profit. Emilia takes it particularly hard when I object to her haunted house idea. I feel sorry, but haunted houses are expensive and high effort, exactly what we are trying to avoid.

"What timeline are we living in," she says furiously, "that you take up all of Dean's ideas but reject mine?"

I roll my eyes, but a boyish smile pushes at Dean's lips as he looks down and away.

By the end of the meeting, it's looking more and more like Fall Festival is going to be a reality. It will be a tight timeline, but it just might work. We've delegated different festival tasks to all the officers with the plan of reporting on our progress by the end of the week. For my part, I'm working on a social media graphic to advertise the festival when Dean plops into the seat next to mine.

"What are your plans for formal?" he asks, twisting at a hoodie string.

I blink, a little surprised at the question. "You realize having *any* plan for formal is contingent on the success of Fall Festival."

He waves a dismissive hand. "It'll be successful," he says easily. "We're working together."

The words are so earnest that something in my chest warms. I blink again. "A bunch of us are going to Emilia's before. She's hosting dinner and pictures," I say. It's a recent plan, formed in the wake of Lisa's decision to go with her team. I hesitate, then add, "I'm going to formal with Andy."

He raises his brows. "Lisa's Andy?"

There's a trace of judgment in his voice that makes me feel

defensive. "It's not like that," I say quickly, hoping to God no one else will think it's like that either. "He's my best friend. That's all."

He nods, but it's like he doesn't quite buy it. Wanting the attention off me, I ask, "Are you going with anyone?"

"I'm asking this week."

"Who's the unlucky girl?"

He grins, dimples flashing. "Katie Nguyen. We're re-creating our freshman-year ask."

I feel a prick of something sharp and unexpected in my stomach. I push the feeling away and clear my throat. "That's sweet," I say.

It does sound irritatingly cute. Katie and Dean are both on our school soccer teams. In ninth grade, he brought flowers and a poster to ask her on the field, not knowing she was planning on asking him at the same time. They dated for about three weeks before deciding they were better off as friends. They've been close ever since.

"I know," he says. "We're totally winning best ask."

Leadership hosts a contest for the best formal proposal each year. The winning couple receives a tacky gift basket and bragging rights.

"Hm," I say. "You're forgetting that I'll be one of the judges." I smile at his startled expression before returning to my laptop screen and its blinking cursor.

Fourteen
Chai and Chats

No," Mindy says. She shakes her head fervently to underline her disapproval, arms crossed across her chest. "Absolutely not."

"Come on," I say. "I look so cute with the ears and whiskers!"

"Arya Khanna, I swear to God I will fire you if you dress up as a cat again this year for Halloween."

"Mindy!" I exclaim. I look up from the display table, where I'm arranging mini pumpkins around our bestsellers of the month, to shoot her an injured look. "Way harsh."

It's true I've been a cat for three Halloweens and counting, but cat costumes are cheap and low effort, so what's not to like? Each year, I don black clothes, eyeliner-drawn whiskers, and the furry ears I've owned since age ten, when Lisa and I were obsessed with the Warriors series and threw a cat-themed joint birthday party. Costume complete.

"I'm showing you some tough love. You're getting embarrassing, hon." When I glare, she adds, "I trust you to find something a little more creative."

"I can go as a leopard?"

"I'm opening applications for your replacement tomorrow."

"Expect a wrongful termination suit within the week."

"Seriously, you can't come up with anything good?" She cups her chin in her hand and muses for a minute. "Inej Ghafa?"

Inej is a brown fantasy heroine I adore, but: "No one would ever believe I can tightrope walk."

"Cece from *New Girl*?"

"Are those really my only options?"

Mindy closes her mouth, chagrined, and I bite back a smile. "I sincerely love my black cat costume. And anyway, we can't all be Mindy Richeys."

Mindy shakes her head, but I know she's pleased. There's very little she prides herself in more than being the absolute queen of Halloween. Belle's always goes way over the top when it comes to decorating for the holiday. It's only the first weekend of October, and in addition to display table pumpkins, we've already got autumnal leaves, fake cobwebs, and golden lights covering every visible surface of the bookshop. Not even Mary Magdalene was spared; glitter-dipped candleholders line her section of the stained glass window.

"Speaking of," I continue, "what are you and Cleo going to be this time?"

Mindy and Cleo have created some spectacular couple's costumes for the past few years. Last Halloween, they went as Edgar Allan Poe and his raven. Mindy spent weeks perfecting what she called her "Poe expression" (really just a despondent frown) before the 31st.

"Oh," Mindy says, suddenly busy at the register. Her fingers drum the countertop. "Cleo's not going to make it this year. She'll be covering a story in Brazil."

I know Cleo is expected to travel often for work, but this

particular trip must be a real disappointment for Mindy. Halloween festivities are everything to her.

"I'm really sorry," I say. "That blows."

Mindy lifts a shoulder in a half shrug. "I get it. It's what her job requires, and she's worked so hard to get where she is today." She looks up and gives me a sad smile. "It's still hard, though. To be far from those you love."

I think of Alina, how heavy her absence was in my heart for three years, and nod. "Yeah," I say. "It really is."

Mindy spends the rest of my shift inundating me with Halloween costume ideas. As attached as I am to my black cat fit, I take the advice good-naturedly. I could work on getting more comfortable with change.

Thursday evening, Andy and I study at Chai & Chaat Café, a small shop best described as a cross between a Starbucks and a Mumbai tea stall. It sits on the outskirts of Chandler's downtown, just a couple blocks away from Belle's. I pop over often during my breaks.

"Hey," I say as we wait in line for our usual order of dahi papdi chaat and steaming masala chai. A knot has been twisting in my belly for a while, and maybe Andy can help relax it. "Have you heard from Lisa lately?"

He gives me a sideways glance. "No, why?"

The knot tightens; Lisa and I have never gone so long without speaking. But I shake my head. "No reason. Just wondering."

"If she's not talking to you, Arya," he says gently, "she certainly won't be talking to me."

He's right, but it still hurts. I feel like collateral damage in the wake of their breakup, and it's not as though I haven't tried to be adaptive. But how many times can I reach out to an unreceptive Lisa before it becomes pathetic?

I wonder if news of my formal plans with Andy has exacerbated Lisa's desire for distance somehow. But those plans wouldn't exist if Lisa hadn't blown me off in the first place, so that hardly feels fair.

"So," Andy says as we take our seats, interrupting my thoughts. "I have some news."

I raise my eyebrows.

"You know the professor I worked with over the summer? From UChicago's biology department?"

I nod, but it's a partial lie. Andy does so many impressive science activities that it's hard to keep track sometimes.

"He offered me admissions advocacy. I heard yesterday." His voice is easy, but there's an unmistakable note of pride there. He rushes on. "It's just a letter to Admissions, and it doesn't guarantee acceptance, but it's a nice opportunity. Especially since he's their first Black department chair, and he wants to mentor *me.*"

"Andy," I say, hushed. "That's incredible."

He tries to shrug. "It's not a big—"

I swat his arm. "Like, wow."

He grins bashfully. "Yeah."

"I'm so proud of you."

"Thanks, Arya." He pauses. "I'm flying there next weekend to tour and interview. I might apply early, just to increase my chances."

"You're going to be a shoo-in."

He gives me a warning look. "Don't jinx."

I knock on my wooden chair for good measure. Then my thoughts catch on the time frame. "Next weekend? That's so quick."

He nods. "It works best for the professor. He's going to let me sit in on some classes." Excitement glimmers in his eyes, and I bite back a smile. The idea of voluntarily taking extra science courses makes me feel nauseous, but this is Andy's version of fun.

"Besides," he adds. "this way I can write about my visit in my essays. The early deadline is only a month away."

"How long are you going to be gone for?"

"Five days," he says. He gives me a pacifying look when he catches my expression. "Relax, I'll be back a whole twenty-four hours before Fall Festival. I would never let you lose my business."

"I wasn't worried," I say, and he laughs at the lie.

We split our order of chaat in half, sipping on chai between bites. Our AP Lit annotations lie abandoned on the table.

"Do you know where you want to apply yet?" he asks tentatively.

I push a piece of spiced potato around on my plate with my fork. "Kind of," I say. "I know I want to stay nearby."

My main consideration while building my college list had basically been which schools would be a bus ride away from Belle's. I've never been very good about change, never craved it like Alina.

"I like Northeastern a lot," I say, picking one of the names on my shortlist at random.

He nods, attentive. "You do give terrier energy."

I give him a bemused look. "Their mascot is a husky, moron. And did you just call me a bitch?"

He laughs and doesn't deny. I flick a piece of chaat his way. It misses.

Fifteen
Shaadi Venues (and Blues)

For Nikhil's birthday, I buy him a box set of Bollywood dramas. We have the films at home, but I don't think he and Alina have copies of their own. I consider it an early housewarming gift; they plan to move to a larger apartment after the shaadi.

We celebrate at the wedding venue: a lovely seaside resort in Chatham, Cape Cod. The party was meant to be a surprise—Alina told Nikhil she wanted to see the site one last time before finalizing decor, all the while arranging for Nikhil's family to fly up from New Jersey for the big day. But Nikhil walked in on her making reservations for eight last night, and she stumbled trying to explain away the number.

"I wanted to do something romantic," she'd pouted after explaining the blunder to me.

Nikhil laughed. "Let's just agree that I'm the romantic one in our relationship."

"We'll lie to our families, though? I don't need anyone thinking I can't pull off something as simple as covertly reserving a table."

"Done," he said, and she beamed.

We open presents in the resort garden before heading to the restaurant. Nikhil's younger brother by a year, Neil (their parents were about as creative with names as ours), passes him a card that reads: *Welcome to Thirty!*

There's a pause. "I'm twenty-five, dude."

"I rounded up," Neil says. Nikhil swats his arm.

"Hey, thanks," Nikhil exclaims after unwrapping my gift. He picks up the DVD of *Mujhse Dosti Karoge,* the movie we watched after Ganesh Chaturthi. "A new favorite," he says warmly, and I hug him tight.

Mamma and Papa give Nikhil a box of sweets, and Rupa Aunty and Yash Uncle give their son a fancy watch.

"So now maybe you will be on time to your meetings," Yash Uncle says. Everyone laughs.

Nikhil rolls his eyes. On his recent visit to San Francisco, Nikhil overslept and arrived late to the very first meeting of his business trip. Nikhil works in something related to computers (I would lose my apartment in a *Friends*-style trivia game if he asked me to name his specific title), which allows him to work from home a lot. I guess he's grown accustomed to creating his own schedule.

Alina's present to Nikhil is a snow globe of the outdoor skating rink where they had their first date. The details are breathtaking.

"Except, um, don't look too closely," she says anxiously. "I didn't realize the artist would give us faces when I asked her to place us inside? So your nose is all wrong—"

He kisses her cheek. "It's magical."

Alina glows.

The restaurant is a small Mexican place within walking distance from the resort. I order a glass of lime soda and a plate of fajitas to split with Alina.

Rupa Aunty supplies the table with enough conversation for all eight of us. She's animated, joyful, and appears to overflow with love.

"Yash and I feel so blessed for the coming union of our families," she gushes as we wait for our meals. She tucks a strand of curly hair behind her ear. Her nails are painted a sunny yellow. "I can think of no two people better suited for each other than my Nikhil and lovely Alina."

Alina looks both deeply gratified and deeply embarrassed by this declaration. She smiles and sips from my soda for the sake of something to do.

"My wife means other than the two of us," Yash Uncle adds on, and Rupa Aunty laughs.

"Yes, yes, present company excluded." She intertwines her hands with Yash Uncle's on the table and squeezes.

Alina locks eyes with me then looks away. I feel it too. There is something uncomfortable and melancholy about watching an older Desi couple so in love. Like a grown-up Bollywood love story. I can't remember the last time Mamma and Papa held hands.

"I will say, though, I worry about your having a wedding in the winter," Rupa Aunty continues. "There is no telling what the weather will be like."

"Cape Cod has warmer winters than the rest of Massachusetts, Aai," Nikhil says. "Besides, most of our events will be indoors."

"I've always loved the idea of a winter wedding," Alina says. "Especially here, by the sea. Nothing could be so beautiful."

The resort Alina and Nikhil chose for their shaadi truly is perfect. Tall, sloping ceilings, spacious ballrooms, and elegant floor-to-ceiling windows that offer views of the water from all angles. Alina plans to string fairy lights through the barren trees bordering the venue to complete her winter wonderland vision.

"Rishabh's sister had a December wedding too," Neil offers. "It turned out just fine."

Rishabh is Neil's boyfriend. They've been together for nearly as long as Nikhil and Alina have. Nikhil actually introduced the pair; he and Rishabh were in a few of the same classes at Columbia.

"Yes, well, I am a mother; I will worry," Rupa Aunty says, not at all reassured by this.

Our food arrives. Conversation stalls as we dig into our meals. I use the pause to check my phone underneath the table. The Leadership group chat has been frantic all weekend. Fall Festival is fast approaching, and we're scrambling to get everything done in time.

I skim through dozens of messages, just gathering the gist of the current group argument. Dean seems to have advocated for country music at the festival and is now defending himself against claims that listening to "horse boy music" and having progressive politics are mutually exclusive. I see a reference to Miley Cyrus's 2009 single "Hoedown Throwdown" and know it's time to turn off my phone.

"Alina, have you and Nikhil put much thought into changing last names?" Rupa Aunty is asking when I tune back in.

"Oh, we're still discussing it." Alina smiles. "I am really proud to be a Khanna woman, though," she says, and my heart warms at the answer.

We talk about Alina's lehenga shopping experience for a while—Rupa Aunty has a million and one questions, most of which are tough to answer without revealing too much in front of Nikhil—and then Mamma announces that she feels a migraine coming on. I look at her bowl; she's only taken a few small sips of her soup.

"Are you all right?" Yash Uncle asks. Concern furrows his brow.

"I will be fine. Thank you," Mamma says. Her shawl is slipping, so she pulls it back up to her neck. "But perhaps it will be better to skip dessert."

Alina and I exchange glances over our plate of fajitas. I narrow my eyes, wondering at Mamma's desire to speed through dinner. Alina shrugs; she doesn't have an answer either.

"Certainly," Rupa Aunty says. "Let us all hurry now so Nandani may have her rest."

"There is no need," Mamma says, but she doesn't push further.

We're back at the resort in twenty minutes. Nikhil's family is staying there for the weekend, so we are here to see them off.

"So nice to see you again, Rajesh," Yash Uncle says, shaking Papa's hand robustly.

"Same to you; sorry to cut short."

They do a man hug, and I try not to smile.

In the middle of the goodbyes, Rupa Aunty finds me and ushers me to an emptier corner of the lobby.

She grasps my hand and beams at me. "I feel as though I am gaining two daughters," she says. "And I am so glad. I have only brothers; I raised only boys." She sniffs like she is fighting tears. Then she smiles even brighter, if that's possible. "So I want us girls to be close friends."

Something inside me is breaking, because how often have

I wished for easy love like this from Mamma? I squeeze Rupa Aunty's hand. "I would like that a lot."

She tilts her head, expression gentle. "You will miss your sister very much, yes?"

My chest tightens. I haven't put much thought into after the shaadi, haven't wanted to, but I know I can't let it be like before. "I'll see her on the weekends. We'll make plans."

She laughs, but she looks close to tears again. "San Francisco is so far to visit often. My heart pains for Nikhil now, and he is just few hours away. I don't know what I will do following the move."

I frown. "San Francisco?"

She pats my arm a little clumsily. "But you are right, we will make plans. Family is forever."

"Aai!" Neil calls from across the lobby. "Nikhil's threatening to rip up my card!"

"You didn't even make it, Neil. I turn twenty-five and all you get me is an inaccurate Hallmark card?"

Rupa Aunty shakes her head and smiles. "My adult boys still acting like children. This is why I need you girls."

She gives a warm smile and walks off, leaving me stunned and alone.

Sixteen

Definitely Not a Country Fan

I'm sure she was just, like, confused," Andy says. His voice sounds fuzzy and distant, swirling in a sea of outside noise. His flight just landed at O'Hare International, and he's finally returning one of my many missed calls from last night.

"Maybe," I say. I've been trying to convince myself of the same thing since my conversation with Rupa Aunty over the weekend. I can't imagine a scenario where Alina decided to move across the country and keep it a total secret from me. Especially not after the dress fitting, after I've let myself hope for true progress.

A group of loud freshmen pass by, and I lift the phone closer to my ear. I'm calling Andy from behind the Leadership building, and it's hard to tell whether his location or mine is obscuring sound more.

"Or you misheard," he continues. "She could have just been talking about his business trip."

"Right," I say, but something twists in my stomach at the

thought. Maybe Nikhil's business trip was a front for, I don't know, signing a rock-solid lease for one of the Painted Ladies.

"I feel like it would have been a bigger topic of conversation at dinner," Andy says. "If they really intended to fly to SF right after getting hitched."

"Right," I say again. I feel guilty as soon as I think it, but I wish for a moment I could talk this through with Lisa instead of Andy. She's always been better at helping me through Alina conflict; messy families are something Lisa and I share. "Besides, Alina hates fog."

"There you go." He sounds like he's smiling. "Listen, I got to hang up, but we'll talk soon, okay?"

"Okay, science boy." Passing period is about to end as it is. "I know you're going to kill your interview."

"Two days away, but thank you." He clicks off. I take a deep breath before slipping my phone into my pocket and entering Leadership.

The room is total chaos. Phones are ringing, papers are strewn across the counters, and poster paint is spilling onto the linoleum next to a half-finished FALL FESTIVAL banner. In the middle of it all, Mrs. Marina sits lazily at her desk, flipping through what appears to be last month's edition of *Vogue*.

I decide the paint spill is most worthy of my immediate attention and hurry over.

"Does. She. Want. Me. To. Look like a PUMPKIN?!" Emilia is exclaiming to Meena, who looks torn between sympathy and laughter.

She decides on sympathy. "So unfair," she says.

"What's going on?" I ask as I look around for a roll of paper towels. I find one on the table across from Emilia and rip off a long strip as I listen.

"My mother made me a formal dress," Emilia says, voice equal parts venom and false sweetness.

I quickly lift the tilted paint can, then lay the paper towel over the blue puddle. "Oh?"

She shoves her phone under my eyes. A dress the color of Kraft Mac & Cheese stares back at me.

"Oh!" I wince. I look up at her. "Well, orange is an autumn color," I offer.

She glares. I try a new tack. "Fall Festival could still flop and then there won't be a formal to wear that dress to at all."

"Trust me, I might just sabotage it myself," she says, and I bite back a smile.

By the time I finally make it to my seat, Dean and Michael are there to greet me.

"Hey, Arya," Dean says as I take supplies out of my backpack. "You're definitely a country fan, right?"

Clearly, the weekend group chat argument carried over to school. I furrow my brows, trying to decipher what, exactly, about me reads "definitely a country fan."

"Come on, tell Michael how you listen to Thomas Rhett every time you have a bad day."

"Who?"

His face pales. "You've got to know who Thomas Rhett is."

I give him a pointed look. "Only white people listen to country music, Dean."

"Well, Kane Brown begs to differ." He leans against the edge of my desk, inches from my open journal. "Anyway, what's our plan for festival setup?"

I narrow my eyes. "Do you mean to say you don't have that sorted already?"

"I thought we could plan together," he says. Then he catches sight of my journal and furrows his brows. He flips through the colorful pages, not spending nearly enough time admiring my doodles and detailed calligraphy. "How many hours do you spend writing in this diary?"

I'm affronted to hear laughter in his voice rather than awe. "It's called bullet journaling, and it's a rather highly skilled task, so of course you wouldn't understand." I swat his hand away from the planner before he can crease the paper.

Unbothered, he stands up straighter. "So," he says, returning to the point. "How are we setting up for the festival, partner?"

He's making fun of me, but I smile at the word choice anyway. "We should have had this figured out days ago. Let's get a plan done this period," I say.

For the rest of the hour, that's what we do. We finish with a few minutes to spare before the bell.

I run into Lisa after school in the parking lot. I stayed late in Bio to finish up an exam I forgot we had scheduled; I have my fingers crossed for a low B. She's all the way on the other side of the lot, basketball bag slung over one shoulder. I only see her because most people have already left by now.

We haven't spoken since that morning in the library, so I jog to catch up to her. "Hey, Lisa," I call once she's within earshot.

She looks up, and something in her expression shifts at the sight of me. "Hi, Arya."

I pause a few feet from her. Now that I'm here, I'm not sure what to say. I settle on: "How was practice?" I lift an arm to my forehead to block the sun, car keys still clutched in my fingers.

"It's at five." My gaze goes to her Nike duffel, so she adds, "I'm cleaning out my locker. This is my conditioning bag."

I nod like that means something to me. "I feel like I've barely seen you since the season started," I say, hoping my voice sounds light and not resentful. I clear my throat. "We should get dinner soon."

She makes a noise in the back of her throat. "Arya," she says. Her face is a mix of disbelief and irritation. "Seriously?"

I step back so quick it feels like whiplash. "Lisa, what's wrong?"

She makes that sound again. "You're asking me what's wrong?"

I pause. "Yes," I say, certain I'm missing something big. "You've been avoiding me for weeks, and you're acting strange now, so I'm asking you what's wrong."

"Well, let's see," she says. Her eyes flash. "My best friend and my ex-boyfriend are going to formal together, and I had to find out through team gossip."

I can't help it; I laugh, but something awful is sinking in my stomach. I had considered and dismissed this reaction, and clearly that was a misstep. Lisa's expression turns to outrage. "That's what this is about?"

She crosses her arms. "Don't even try to tell me I'm overreacting."

"You *are* overreacting." She looks furious, and now I'm starting to get mad. "I don't see Andy that way. That's not something I ever thought I'd need to clarify to you. As for not telling you first, which of the zero times we've hung out recently should I have done that?"

Her nostrils flare. "A text would have been fine, thanks."

"Well, you've been dodging those too." There's a pause. "You broke up with Andy, Lisa, so how come I never see you either?"

"*He* broke up with *me*, Arya," Lisa corrects, her voice firm.

I try to backtrack. "You're right. I'm sorry. I just meant—your breakup with Andy shouldn't alter *our* friendship, right?"

"I really don't know now. A real friend wouldn't have been

so careless with my feelings. A real friend would have stuck by my side."

I take another step back, stung. "I wanted to do that, Lisa. But you pushed me away. You said you needed distance."

"From *Andy,*" Lisa says. "But I guess that's proven to be the same thing, hasn't it?"

I blink twice. "I really didn't think Andy and I going to formal together would be such a big deal. It wasn't a secret, either. It would have come up if I'd seen you more. And I've tried to see you more." I stop because my voice is starting to waver. I don't know the last time, if ever, I fought with Lisa like this.

"Besides," I say after a beat. My voice is clipped, and resentment is starting to seep in. "The only reason I'm going with Andy is because you decided to go without me."

Lisa scoffs. "Oh, so this is all my fault, actually."

A lump is rising in my throat, so I don't respond. Lisa's mouth hardens. "You know, it's whatever," she says, but her expression is still set in a way that makes clear it most certainly is not whatever.

I swallow. "Are we going to be okay?"

She lets out a slow breath. "I think we just need some space from each other right now," she says, as if space isn't all we've had for the past several weeks.

My throat feels tight. "If that's what you want."

She gives a stiff nod, and I back away. Moments later, she drives out of sight.

Seventeen
Always Wanted to Be Your Friend

Tuesday morning arrives with heavy rainfall. I brought home the Fall Festival banner yesterday to finish up myself, and I'm forced to make two trips to my car to save my hard work from the downpour. I'm still drenched by the time I plop down in the driver's seat, socks damp and squishy under my feet. I need to order new rain boots.

Gloomy weather to match a gloomy week. I haven't allowed myself time to fully process my fight with Lisa, and I'm tiptoeing around both Mamma and Alina at home. Dinner with the Joshis left Mamma in one of her moods, and I'd rather not speak to Alina just to hear a confirmation of Rupa Aunty's words.

I split my time outside of class between Belle's and Mellie's. I'm at the latter under the pretense of studying (since midterms are next week), though my coffee shop evenings are admittedly spent watching Netflix through headphones on low brightness so the battery doesn't drain. Self-care is important.

Emilia notices something is wrong during lunchtime. We're

eating in Leadership instead of at our usual table with the goal of accomplishing festival prep tasks, and I'm stuffing paper towels into my boots to try to fix the wet-sock situation.

"You okay?" Emilia asks. "You've seemed kind of off lately."

I wish she would speak softer; Dean glanced up at her words from the table over. "I'm fine," I say because I don't want to discuss Lisa just yet. Done with the boots, I sit up straighter in my seat and give her a small smile. "Just tired. Midterms and all."

She nods, satisfied with my response. Candace and some of our other friends skipped lunch today to go to a Physics study session—grades are on everyone's mind.

"I totally get it," she says. "I need a ninety-four on my Chem exam to bring my grade up."

I make a sympathetic face. "Lewin is the worst," I say. I had Chemistry with him sophomore year, and all I learned was how to fall asleep undetected during lecture.

"The *worst,*" she agrees. We spend the rest of lunch complaining about bad teachers and classes, festival tasks forgotten.

I feel a little bad for lying to Emilia. She's been nothing but kind to me, and maybe she'd give good advice on how to resolve conflict with Lisa. But I haven't had time yet to sort out my own feelings (a tangled mess of guilt and frustration and bitterness), and I don't want to involve anyone else before I've had a chance to do so.

I've kept the information from Andy so far, too. I'll tell him when he returns, but every time we've spoken on the phone since the fight, he's seemed joyful and excited, and I haven't wanted to ruin that.

During passing period, I run into Lisa. It's startling because I've worked hard to prevent exactly this situation, literally creating a new path to my classes to avoid any accidental encounters. But there she is, dawdling outside the science building with one of her teammates.

We see each other at the same time. And we look away almost immediately. My stomach feels hollow as I walk quickly past her on my way to Bio.

I've never been in a relationship before, so I don't know what breakups feel like, but I imagine something like this. It's hard to believe that I'm no longer on speaking terms with the same Lisa I grew up with, the same Lisa who has been a constant in my life for as long as I can remember.

The next day, I go to the bench behind the history building instead of heading to the library like I do most mornings. It rained hard last night, and water droplets still cling to the wood, so I lay my coat over the bench before sitting.

I'm being a complete coward, but I don't want to chance a brush with Lisa before class. I push in my headphones and decide to review my Civics notes for next week's exam. I didn't get much of a chance to study last night. My shift at Belle's was long and tiring, full of disgruntled customers. I fell asleep pretty much immediately after arriving home.

A few minutes into my reading, I hear someone call my name. I pull out an earbud to see Dean standing nearby. "Is this seat taken?" he asks. If the oddness of this encounter strikes him, he doesn't show it.

I wonder at how pathetic I must look, studying by myself in an unfrequented corner of campus. I wonder what he's doing here. Then I realize he asked me a question, and I shake my head. He sits down against the opposite wooden armrest so that we are facing each other.

"I have to study for Civics too," he says conversationally, nodding at my binder. I'm grateful he doesn't comment on the picture in my cover sheet, a headshot of Harry Styles with the quotation box: *Hey, Girl, Keep Studying—I Believe in You.*

"Oh," I say intelligently.

Then: "You look really pretty today." His voice is clear and sincere.

My heart jumps quick to my throat. I hope to God I'm not blushing. "Thank you," I say, and it comes out puzzled. I did a rush job on my makeup this morning. I decide the new mascara I splurged on was a worthy purchase.

He smiles a little, dimples appearing, as though he knows the effect he has on me. "Do you feel ready for Fall Festival?" he asks.

I sit up straighter against the armrest. "Mostly," I say, meaning it. "I think we might just pull this off."

We're only a few days out now, and everything has been going according to plan. I confirmed setup times with the owners of the portable pumpkin patch yesterday, and Dean sent the group chat a receipt of our cakewalk order from Merri Berry Sweets last night. The junior officers are on top of decor, and best of all, early ticket sales are already up to eighty attendees. We're expecting to at least double that number by the day of.

"I think so too," he agrees. "See what happens when you put your faith in me?"

"Team effort," I correct, and he gives a half shrug.

"Georgia's really excited for the festival," he tells me. "She's spent weeks planning her Dragon Witch costume. She can't wait to show it off at the contest."

"Incredible taste," I say. I finished the latest Dragon Witch installment over the weekend, and the characters have been living rent-free in my mind. "I knew she was my favorite Merriweather sibling."

"You hardly know her, Arya."

"She had slim competition to begin with."

He rolls his eyes, and I smile. We fall into an easy silence. I feel hyperaware of how close we are seated and try to ignore the realization. I return to my notes, highlighting important info with a pink pen, and he pulls out his laptop, typing away on his keyboard.

"Dean," I say after several minutes have passed. He looks up, eyebrows raised. "Why are you here?" The curiosity hasn't faded, and it seems too unlikely that he just happened upon me.

"I got to class early," he says. "I thought I would study."

"Do you study here often?" I ask, and the corner of his mouth tilts up, caught.

"Do you?" he counters.

I don't say anything. I wonder if he knows about Lisa. Wonder if he's guessed. I remember his reaction when I told him Andy and I were going to formal together and think he must have anticipated this.

"I saw you walk back here," he admits.

I sit up straighter. "You followed me?"

"Not followed," he says quickly. "I just wanted—" He flattens his hair. It's dark and damp from light morning rain. "I thought maybe you'd want company."

My face feels warm. "Oh."

He picks at his jacket sleeve. "You've seemed a bit lonely this week."

There's a pause. My face grows warmer. "Lonely?"

He looks alarmed, then regretful. "I didn't mean—" He breaks off. "I just thought you could use a friend."

I swallow. "You came here because you thought I was lonely?" I am mortified to discover my eyes feel hot.

"And I thought you could use a friend." His brow furrows,

119

like he doesn't understand why I'm upset. "I've always wanted to be your friend, Arya. You've just never let me."

Dean Merriweather feels *sorry* for me. The thought hits me in the gut.

"I'm not lonely." I rush to my feet. I think of how he told me I looked pretty earlier and wonder if he only said that because he felt sorry for me then too. I cross my arms tight across my chest. "And I don't need your company."

Dean doesn't flinch, but a light blush rises to his cheeks. His eyes darken. After a beat, he says, "Have it your way, Arya." His voice is impassive. He gathers his things, and within seconds, he's out of sight.

Inexplicably, I feel a million times worse when he's gone.

I sink back down on the bench, my legs wobbly, my heart going fast. My fingers itch for my phone. I think of calling Andy or Alina, but he's far and busy, and she might be packing for a life far away from me, so I just sit here and breathe and try not to cry.

Eighteen

Henna and Heartache

"*orse v. Frederick,* 2007," Emilia says. She taps a gold acrylic nail (her Fall Festival manicure) against the desk impatiently.

"Hm?"

She sighs, exasperated. "*Morse v. Frederick?*"

I blink twice, looking at her. We're in Leadership, and Mrs. Marina gave us the hour to prep for midterms. Fall Festival is two days away, and there's no more work left to do until setup tomorrow evening. Emilia and I have been studying for Civics together, reviewing flash cards on First Amendment case law, and it's safe to say I've been more than a little distracted.

"Sorry," I say, meaning it. "Um, Bong Hits 4 Jesus?"

A high school student had received suspension for holding up a banner featuring those four poetic words across the school campus. If I remember right, the Supreme Court case dealt with whether the suspension violated the student's free speech.

"That's the case context," she says. "What was the decision?"

"Educators can restrict speech that promotes drug use," I say, recalling the ruling as I speak. "Is that right?"

"Yes." She turns to pull another flash card from her box.

I use the pause to sneak a glance at Dean. He's across the room, studying with Michael and Lacey. Michael says something that makes Dean smile, deep and boyish. I think of how handsome his smile is. Then I think of our conversation this morning and guilt knots in my stomach.

"Something happen with you and Dean again?" Emilia asks, following my line of sight, and I snap back to face her.

"Again?" I echo.

She gives me a look. "You guys are always fighting,"

I pull my arms deeper into my sweater. The room feels drafty. "Not always." It comes out defensive, and she laughs.

"Pretty much," she says.

"Not this time," I lie. I don't want to talk about Dean. I clear my throat. "I know I've been a little scatterbrained today. I guess there's just a lot on my mind."

She nods. Then her eyes widen. "Oh," she says. She lowers her voice. "I know about what happened with Lisa."

My brows go up. "You do?"

Her nose scrunches up in sympathy. "I heard from Candace," she says. "Who heard from Katie Nguyen, who heard from Clara Armstrong." She pauses. "Who heard from Lisa, obviously."

Clara Armstrong is the post on Lisa's basketball team.

"I didn't know so many people knew," I say finally. I curl a strand of hair behind my ear. At least a benefit of the story going around is that I'm not required to recount it myself. I frown as I realize the drawback—I don't know what the story going around *is*. "What did you hear?" I ask Emilia.

She looks down and picks at her manicure. "Well, Clara told Katie she thinks you and Andy are sneaking around." My mouth drops, and Emilia hastily adds, "Everyone knows that's not true, though. Clara just loves to stir the pot."

I shake my head, disbelieving. It's a ridiculous rumor, and even more ridiculous is the thought of Lisa, who knows us so well, giving it any credence. I take a deep breath and remind myself that Clara has always been a gossip—she was responsible for multiple rifts in our middle school Girl Scout troop—and most people with sense have long learned to take her intelligence with a grain of salt.

"I'm sure it'll blow over soon," I say with more confidence than I have.

"I'm sure," Emilia agrees. "Time will sort things out with Lisa." She gives me a smile. "You guys have been friends for so long. This is probably just really sensitive for her. The split was pretty recent, after all."

"Right," I say, with a little less confidence this time. I straighten up and take another long breath. "Okay, let's keep going."

She tilts the box to me, and I pick a flash card out. *"Texas v. Johnson,* 1989."

"Flag-burning case," Emilia says smoothly, and then she dives into the particulars.

That night, Alina knocks on my door. I've been shut in my room when I'm not at Belle's or Mellie's, citing midterms as the reason I'm not to be disturbed. It's worked for the most part, but the ruse was bound to fall through at some point.

I sit up quickly on my bed, where I've been rewatching an episode of *The West Wing* on my laptop. I grab a nearby textbook and close out of the Netflix tab for good measure before calling, "It's unlocked."

Alina enters. "Hey," she says. She's wearing the cloud-patterned pajamas I sent for Christmas a couple years ago, and her hair is twisted into a bun on the top of her head. "Still working?"

I nod my head, and she makes a disappointed face. "I feel like I've barely seen you this week," she says. "I thought we could have a movie night. But I totally get if you're busy. Exam season is the worst."

Shame twists in my belly. I've been avoiding her for days now. "I guess I could take a break," I say. "I mean, I've been reading for hours." I wave at the Bio textbook open on my lap. I hope it escapes her that it's turned to the index.

She lights up. "Perfect," she says. "It'll be just the two of us, too. Nikhil had a long day, so he's already asleep."

It's only ten p.m., but Nikhil's never been a night owl. "Sounds good."

"I'll get snacks ready?" she asks, and I nod.

"Wait," I say as she turns to leave. My heart starts to pound, and I wish I had the foresight to rehearse how to ask her about Rupa Aunty's words. "I've been wondering," I begin. "What are things going to look like after the shaadi?"

Her brows pull together. "What do you mean?"

I lick my lips. "Is it going to be like last time?" It's all I have the strength to ask, and thankfully, she understands my meaning.

"Oh, Arya." She sits down on the edge of my bed. "No, it won't." She squeezes my hand. "I was young then. Young and angry and foolish. I won't repeat those mistakes."

My stomach starts to loosen. "You promise?"

"Cross my heart."

It's not an answer about San Francisco, but that's not the question I asked. I don't have courage to get clarity on that just yet. "I'm glad," I say, squeezing her hand back. "You are still young, though," I add. "Like, practically a child bride."

Her expression turns to outrage. "I turned twenty-three in June. That's three years older than Mamma was when she got married."

"I'm just saying. You're barely the age of a college graduate." I pause, feigning confusion. "No, that can't be right—"

She gasps, then glares. She swats my leg. "Just for that, I'm picking the movie tonight."

A half hour later, we're curled up on the living room couch, bowls of popcorn and strawberry ice cream balanced on our laps. We are both wearing sheet masks, the animal print kind— Alina's is a tiger, mine is a panda. The beginning credits of *You've Got Mail* are playing on the television screen before us.

"This is cruel and unusual punishment," I say. "I work at an indie bookstore. This movie is my greatest fear dramatized."

Onscreen, a young Meg Ryan opens her children's bookshop for the day, blissfully unaware that she will be out of a job in a few short months.

"Hm," Alina says, clearly enjoying herself. She scoops a bite of ice cream from her bowl. "I hadn't thought about that. I just picked it for 1998 Tom Hanks."

"You're evil," I say, and Alina blows me a kiss, looking ridiculous in her tiger mask.

If Belle's ever closes down, I would never forgive—let alone fall in love with—the soulless capitalist responsible for its closure. Not even if he looks like 1998 Tom Hanks. Maybe if he looks like 1998 Tom Hanks.

"So," Alina says, smoothing the crinkles in her face mask as she turns to face me. "I've decided that I want to do my own mehndi for the shaadi. You'll help me practice tonight?"

I give her an astonished look. "What do you mean, do your own mehndi?"

125

"Not both arms, obviously," Alina says, as though this is the issue. "I could never do both. Just my left."

I shake my head, bewildered. "The henna artist is going to loathe you," I say.

"Well," Alina says defiantly. "She can wipe her tears with the thousand-dollar check I'll be writing her." I start to open my mouth, and Alina snaps, "Don't you dare make a comment about how Mamma and Papa are paying."

"I'm hardly that predictable," I say, indignant, even though that's exactly what I was going to do.

"I just want to write Nikhil's name in mehndi myself," she explains. "That's important to me."

It's a tradition in Desi weddings for the groom's name to be hidden somewhere in the bride's mehndi. Post-wedding, the groom is meant to search for his name. It's said to be a predictor of success in marriage if he finds it quickly.

"Okay, that'll be sweet," I say. "Don't tell Mamma yet. What do you need my help with?"

Alina beams and holds up a henna cone.

I rest one hand on Alina's lap and use the other to spoon ice cream into my mouth while the movie plays. Alina swirls mehndi on my palm as Meg Ryan falls in love with Tom Hanks through a vintage version of email.

"Done," Alina announces ten minutes in. I look down and my mouth drops open. She's drawn a neat row of penises on my wrist.

I jerk my arm away from her. "Alina!" I exclaim. I pull my hand up to examine the damage and immediately regret it. The design is worse close up. "Seriously, are you a middle school boy?"

She's laughing. "I meant to draw flowers," she says. "Truly. But I was partway through the first one and thought this might be . . . more fun."

"More fun." I glare at her.

Her laughter dies slowly. "Well, *I* thought it was fun. Nice to know I still have my henna talent." She stands, stacking her empty bowls together as she does. "I'm using my bride card," she calls as she walks to the kitchen. "You're not allowed to be upset with me!"

"Card declined!" I call back. She doesn't respond.

I pause the movie and use the break to peel off my panda mask, which I've kept on for far longer than the packet said to. Then I use a napkin to wipe off the mehndi. Unfortunately, it has already started to set. Pale orange penises line the base of my wrist.

I place my bowls on the coffee table, toss away the trash, and wash my hands in the bathroom. When I return, Alina is curled on the couch, blankets drawn up around her.

"It'll fade," she says before I can speak. "Since you washed your hands right after."

I cross my arms and start to reply, still irritated, but she has the nerve to shush me. "I want to finish the movie before morning," she says sweetly.

I elbow her when I sit down. She leans her head on my shoulder. We watch in silence.

Something shifts in me at the halfway mark of the movie. Meg Ryan's character is trying desperately to save her shop, and her life continues to implode around her. There are moments where she makes matters worse for herself too. I find myself fighting tears as I watch.

"Arya," Alina says gently after a while. "Are you okay?"

"I'm fine," I say, even as I blink back fresh tears. "Why do you ask?"

She frowns. "Well, because of that." She points to my blotchy face, and I don't have the energy to feel insulted. "At first I thought it was because Shop Around the Corner closed, but, honey, we're getting to the happy part, and you still look like you're about to cry."

Onscreen, a fluttery Meg Ryan waits for her mystery man in a blooming New York City flower garden.

I can't hold back anymore. Tears spill out of my eyes, fast and thick.

"Arya!" Alina exclaims. She rushes to pause the movie then turns to face me. "What's going on?"

I wipe at my cheeks. "I feel like I mess everything up," I blurt, thinking of Lisa and Dean. "And the penis mehndi isn't fading like you said it would!" I hold up my hand to show how the phallic design has gotten darker. Alina's mouth twitches, but I continue. "And my period starts tomorrow and my festival dress is light."

I chose my favorite of Mindy's many costume suggestions—Princess Belle, our bookshop's namesake—which means I'll be wearing a pale yellow sundress for Fall Festival. I agreed to the idea without bothering to check the menstrual calendar on my phone.

"Double up on panty liners for the festival," she says. "And foundation will cover your wrist dicks." She tilts her head at me, concern lining her features. "But let's talk about the first thing. What do you mean, you mess everything up?"

I take a shaky breath, and then I'm telling her all about my fight with Lisa and how I lashed out at Dean a few days later. She listens attentively, not interrupting once. When I finish, she folds my hand in hers.

"So you've made mistakes." Her voice is tender. "Everyone makes mistakes. Instead of beating yourself up, take the steps to make amends and resolve conflict."

I use a corner of the blanket to wipe remaining tears. "How?"

"Well," she says. "It's a little harder with Lisa. You could have been more careful about formal and Andy to begin with, since it's clear this is still a tough topic for her. Just because someone seems okay doesn't mean they are. You should've spoken with her before she had a chance to learn from others and the truth got twisted."

I nod; this is what I have been thinking lately too. I was so absorbed in trying to salvage my formal plans, to make the most of my changing friendships, that Lisa's hurt became an afterthought.

She continues. "I think it'll be productive to apologize, but then give her the space she asked for. You need to let her figure things out. I'm sure she'll come around soon."

I'm less sure than Alina, but it's soothing to have someone tell me what I want to hear, so I don't correct her. I sit up straighter. "And with Dean?"

She gives me a look. "That's more black-and-white. You were so in the wrong. Especially after he said he's always wanted to be your friend."

"That was definitely a lie," I say. "He's constantly rude to me. He makes fun of me all the time."

"Little boys pull little girls' pigtails because . . ."

"Don't romanticize toxic behavior," I scold, and she rolls her eyes. "Besides, neither of us is very little anymore."

"You've engaged in just as much toxicity as he has, my girl," she says, and I'm quiet, because she's right. "More, this time around." She tilts her head at me, fighting a smile. "By the way, is Dean cute?"

My cheeks go warm. "What does that matter?" I pluck at a loose thread on the couch cushion. "Yes." The word pushes out. I put my face in my hands. "What do I do?"

"I think you should make a nice gesture. Something to show

you value him, something to show you've *always wanted to be his friend* too."

I shove her. She laughs. "It's all going to work out, Arya. Okay?"

My heart feels warm in my chest. "Okay." I have missed this, Alina being my sister and advisor in one. There have been too many moments lately where I have had to be that for her. I lean into her, tucking my head in the space between her ear and her shoulder.

"Let's return to the movie? I think Meg Ryan deserves some joy right about now."

I smile. Alina presses play.

Nineteen
Mujhse Dosti Karoge?

No streamers." My voice comes out strangled. "Please."

Ned, or maybe Nathan, furrows his brow. "But I picked these up at Party City," he says. He holds up the plastic-wrapped packets of butter-yellow streamers, discount stickers still taped to the front. "They come with hooks and everything."

"Let's stick with the decorations that Meena and Lacey made. They have enough." I force a smile. "Maybe you can go ahead and help with setting up the cakewalk area?"

Ned pulls a sour face, but he doesn't argue. He heads in the direction of the cakewalk numbers, which Candace drew with chalk markers on one end of the courtyard. Relieved, I hug my clipboard to my chest and glance around.

Unsolicited decor suggestions aside, we've done a solid job with festival setup so far. The banner I labored over hangs above the courtyard stage where we'll hold our costume contest, and Meena's glittery handmade signs announce all the offered activities to our attendees, from the pumpkin patch to the face-painting booth to our last-minute amateur haunted house—Emilia got her way in the end, after offering to fund and organize the event herself.

It'll be in the small gym, and it's not quite a haunted house so much as a haunted hall, but Emilia is positively giddy with anticipation. I'm pretty excited to see the end result myself.

We've marked off the area where we'll hold the pumpkin patch, and junior officers are setting up tablecloths and floral arrangements in the seating area, where festivalgoers can enjoy their concessions purchases and cakewalk winnings. By the stage, Dean readies the sound booth. We asked a junior on the theater's sound team to deejay in order to save money. She'll be working with preapproved music selections, but she's running for student council in the spring, so she agreed.

Suddenly, there is a terrible screeching noise. Wincing, we all turn to the sound booth. "Sorry," Dean says, voice too loud, fingers stuffed in his ears. "I twisted the wrong thing." Our eyes meet, and he looks away.

We've barely exchanged two words all evening. I wanted to speak to him when I first arrived, but he was already busy with deejay setup, and I haven't gotten an opportunity since.

I sink down on a cushioned seat by the parking lot. It's the space we've designated for admission tickets, and tonight, it functions as my workspace. I have a list of festival preparation tasks pulled up on my laptop to tick off as we make progress.

I'm done delegating for the moment, so I pull out my phone to check for new messages. I have one from Andy telling me his plane just arrived at Boston Logan and one from Emilia with a picture of the pumpkin-colored dress, asking if the outfit is as terrible as she fears.

My stomach twists at Andy's text. I write back asking him to FaceTime when he's settled at home; I'll have to tell him about Lisa tonight. Then I send Emilia reassurances that she will totally be able to pull off the look with the right accessories and don't let myself feel guilty for the lie.

Dean walks my way a few minutes later. I rise quickly and clumsily to my feet, realizing too late that he was probably heading to the parking lot to pick up extra supplies from his car.

I'm committed now, so I step forward and smile. "Dean," I say, voice bright. "Hi."

He slows before me, eyes shifting to the lot, probably trying to determine whether he can still leave. He must decide against it, because he turns to me, hands stuffed in pockets. "Hi."

There's a pause. I curl a lock of hair behind my ear and take a deep breath.

We speak at the same time.

"I wanted to—" I start.

He says, "There's a penis on your wrist." He tilts his head and frowns. "Multiple, actually."

"Oh," I say, face burning. I give a short laugh, hating myself for not covering the mehndi with foundation this evening. "Thanks." This is so not the appropriate response. "Um, my sister made it."

I want to eat my words. Dean looks like he's not sure if he should laugh. He coughs instead.

"How's the sound work going?" I ask, wrapping my arms around my chest so my hands are hidden.

"Fine," he says. I wait, but he doesn't add anything, and I realize this is all I'm going to get.

"Ned wanted to hang yellow streamers." I raise my brows in a *Can you believe?* way.

"Nathan."

"Right." I cross my arms tighter. "Look," I say. I take another long breath, steadying myself. "I'm sorry for lashing out at you that morning. I was really unkind to you."

He is silent, so I go on. "It's a bad habit of mine. To pick a fight with you when I'm upset about something else. But that's not okay, so I'm working on it."

His brows lift at this. Then he gives a nod, but he still doesn't speak. I try a different angle. "You said you've always wanted to be my friend."

Now his cheeks flush. "I meant—"

"I feel like you've done a really poor job of showing that," I interrupt. "Like, really poor. With the haircut thing and calling me your 'assistant' and so much else, I can't even remember right now." I clear my throat. I've gotten off topic. "But, truly, I would like for us to be friends too."

He shakes his head, marveling. "You are reliably bad at apologizing."

I hold my hand out to him. "Will you be my friend, Dean?" I ask, like I live in a Bollywood movie.

The corner of his lips twitch up. "Is this a business deal?"

"It's a truce."

After a moment, he steps forward and takes my hand. His skin is rough and warm against mine.

"You know you have to be nice to me now."

"And you have to be nice to *me*."

He smiles, just barely, and I release him. He flexes his hand. My fingers feel cold.

"I have something for you," I say before I can lose the nerve. I walk to my bag and pull out the glass container I packed so carefully earlier today. Returning to Dean, I pass him the box. "Here."

He opens the lid. Chocolate squares stare up at him, and a sweet scent wafts through the air. He looks back to me.

"You made me brownies?"

Something about the way he's asking makes the gesture sound

so intimate that I fluster. "From a mix," I add quickly. It seemed like a good idea at the time. I wanted to act in the spirit of Alina's advice, and our evening at Mellie's made brownies seem an appropriate choice.

For some reason, he laughs. "Betty Crocker?"

"Ghirardelli."

"Glad to know I'm worth the extra dollar."

I nod. "They're good," I say. "I tried one. Four, I mean."

"Well, thanks, Arya."

"Sure." And then we're just standing there, looking at each other, so I say, "I should get back—" I glance at the admissions table, where I was moments before, doing absolutely nothing productive. "Lots going on, you know."

He starts. "Yeah," he says. "Same here." He makes like he is about to leave, then stops, then begins again.

He glances back at me as he walks out of the courtyard, and something about the look makes my heart squeeze in my chest.

Twenty
This Really Is a Beautiful Friendship

Alina turns the penises into an elaborate floral pattern with a few more swirls of henna. I squeeze drops of fresh lemon on the design so it will darken and last, then slip my hands into a pair of old socks so I can sleep with the mehndi on.

In the morning, I do my makeup before twisting in silver jhumke and donning the yellow sundress that I bought from Target last week to complete my Belle transformation. I'm going for a Desi Disney Princess look this Halloween. I hope Mindy will be proud.

I pick up Andy from his place on my way to campus. Fall Festival doesn't officially start for an hour, but I want to be there early to make sure everything is in order.

Andy's costume (if you can call it that) is one of his usual fits paired with a Joker mask.

"Someone is comfortable placing last in the costume contest," I quip when he gets in my car. He flips me off, looking ridiculous in the mask, and I laugh as we drive away.

I filled Andy in on the Lisa situation after he arrived home from Chicago yesterday. I was nervous to tell him, but he was a comfort, listening and telling me with conviction that Lisa and I would mend things soon enough. Then we spent a good hour bashing Clara Armstrong and her big mouth. By the end of our talk, I felt remarkably lighter.

Lisa's basketball team has an away tourney this weekend, so she won't be at the festival. I only learned through her Instagram story; neither of us has reached out to the other since our parking-lot fight. I have mixed feelings about her absence—I'm glad to avoid conflict a little longer, but it still feels strange to not have her by my side.

Emilia greets us at the admissions booth. She's dressed as Lady Gaga in her infamous meat-dress outfit for the night, and the costume suits her surprisingly well.

"You're both here!" she exclaims. "How was Chicago?" she asks Andy.

"Really incredible," he says, and I swell with pride. Andy's account of the interview portion of his visit was modest, as expected, but I feel confident he'll be settled into the UChicago dorms this time next year.

"Hi, Em," I say, giving her a quick hug. "You look fantastic."

She beams. "Thank you, thank you," she says. "I better place in the contest. These meat strips are *so* uncomfortable."

"You have our votes," I say, and she smiles deeper.

Emilia's done with her haunted-house setup, so she sits down at the booth with us while I try not to fret about the evening. Guests won't arrive for another half hour, so the courtyard is empty aside from council members doing last-minute decor. A quick glance at the cakewalk space tells me everything is ready, with the pastries arranged in half moons on the table.

Dean must be here, though I haven't seen him. He was responsible for bringing over all the sweets from his mother's shop. I pull out my phone and consider texting him.

But Dean isn't away for long. Moments later, he plops into the empty seat beside Emilia. He gives me an almost-smile, and I put my phone down instinctively, text thankfully unsent. My sleeve slips and I tug it back down.

"Hey, Dean," Emilia says. She frowns. "What are you supposed to be?"

Dean is wearing joggers and a windbreaker, clothing indistinguishable from his usual attire if not for the addition of a black whistle slung around his neck.

"I'm a soccer coach," he says. The "duh" is silent.

"Oh," Emilia says. "Like the guy from *Bend It Like Beckham*."

I stop fidgeting with my dress. Emilia did not just reference the only movie ever made in which a soccer coach falls for a Punjabi girl whose older sister is getting married.

Dean looks puzzled. "Never seen it."

Emilia clucks her tongue. "Shame," she says, a smile curving on her lips. I kick her under the table. She kicks back.

Dean looks even more puzzled. I decide it's time for a subject change. "Which pastries did you end up bringing?"

"Lots of festive things," he says. "Pumpkin tarts and pecan pies and caramel apple cheesecakes." He pauses, lips twisting down but eyes still merry. "No brownies, unfortunately."

I smile in spite of myself, my chest going funny and warm. "We'll persevere."

There's nothing more to do until Mrs. Marina stops by for a cursory check-in, so Emilia begins filling in Dean on the details of her haunted house, which has come together rather splendidly. Andy nudges me in the middle of the narration.

"I might be seeing things," he says, voice low to not interrupt Emilia. He's pushed his Joker mask up so it sits flat on his head, casting his face in shadow. "But did you just smile at Dean Merriweather?"

My voice goes defensive. "I've smiled at Dean before."

"Only ever in a hateful way."

I roll my eyes, but it's not like he's that wrong. I pick at my manicure as I explain. "We're friends now, actually," I say. The words sound ridiculous even as they leave my lips.

His brows go high. He starts to laugh when he realizes I'm serious. "Just how many lifetimes was I gone for?"

I'll fill Andy in later, but for now, I settle for swatting his shoulder.

Nikhil and Alina arrive ten minutes prior to opening. The line for admission winds down the length of the parking-lot sidewalk, and Alina texts me twice begging to cut, but I'm too thrilled about there being a line at all to oblige her.

Alina is Frida Kahlo for the evening: flowers in her hair, shawl draped around her neck, and paint supplies strapped to her waist. Nikhil, predictably, is still in his work clothes.

Mamma and Papa are absent, but I try not to dwell. Mamma has hardly left her room since the Joshi dinner, and Papa had a work event. But the rest of my family is here, and I'm grateful.

"Thoughts on the makeup?" Alina asks as I secure an orange admit wristband on her hand. She gestures to her brows, which are connected by expertly drawn eyeliner baby hairs. "I really tried to get in character."

I peer closer and pretend not to notice a thing. "You look the same as ever," I say.

Alina gives me a withering look. "For that, I am going to be *so* annoying to your friends tonight."

With that, she grabs Nikhil's hand and steers him in the direction of the haunted house, and I say a silent prayer for Emilia.

An hour into the festival, I trade spots at the admissions booth with another officer and allow myself a stroll around the courtyard. My first stop is at the concessions stand for some hot cider—generously supplied by Mellie's for the evening.

I drink as I walk, cider spreading warmth through my belly. We've sold two hundred tickets so far, which means we've officially earned enough to keep our autumn formal venue. With the added money from festival events, we just might pull off the annual dance without any financial stress. The Leadership group chat has been celebrating since I sent in a picture of our sales ten minutes ago.

I finish my cider as I reach the cakewalk table. We have pastries for purchase on one end, so even those who lose the game can enjoy the treats, and the frosted pumpkin tarts are calling my name. I'm tugging my wallet out of my purse when I hear a voice behind me.

"Oh, I *strongly* recommend the tarts."

I twist around to see Ms. Merriweather, gray-brown hair pulled back with a sparkly orange headband. Her eyes widen with surprise, and her smile lines deepen in recognition when she sees it's me.

"Arya, hi. It's so wonderful to run into you."

She steps forward for a quick embrace even though we've only met a few times, and I hug her back. Ms. Merriweather, along with Lisa's mom, is a member of the local temple's Divorced Moms Book Club, which hosts meetings at Belle's every so often, and we've spoken in passing there. I've seen her at a couple Leadership events over the years as well, but nothing beyond that.

"It's great to see you too," I say when she pulls away. The smell of sugar lingers; she must have arrived straight from her bakery. "And thanks so much for sponsoring the cakewalk—really, we're all so grateful."

She waves a hand, but I can tell she's pleased. "I was glad to," she says. "Especially since it means Dean will be working extra hours at the shop."

I laugh, and she continues. "I've been so happy to hear that you and Dean have grown closer this year. He's always spoken so highly of you."

I'm so struck by the idea of Dean talking about me to his mother that I almost miss the substance of her words. "He has?"

Now she laughs. "Ever since ninth-grade Leadership. I remember that first project of yours, a commercial or something. He couldn't stop talking about you. He thought you were so impressive."

I remember the project, though rather differently. Dean and I were paired up to create a video advertisement for a school event, and we fought at every stage of production. He spent the whole time undermining my judgment and acting superior. Dean and I went to different middle schools, so the assignment was our first real interaction and laid the foundation for years of mutual dislike. It's startling to hear Ms. Merriweather's version of the tale.

She must take my silence as disinterest. "I'm rambling, forgive me. I love your costume, by the way. Belle has always been my favorite princess." She turns to go, then pauses to add, "Definitely get the tart!"

I'm still thinking of Ms. Merriweather's words when I go to relieve Emilia from her post at the haunted house. Those who wish to enter the costume contest are lining up by the stage, after which we'll vote on social media, and Emilia has been waiting for this all night.

Emilia breaks off a piece of my pumpkin tart in lieu of hello. I allow it, even though I definitely haven't forgotten her earlier behavior.

"Em," I say as she brushes tart crumbs off the blouse of her meat dress.

"Hm?"

"*Bend It Like Beckham?*"

She sighs and smiles. "Such a great film."

I elbow her as she exits.

At the end of the evening, I revisit the concessions stand and the cakewalk table for leftovers. There isn't a wide selection, most of the good things are long gone, but I still pile kettle corn, caramel candies, a lemon pudding cup, and two cranberry scones on a paper plate. Then I go find Dean.

He's sitting on a bench in the pumpkin patch, scrolling social media. He puts his phone down when he sees me.

"Hi," he says. His eyes travel quick to my dress and back up. He slowly removes his feet from where they were resting on the bench beside him. I realize he is making room for me and sit down, movements inelegant.

"What's this?" he asks, nodding at the plate in my hands.

"Think of it as charcuterie," I say.

"Charcuterie is supposed to have cheese," he says. He pauses. "And crackers. And cured meats."

"A poor man's charcuterie, then."

He smiles and plucks the cherry from the pudding cup, handing me a spoon and taking the other for himself. "I like the new henna," he tells me after finishing his cherry.

"I liked the original," I say. I stop when it registers how dangerously close I am to making a dick joke.

He looks amused. We fall quiet, and I take a bite of the creamy lemon pudding.

"I saw you with my mom at the cakewalk earlier," he says, breaking the silence. He plucks at the whistle around his neck. "What did you guys talk about?" he asks. His voice is casual, but his hands are nervous, moving from the whistle to his pockets to his hair.

I'm not entirely sure how to reply, since I'm still trying to unravel Ms. Merriweather's comments myself. "Not much," I say finally. "She said Belle is her favorite princess."

He nods. "My favorite was always Ariel," he says.

"Because she can't talk?"

He shakes his head, dimples deepening. "I wish *you'd* learn that skill."

I bite back a smile. "We did well with the festival," I say. "We earned more than enough money, and it seems like everyone had a great time."

It really was a lovely, busy night. The pumpkin patch was always packed, and the cakewalk line was never ending. Emilia, Georgia, and a PTA mom whose name I don't recall all placed in the costume contest (in reverse order), and during my breaks, I took part in the festivities too.

"We did great," he agrees. "Though I do wish Michael had passed along the songs we agreed upon."

Michael Wilson was responsible for providing the music list today, and if I recall from the most recent Leadership group chat argument, he refused to include any of Dean's country choices. I'm Team Michael for this one, but I keep that to myself.

"There's always autumn formal," I say, and this makes Dean smile.

"Yes," he says. "Because of tonight, there is."

We spoon more lemon pudding from the cup. It's far better than I expected, sweet and tangy on my tongue.

"Arya," Dean says. He shifts to face me on the bench, figure illuminated by lamplight. "About your bad habit. You said yesterday that you pick fights with me when you're upset about something else. What was the something else?"

My brows rise at the question. There's so much care in his voice that I feel it warm in my chest. "There's a lot going on at home, I guess. Wedding stress, maybe," I say. It's a truth, and I could stop there. I don't. "Sometimes I worry that my sister and I aren't friends anymore. Not like we used to be."

It's the fear I haven't allowed myself to voice since Alina has been home. For years, I thought Alina returning would solve everything, do away Mamma's hurt and my loneliness, but it's done none of that. If anything, it's just exposed how much things have changed since she first left. My conversation with Rupa Aunty was a reminder of the resentment that I still hold for my sister, that I maybe always will.

"And Lisa and I had a bit of a falling-out," I add. It's a sharp subject change, but Dean doesn't press me. I clear my throat. "But those aren't excuses, and I know it. Believe me, I am very committed to our new friendship."

A smile touches his lips. He tilts the near-empty pudding cup, asking if he can have the last bite, and I allow him. He spoons it up and sighs, content. "This really is a beautiful friendship."

Intermission

On the first of November, during a particularly painful Leadership lecture, I tug my journal out of my backpack and write.

Mrs. Marina will not stop talking. Hopefully it looks like I am taking notes. Anyway.

I keep thinking about that moment in my favorite Bollywood films. You know, *that* moment. When the heroine is walking through mustard fields to get away, to clear her head. And then all of a sudden the hero appears, and they are transported to like, the Swiss Alps, and it rains and they dance and he sniffs her neck and it is all so much better, it is all perfect.

I'm rambling. But what I mean to say is—I would give anything to Bollywood-dream-sequence escape everything going wrong in my life. Because there is so much going wrong in my life. I wish

Someone clears their throat loudly. I snap my head up to see Dean looking terribly amused beside me. "You want someone to sniff your neck?" he whispers, voice low enough to avoid being overheard.

Heat crawls fast up my face. "Were you just reading my *diary*?"

He cocks his head. "I thought it was a bullet journal."

"*Dean.*"

"It was hardly an effort. It's in my direct line of sight. You should take better care in the future."

"I will kill you one of these days, really, I swear."

He has the nerve to shush me. "Less death threats, more listening." He nods to Mrs. Marina still presenting before us.

I comply only to avoid potential discipline; this is one of the few times Mrs. Marina has taken an active role in class, after all. But the sound of pencil scratching paper returns my attention to Dean.

Below my entry, familiar, boyish lettering spells out: *You deserve your Bollywood moment, Arya Khanna.*

Arya's Bollywood Drama Recommendations

- *Dilwale Dulhania Le Jayenge,* 1995
  Practically invented the Bollywood dream sequence.

- *Kuch Kuch Hota Hai,* 1998
  Best friends to lovers meets second-chance romance? Say less.

- *Kabhi Khushi Kabhie Gham,* 2001
  Watch with tissues.

- *Jab We Met,* 2007
  There's a reason Shahid Kapoor was voted Asia's Sexiest Man Alive.

- *Yeh Jawaani Hai Deewani,* 2013
  A modern classic. <3

Act III
Something Blue

Twenty-One
Checkmate

After an evening shift at Belle's, Nikhil and I play a round of chess during dinner. Neil mailed him a glass set last week, guilted into purchasing a real birthday gift for his older brother by Rupa Aunty. We sit on the living room floor, bowls of fresh sabudana khichdi balanced in our laps as we play.

"God, you guys are dorks," Alina says. She's on the other side of the living room, stuffing clothes into an already overflowing suitcase. Tomorrow, she heads to New York for a couple days, meeting with the organizers of the gallery's spring showcase to discuss her commissioned piece.

"Hey, chess is a sport," Nikhil says. "A mental sport," he clarifies. He slides a bishop across the board to take my knight.

"It's like you're determined to prove my point," Alina says, shaking her head.

I move my queen forward to capture the offending bishop. "Don't mind her, Nikhil, Alina's just bitter she lost every chess match we've ever played."

A sock hits me in the back of my neck. I nearly drop a

spoonful of sabudana on the floor. I whip my head around to face her. "Alina!" I exclaim.

"Oops," she says.

I glare. "I can't wait for you to leave." She blows me a kiss.

"Check," Nikhil says, moving his rook forward.

I gasp, turning back to the board. "The bishop was a distraction!"

He grins and taps the side of his head. "Mental sport."

I frown, trying to figure a way out. I move a pawn to guard my king as a temporary defense.

"So, Arya, Sheila's going to teach me Sangeet choreography in New York," Alina says. Her voice sounds strained with effort; she's in a kind of downward-dog pose, pushing on the open suitcase to create more space. "We'll record the routine and then you can learn from the recording. Sound good?"

I furrow my brows. "But we haven't even decided on an interval yet."

Our Sangeet song, "You Are My Soniya," as most Bollywood classics go, is nearly six minutes in length. Neither Alina nor I have that kind of stamina, so we're going to select a minute-long portion to perform our routine to.

"Never mind that. Sheila and I are going to settle on it first thing."

Alina is staying at Sheila Jawani's place for the duration of her trip. Alina and Nikhil broke their lease when they moved home for the fall, so it's the best option. I know Alina must miss the city and her gallery job; she's been on leave the past few weeks to wedding plan and brainstorm for her project, only doing the occasional remote task. A few days in New York will be good for her soul.

Alina stands up from the suitcase, brushing her hands off,

and gives me a meaningful look. "You just create time in your busy life to learn how to dance."

"I'll make time," I say, and I mean it, though it'll be a challenge. Festival planning is complete, but formal planning is here to replace it. Early deadlines for college applications are fast approaching too, so the rest of the semester is bound to be super hectic.

"What Sangeet song did you decide on?" Nikhil asks conversationally. He keeps his eyes on the chessboard as he speaks.

"I'd marry someone else before I told you that," Alina declares hotly.

"Cute." A smile curves on his lips. "You guys should pick up the pace. Neil and I started learning choreo last week."

"I'm not worried," Alina says, though every muscle in her body tenses. "My team plays to win."

I feel gratified by her vote of confidence. I decide to never tell her how often I tripped over myself on the Roka dance floor.

"Our wedding isn't a contest, babe."

"Sangeet night it is."

"If that's the case," Nikhil says, tilting his head at Alina, "let's make things interesting. Whoever pulls off the better routine gets to pick our honeymoon location."

Alina's brows fly up. She and Nikhil have been squabbling about where to go on their honeymoon next spring for weeks. Alina desperately wants to explore and sightsee, while Nikhil just wants a relaxing beach trip.

"Fine with me," Alina says. "But don't be a bad sport when I'm booking flights to Peru."

"We're going to the Amalfi Coast, and that's settled."

"Hey," I say, twisting to face Alina. "You sure you don't want help with choreography?" I'm invested in this dance challenge now, and if I can contribute to our success, I want to.

"Super sure." She bites back a smile when I shoot her a dark look. "Let's please accept this is not one of your strengths and move on."

I'm about to grumble a retort when Nikhil says, "Checkmate, Arya."

There is triumph in his voice. My mouth drops as I turn to look at the board. Another sneaky bishop move is to blame.

"I hate this dork sport," I groan, and Alina laughs.

Monday is a special morning. Every year, Mellie's releases their holiday favorites menu on November 5. And every year, I wake early and wait in an enormous line to collect the chestnut latte and sugar plum cake I've spent the last ten months dreaming about. The first sip is heaven on my tongue.

I finish my drink during Literature; Andy steals sips when I'm not looking. But I'm still savoring bites of cake as I wait for Mr. McMoore to start the Civics lesson. I'm doodling in my planner, Mellie's bag set out in front of me, when the last piece vanishes before me.

My eyes snap up. Dean's brushing cake crumbs from his hands. A strangled sound escapes my lips. "You did not."

His eyes widen. "I didn't think—" He pauses, finishes swallowing. "I didn't think it was a big deal. It's just cake."

"Just cake?" I want to shove him. "I waited twenty minutes to order this morning."

"Relax, Khanna, I'll buy you another piece." His fingers drum against the desk. "Anyway, are you free sometime this week?"

"For what?"

"I thought we could get started on formal prep," he says.

"Yes, fine." Fall Festival was only two days ago, but we need to start placing orders with vendors now to make sure autumn formal goes off without a hitch. At least the stress of the job is much lower now that we know we can afford the dance.

He smiles, dimples cutting into his cheeks. "Nice."

I narrow my eyes. "I'm not going to do all the work." He's still smiling, so I add, "I mean it, Dean. Workload will be an even split."

He tilts his head. "I feel like we've had this conversation before," he says. "You might remember; it ended with you apologizing."

I'm about to snap back, but he continues. "I thought we could hang out after getting some work done," he says.

Some of the fight leaves my body. "Hang out?" The words sound foreign on my tongue.

"Yeah," he says. His voice is easy, but his fingers are fiddling with my planner. "Friends hang out together," he reminds me.

"Right," I say. "That's true." I clear my throat. "Um, I can do tomorrow. I have work till six, but you can meet me at Belle's after, and we can walk over to Mellie's."

"Hey, I'll buy you your cake then."

"I want a drink too," I say. "Chestnut latte, no whipped cream, medium." I frown. "Make it a small. I won't sleep if I have too much coffee so late."

He makes a sound in the back of his throat. "I'm not your *barista*," he says.

"This is the price of my friendship," I say.

He ducks his head to hide a smile. "Then it's a date," he confirms, and he's gone before I have a chance to parse the words.

Papa and I watch an episode of *Friends* during dinner. We curl up on the couch, comfy and relaxed, bowls of soupy Maggi noodles fresh from the stove wobbling on our laps. Nikhil's meeting friends in Boston, and Alina left for Sheila's this morning, so it's a rare moment of togetherness, just the two of us.

We pick an early episode, one before Ross and Rachel ever kissed. Papa laughs in time with the laugh track. I slurp noodles from my bowl as we watch.

Halfway through the episode, I hear Mamma's voice carry from upstairs. She's talking loudly on the phone, clearly agitated. The ceiling is too thick for me to make out what she's saying, but I doubt I would understand regardless. The words sound Punjabi, and Hindi is the only Indian language I speak fluently.

"What's going on?" I ask Papa after a few more minutes of this.

Papa sighs. He swirls his spoon in his bowl. "Today is your nanaji's birthday."

"Oh," I say. My brows draw together. "Isn't that a happy thing?"

"Last week, he said he will not be coming for Alina's shaadi."

"Oh," I say again, and then I get it. Mamma has been trying to convince Nanaji to live with us ever since my naniji passed away. But Nanaji will never quit the home he once shared with his wife. He hasn't visited Boston, hasn't even left Punjab since her death. Mamma must have thought Nanaji would make an exception for Alina's wedding, and that once here, it would be easier to convince him to stay for good.

"Is Mamma—" I lick my lips. I'm not sure what I'm trying to ask. "Is Mamma very upset he won't be attending?"

"Yes." He rethinks. "Maybe." Papa pauses again. "I don't think your mamma ever expected that he would come."

I frown, bemused. "Then why are they fighting?"

The laugh track sounds on the television. Papa's expression

Arushi Avachat

is tired and gray. "He is a sad person," Papa says finally. "Sad all the time, sad like your mamma. They don't know how to help each other. This is why they argue."

Nighttime must make his tongue lazy and loose, because Papa has never spoken to me like this before. Then again, I've never asked questions like this before.

Papa turns back to the television, spoon scraping the bottom of his bowl for more Maggi. A moment later, I turn back to the screen too.

Not for the first time, I wonder if Papa is a good husband. I think he is a good man, but I wonder if he has the capacity or the will to take care of Mamma like she needs. He is either at work or at his flower garden or otherwise away.

Though, by that metric, I'm not a very good daughter. Mamma and I don't spend much time with each other. It's mostly my doing; I tiptoe around her when we're both at home. I picked up the habit in the early weeks of Alina's absence, when Mamma was sadder than I have ever known her, and it's stuck since. Maybe I'm cruel to think so, but I feel she's too unhappy to be good company.

The episode ends. Papa looks to me. "Another?" he asks.

I set my empty bowl on the table beside me and nod, pulling the comforter up to hug my body.

Twenty-Two
The Not-Date

So," Andy says, brow furrowed. "Is it a date?"

"No," I say. "Definitely not." He looks unconvinced, so I add, "I'm sure it was a figure of speech. We're just doing Leadership tasks together. Like you and I do for Lit." I'm feeling kind enough not to remind Andy that I mostly do our partner Literature assignments myself. "Those aren't dates."

"Hm, Clara Armstrong disagrees."

I give him a dark look, and he laughs. "I told you," I say, folding my hands neatly on the table before me. "Dean and I are friends now."

"That's all?"

I pick at my chipping nail polish. "That's all," I say, and Andy smiles, shaking his head.

There's a part of me that wishes he would press the matter, like Lisa surely would, but he doesn't. The truth is I want someone to analyze Dean's behavior for me, to tell me how to act around him. But that was always Lisa's area of expertise, and it's not like I can reach out to her anymore.

I ignore the tightness in my stomach and return to my laptop. It's Tuesday morning, and we're working on college essays in the library before class, though neither of us has done more than pull up our Google Drives. I decide to be the responsible one and click on the folder titled: college apps </3. Then I switch over to the Sephora tab open on my browser and add a new blush palette I definitely can't afford to my cart.

Two impulse buys later, I look up from my screen. "He told me I looked really pretty," I say. The words come out rushed.

Andy glances at me. "Who?"

"Dean," I say. I twist a lock of hair behind my ear. I've run that moment through my head more times than I care to admit. "Two weeks ago."

Andy nods. "Was it dark?"

I hit him. He grins. "He's going to buy my order today, too," I continue. "At Mellie's." I twist at my hair again, anxious. "That doesn't mean anything, does it?"

"Do you want it to mean something?"

"No," I say quickly. I blink. "I don't know," I say. I let out a huff of air. My relationship with Dean has never been more confusing. After years of professed mutual dislike, it's strange enough to think of Dean as my friend. But then there are those little things that make me question whether that label is exactly right either.

Andy does a cross between a laugh and a sigh. "Try not to overthink." He pulls an apologetic smile. "I'm sorry if I made you overthink."

"Right," I say. I am so overthinking. "It's really nothing. I'm sure everything will be fine," I add, and I try to make myself believe it.

That evening, I read Dragon Witch fan fiction on my phone as I work the Belle's register. It's been a slow day, and I'm getting to a particularly climactic scene when the door jingles. I look up and see Dean at the entrance, dressed in joggers and a navy Abigail Adams High half zip. I straighten immediately, knees knocking on the wood of the counter in my hurry.

He smiles. I wonder if he noticed the blunder. "Hey, Arya."

"Hi, Dean." My knee throbs. I try not to wince from the pain. "You're early," I say, puzzled. I glance at my phone to confirm my words. Sure enough, I have almost twenty minutes left on my shift.

He nods, but he's not looking at me anymore. He's by a window, squinting up at a stained glass portrait of a biblical supper scene. "My mom let me go from the bake shop early. I thought I'd head over," he says. He glances around the rest of the shop, then turns back to me. "I've wondered," he says, "what's with all the Jesus art?"

"We used to be a church." I frown. Mindy usually tells our customers the Belle's origin story. "You've been here before."

"Actually, the reading with Georgia was my first time inside."

"Oh," I say, oddly insulted. "Where do you get your books, then?" Belle's is the only bookshop in Chandler; local competition isn't something we've ever had to deal with. We stock all the school reading lists too, so most Chandler students pay us a visit each fall.

He shrugs. "From Amazon, mostly," he says.

A loud noise sounds from the back room. I turn and find an irate Mindy picking fallen books from the floor.

162

"What was that?" Dean asks, brow furrowed. He's reached the register, so he leans his head to see what's going on behind me.

"You said the *A* word," I whisper. Mindy's hate for Amazon knows no bounds. Her Twitter is full of #BoycottAmazon threads, and she once drove to New York City on short notice to attend a night-long protest outside the billionaire owner's home.

His eyes widen in understanding. "I have been meaning to cancel my Prime subscription," he adds loudly. Mindy's grumbling fades, and I bite back a smile.

The corners of his mouth push up. He rests his arms on the countertop, inches from me. His fingernails look freshly cut.

I step back. "I still have fifteen minutes left on my shift," I say. "We get pretty busy around this time," I add.

There are exactly two other people in the shop. Dean lifts a brow, but he doesn't call me out. "You need some help?" he asks instead. "I could even be your assistant. Little role switch for the day."

"You know I can have you thrown out, right?"

His eyes are bright and mirthful. I wish he wouldn't mill by the register. My fingers feel restless. I open and close the cashbox for the sake of something to do.

"I'll be your customer, then," he says. "What are some Arya Khanna recommendations?"

I stand taller, switching into bookseller mode. "Well, what kinds of books do you usually read?" Provided with a favorite genre or trope, I can usually find something enjoyable for any reader.

"I haven't read for pleasure in a while," he says. He shifts his stance, as if nervous for my reaction, but I'm not judging. "I was a huge fan of Encyclopedia Brown as a kid, though," he adds.

"The boy detective?"

He flashes a smile. "Terrific stories. My dad's favorite too. We would read them together and try to work out each mystery before the reveal."

It's a sweet memory, but I'm still surprised by the admission. Dean doesn't talk about his father much. His dad left when he was young, something I only know because of Ms. Merriweather's membership in the Chandler temple's Divorced Moms Book Club. I've overheard bits of their conversations during my shifts.

"Did you ever figure them out?"

"Not once."

A smile pulls at my lips. I wonder how to phrase my next question and decide to just come out with it. "Do you see your dad much?"

If my curiosity is an overreach, Dean doesn't say so. But I can tell he dislikes the topic by the way his eyes flit away. "Not really," he says. "He and his wife live in Portland. So just on holidays and school breaks."

I nod, and Dean takes the chance to redirect the conversation. "What books have you been reading lately?"

"A lot of historical romances," I answer honestly, and the corner of Dean's mouth quirks. I know he's thinking of the raunchy cover on the book I was reading the last time we met for school, but I refuse to feel embarrassed. "I'm also about to begin my annual *Pride and Prejudice* reread. But you'll have read that already."

Pride and Prejudice is part of our freshman-year English curriculum, and I've reread it every winter since. It's a familiar routine that never fails to bring comfort.

Dean ducks his head, and my eyes narrow. "It was required reading," I remind him. He looks up, guilty eyes, and my mouth drops. "You didn't!"

"I did," he says. He sees the look on my face and rushes to explain. "It was the middle of soccer tryouts, and my mom's bakery was preparing for the anniversary. I had zero spare time, and SparkNotes is a terrific resource."

I shake my head violently. "I can't believe what I'm hearing. This is one of the greatest books in the English language."

He looks unconvinced. "Says who?"

"Says everyone." I shake my head again. "Beyond, like, the social commentary or whatever, it's a blueprint for enemies-to-lovers romance. Plus, the longhand letters are everything."

He raises a dark brow. "Enemies to lovers?"

I don't know why he's fixating on that part of my rambling. "And the letters. I love the letters. *Pride and Prejudice* was originally an epistolary novel, so the letters that made it through to the final draft are incredible."

He frowns. "A-pistol-what?"

"Epistolary," I repeat. It's my favorite Jane Austen fun fact, first gleaned from Mindy. "It means narration entirely through letters and journal entries and the like."

"Ah," Dean says. "So, *Diary of a Wimpy Kid.*"

"I guess." I don't love having my favorite romance novel of all time categorized beside the Cheese Touch book.

"Now, *that* is one of the greatest books in the English language."

I roll my eyes. "Anyway. The letters in Austen novels are so special. *Persuasion* has them too. I just love the idea of someone physically writing down their feelings for another person to read." I feel a little silly for gushing, but Dean is attentive. "I wish people still wrote longhand letters."

He's beginning to respond when Mindy appears at my side. Dean quickly pushes away from the counter. "Taking a break from unboxing," she says. Her bright blue hair is pulled back with a floral headband today, and her nails are still painted a Halloween orange. "Wanted to wish you goodbye."

I am skeptical of these intentions, and my skepticism is confirmed when she turns to smile bright at Dean. "I'm Mindy," she says. "Welcome to our shop. I heard you're a first-timer."

"I don't, um, support Amazon." He nods as he speaks. "For the record." He clears his throat, regaining some of his usual charm and composure. "I'm Dean Merriweather, by the way, Arya's friend from school."

"Yes, I've heard a lot about you." Her smile deepens when Dean's eyes jump to me. My cheeks flush dark. "Bad things, mostly," she says, and now Dean flushes. Mindy seems to be thoroughly enjoying herself. There is an extended pause before she speaks again. "But, more recently, some good things too."

He looks gratified by this, if still a little disconcerted. He looks at me, eyes questioning. I am too mortified to maintain eye contact.

"Would you look at that?" I say to Mindy, false sweetness coating my voice. I gather my things as I speak. "It's already six."

"Time really flies," she says, shaking her head. "You kids work hard," she continues. "Dean, come back soon, okay?"

He makes an incomprehensible sound that is certainly not agreement. I glare at Mindy as I follow Dean out the entrance. She winks in return.

Twenty-Three
Practice Makes Perfect

I tilt my head at the laptop screen. Next to me, Alina makes a horrified sound in the back of her throat.

"No," she says. She shakes her head back and forth like a broken bobblehead. "No, no, no." She squints harder at the footage. "What is my body *doing*?"

It's Thursday morning, and we're practicing for the Sangeet before I have to leave for class. Sheila texted a solo recording of the finalized choreography last night; she and Alina had been unable to get a good shot of the routine while they were together in New York. I'm beginning to understand why. We filmed our first full run-through of the dance and the replay so far has been a total shit show.

"Malfunctioning," I suggest.

Alina ignores me. She pauses the video and wrings her hands. "What am I going to do?"

"Invest in a better sports bra?" This time Alina responds with a shove.

"My boobs are not the problem." She sniffs as I grasp at the coffee table to regain my balance. "Won't be, anyway. My Sangeet lehenga has a very supportive built-in."

I rub my shoulder where it's smarting. "Well, good."

"But the rest of it—" She breaks off to cover her face and groan. "I can't look like that at my wedding." Her voice grows indignant. "And there's no way I'm letting Nikhil win and make us spend our honeymoon at some *beach.*"

I'm torn between sympathy and amusement. Alina is a truly terrible dancer; her movements are somehow both stiff and floppy, and she has zero understanding of rhythm. But I decide she needs some comfort. "You'll get better. There's still a lot of time before the shaadi."

She shoots me a resentful look. "How did you pick it up so quick?"

"Natural talent, I suppose." Alina glares, and I suppress a smile. The truth is Sheila plucked our Sangeet steps from familiar, famous Bollywood dance routines. I didn't need to learn much that was new. "Oh, Alina, I just watch more Bollywood films than you. It's not deep." She's still sulky, so I add, feeling generous, "Besides, I have lots to improve on too."

She nods at this. "That is true. Your footwork was all over the place." She rolls her shoulders back and releases a slow breath. "Okay, I feel better."

I shake my head. "Happy to help."

"Let's play the song?" she says, turning to me. "No dancing, just listen through. I think that might be useful."

"Pay attention to the beat, won't you?"

She elbows me. I switch over to the Spotify window on the laptop to click play on "You Are My Soniya."

I'm still so glad Alina went with my suggestion for our Sangeet number. The song is fun and sexy, as per her requirements, and Sheila chose my favorite section to perform our routine to. I signal to Alina when that interval begins.

Alina loops her arm through mine after the music ends. "Once more," she says. "Music video this time."

This is definitely not a productive use of practice, but I don't feel like denying the request. The music video is pretty fabulous. Alina pulls up the tab. We watch it twice before running through our dance again.

We have a work period in Leadership today. Mrs. Marina definitely meant Leadership work, but I spend the hour editing my Northeastern application instead.

I don't feel guilty, though. Dean and I accomplished a lot during our Mellie's trip Tuesday, and we're planning to meet again next week, so we're very on top of formal prep. A little *too* on top of, even. Dance planning is pretty low-stress now that we have the needed funds. We don't need nearly as many out-of-class meetings as we have planned, but I don't feel like reminding Dean of that.

"Northeastern, huh?" Emilia asks, leaning over my shoulder to look at the screen. I have the English department's faculty list pulled up to try and make my essay on "world-renowned professors" sound less insincere.

"I think," I say. I twist my necklace. "Mostly because I look good in red," I add.

She laughs. "Are you going to apply early?"

"I'm considering," I say, meaning it. I was being glib when I told Andy Northeastern was my top choice all those weeks ago, but more recently, it has become one. "I would only apply early action, though. I'm not sold enough to commit to a binding decision."

She nods, then leans forward, confession-like. "I'm applying early decision to Tufts," she says. "I don't want to jinx myself by telling too many people. You're the seventh to know, so, lucky number. But anyway, I'm submitting my application tomorrow."

"Em, that's so exciting!" I exclaim. "I have so much faith in you." I knock my knuckles against the wood of the desk when her eyes flash with warning.

She seems satisfied with the protective action. "Thanks. I mean, my grades and scores are well within their range, my major's History, so not too impacted, and I think applying early shows how much I like their school, right?"

Her words are rushed and anxious. "Definitely," I say, hoping I sound reassuring. "There's no doubt you'll be a strong applicant." Her eyes flash again, and I knock the desk once more. "No jinx."

"Hey, I was considering Tufts too," Dean interrupts. He's by Lacey, just across the table, but his head was bent over a Chem assignment moments ago, so I didn't know he was listening. "Probably going to apply early to BU, though."

"You heard?" Emilia's tone is stricken. "No, no, that's eight people." Her voice rises. "There's nothing lucky about the number eight!"

Dean looks alarmed. I turn to Em. "Were you counting yourself in the original seven?"

She stops panicking long enough to count. "I think I was," she says slowly.

"There you go," I say. "Crisis averted."

"Actually, I heard too," Lacey says from next to Dean. She pulls a guilty face. "Sorry, it carried over."

Emilia begins to moan again. I give Lacey a look like *Why would you admit that?* She scrunches her face in apology.

"Eight is plenty lucky—" I start, but Emilia cuts in.

"Wait," she says, pulling her hands away from her face. "I was also counting my pastor, and since she's like a messenger of God—?"

"Good point," I say, encouraging. "I don't think she counts."

Emilia sinks back in her seat, relief lining her expression. "I'm going to be so glad when this is all over."

We all murmur agreement before returning to our screens.

Dean waits for me outside the door when the period ends. He's been doing that often this week, walking with me to my next class even when his is in the opposite direction. I try to act like this new routine is the most natural thing in the world, but inside my muscles are turning to Jell-O.

He has pumpkin macarons for us to snack on as we walk, two-day-olds from his mother's bakery. The anniversary of Merri Berry Sweets's opening is this weekend, and Dean has been helping out overtime to prepare for their annual celebration.

"Hey," Dean says when we reach my statistics class. We're dawdling outside the doors, students rushing past on both sides. "You should come. If you'd like."

I raise my brows. "To your mother's party?"

"It's a community event," he clarifies. He scratches his neck, flushed. "Everyone's welcome. Katie and Kevin will be there, and we're thinking of watching a movie in the event room, so it should be fun."

"Oh," I say. "I might have to work," I remember. Sundays are always busy for Belle's. I could probably slip away anyway; Mindy is never too much of a stickler about my work schedule. But on second thought, I don't know if I'll enjoy a whole evening with Dean's friends, none of whom I know very well. "I'll definitely let you know."

He nods, a half smile curving on his lips, and I watch him walk back the way we came, on his way to a class on the other side of campus.

Twenty-Four
Diwali Drama

Diwali falls late this year, on the second weekend of November. Alina and I spend Friday afternoon making a rangoli on our front porch. Rangolis are beautiful floor art designs typically made with bright-colored powder. But we forgot to pick up materials on our last trip to Bharat Bazaar, so we make do with kitchen spices: red from chili powder, yellow from turmeric, white from salt.

I have no artistic ability, so for the most part, I sit back and watch Alina, passing her supplies as needed.

"We'll use these," Alina says when she's finished with the swirly powder design. She holds up a handful of candleholders, each one bright and bejeweled. "To add some more color."

"Good thinking," I say. Normally, we place plain gold diyas in our rangoli. But these vibrant pieces are a perfect complement to the simplicity of this year's design.

I nod at the pink-and-yellow diya Alina is positioning in the center of our finished rangoli. "Is that from our last India trip?" We haven't been back in years, but I remember admiring similar candleholders at a market in Jaipur once.

"Close," she says. "Anthropologie."

Inside, Mamma hums to herself as she works in the kitchen. Three separate pots simmer on the stove, and she breaks from rolling sweet besan ladoos to give each pot a haphazard stir every few minutes, adding imprecise amounts of salt and garam masala to the dishes as she sees fit.

Mamma starts when I turn the sink on to wash my hands. I've been observing for a few minutes, but she must not have noticed.

"I can help with the ladoos," I offer from the sink. Ladoo-making is a very low-skill task, especially since the crumbly dough has already been prepared. There is nothing left to do but roll balls and sprinkle coconut shavings on the finished products. We'll serve them to guests for dessert tonight.

Mamma's expression is anxious but shining. After a moment, she nods. "Be gentle," she reminds me when I dry my hands and move to the counter. She watches as I make the first few ladoos, then turns back to the stove after my work proves satisfactory. She resumes humming, an old Hindi tune I recognize this time.

Diwali might be when my mother is most alive. She's always busy and moving; there is always someone to call, something to cook. But there is also a heavy pressure to functions like tonight's. Hosting is a duty Mamma takes very seriously, but at some point, her role as polished homemaker morphed from truth to presentation. I wonder if she ever fears being caught.

Mamma and I work side by side for the next half hour. I sneak bites of ladoo and coconut when she isn't looking.

I dress in simple white-and-pink salwar kameez for the evening. My chunni is a gold-petal piece that adds grace to the ensemble. I drape it over my right shoulder and fasten with a safety pin, then accessorize with dangly golden jhumke and a choker to match. I'm securing a complementary tikka to my hair (trying to set it so it's not too high up on my forehead but also not falling below my eyebrows), when my phone buzzes with a text from Dean.

I let the tikka drop to my vanity. It's a picture of *Pride and Prejudice,* with the caption: Decided academic honesty matters to me.

My mouth drops. I can't believe he followed through on my book rec. I heart react to the photo and type back: three years late but so proud. I send a string of exclamation marks to really underline my delight.

My phone buzzes again moments later, but Mamma appears at my door and I'm unable to check. She's wearing a royal blue sari and elegant silver jewelry, but her face is bare. Her hand rests on the door frame. "You will do my makeup?" she asks.

I lift my brows, surprised. "You don't want Alina to do it?" Makeovers are Alina's territory, and though Mamma's asked me to help her get ready for events in the past, that was when Alina wasn't home. Now that she is, I wish Mamma would return to convention and try harder to be close to Alina.

But Mamma shakes her head, and since it's Diwali, I don't press her.

Mamma takes my place at the vanity. I shift my tikka to the side of the table for later. "What would you like?"

She lifts her hands. "Zyada kuch nahin," she says. "But very pretty," she adds, which means nothing at all. I interpret it as she wants something glam but understated.

Five minutes in, under the guise of reaching for a new brush, I check my phone. I have two texts from Dean. The first is an eye-roll response to my message, and the second reads: Promise I did not buy from Amazon.

I smile, probably a little too wide and foolish for such a small text, then ask, from Belle's?

He replies in moments: Barnes & Noble.

I write back: baby steps. The typing bubble appears. I tap the side of my phone as I wait for his message.

Then Mamma opens one eye and I jump. "Kya hua?" she asks, impatient.

I am quick to set my phone on the counter. "Sorry," I say. I clear my throat. I hope I'm not blushing. "Left eye is almost done."

Deepti Aunty is the first to arrive. Her husband, Manav, and their daughter, Shruti, follow in the door after her. I haven't seen Shruti since last Diwali, and she's changed her hair since then. It's shorter with layers and streaky caramel highlights.

She hangs back as Deepti Aunty embraces Mamma and Papa before engulfing me and Alina in her arms. "My girls," she says, beaming. "Looking so nice. But, Arya, you still haven't learned to put on tikka correct, no?"

My hand flies to my hairline. I had been really proud of my tikka placement. She laughs joyfully. "Trick is to hide pin beneath the hair. My Shruti has mastered long time back."

I want to retort how I don't plan to take beauty tips from a girl with such a mediocre dye job but bite my tongue. Shruti hasn't done anything to deserve my snark.

Instead, I say, "That's helpful advice."

She looks back at her husband, who's removed his shoes and is now wobbling over to the living room with a large foil-wrapped tray. "Oh, someone must help Manav with this dish. We have brought specially made ladoos for all."

Beside me, Mamma stiffens. Even Alina widens her eyes at the obvious slight. Mamma has supplied our Diwali dinner guests with her homemade ladoos every year for as long as I can remember. It's a tradition she is well known for in our circle of friends.

"So very thoughtful," Mamma says. Her smile is plastic. "But you need not have gone to so much trouble. We have made ladoos here as well."

"No trouble, Nandani, no trouble. These are best ladoos, favorite recipe, only try and see."

Mamma looks like she would rather eat glass. Papa rushes to Manav Uncle's aid, and Deepti Aunty proclaims him her hero.

We take our seats on the living room sofas as we wait for the men to return from the kitchen. Alina crosses and uncrosses her legs. I know she feels unguarded in this company without Nikhil by her side. He's still upstairs, on the phone with his grandparents in Pune to wish them a happy Diwali. She glances to the staircase every few moments.

"Lovely rangoli outside," Deepti Aunty says. "Who is the talented artist?"

Alina lifts her head warily, as if anticipating a trap. "Arya and I made it," she says, voice careful. I pinch her leg at the lie, and she struggles not to flinch.

"But of course. Looking nice, though I must say colors are very plain; we are used to so much brightness. I thought at first this must be unfinished!" She laughs, delighted by her own joke. She quiets and smiles. "You will learn, I am sure."

The conversation shifts, but Alina's expression stays mutinous. "I can't believe I relented and gave her a shaadi invite," she says to me under her breath.

I squeeze her arm, sympathetic. "Everyone makes mistakes."

"Her wedding gift better be fabulous." We clink water glasses to that.

Nikhil walks into the living room then, and Alina sighs

in relief, but his arrival turns out not to be the blessing she wished for. Deepti Aunty takes the opportunity to warn Nikhil and Alina about the dangers of a December wedding and how she was certain the invite listed the date wrong because could anything be worse than snowy weather on their big day, and hadn't they put any thought into the comfort of their guests?

Alina takes to looking toward the front door, praying for the entrance of other families to free her from Deepti Aunty's condescension.

Dean live-texts *Pride and Prejudice* commentary during Pooja. He's at a soccer tournament today, so he's reading in the space between games. Boys' soccer at AAHS doesn't officially start until January, but the preseason scrimmages began last week. Dean's had to watch film with his team during lunch the past few days.

I attempt discretion as I respond, covering my phone screen with my chunni and glancing down as little as possible, but my texting doesn't escape Preeti Aunty's notice. She is Mamma's closest friend in our circle of families and is seated right next to me and Alina.

I am texting back a furious reply to Dean's latest hot take (wish she'd accepted Collins; fuckin love that guy) when Preeti Aunty's delicate, musing voice interrupts me.

"Something more important on your phone than God, beti?" she asks.

I drop my phone in my lap. I wonder how scandalized she would be if I said yes. "Not at all." I fold my hands together and turn to the home mandir.

Pooja drags on for another quarter hour, and then it's time for dinner. I load my paper tray with bhatura, chole, and raita before making my way to the family room, the designated kids' space for the night. I plop down on a cushion next to Nikhil, who's turning *Frozen* on the television for the two twin boys across from him. They are some relation of Rakhi Aunty's, and they are both dressed in matching blue kurtas for Diwali.

Alina leans over and breaks off a piece of my bhatura before I can swat her hand away. "Finished mine already," she explains through a full mouth.

"Get some more, then," I snap. "And get some manners," I add when she wipes her lips with the back of her hand. She makes a face at me in response.

"Don't you feel embarrassed?" I ask. "Sitting here with the children for dinner. You should know that Shruti's drinking chai with the adults in the next room."

"Hush, Arya, the movie's starting." Alina turns to the screen, where young Elsa is shooting snowflakes from her fingertips. Smiling, I get comfy in my cushions and watch too.

We're nearing the halfway point of the movie when Shruti makes an appearance. Nikhil's in the kitchen, getting movie snacks with the twins, so it's just the three of us. "Hi, girls," she says, sounding more like an aunty than someone our age. "It's been way too long."

Alina pulls an almost-believable imitation of a smile. "Shruti, hi."

She leans against the side table and glances at Alina. "You moved back with your parents, right?"

Alina's smile thins as she nods. "Just for shaadi season."

Shruti shudders, like she can't imagine anything worse, and tucks a black-blond lock of hair behind an ear. "I would just *die,*" she says brightly, "if I had to live at home again."

"Where are you staying now, a hotel?"

Shruti's mouth opens and closes. Then she simpers, resembling Deepti Aunty in the most frightening way. "You understand the difference between a weekend and four months, surely."

Nikhil and the twins return before Alina can reply, cradling bowls of popcorn and mithai, and Shruti takes the opportunity to excuse herself, presumably returning to wait on the adults in the next room over.

"Family of monsters," Alina whispers when Shruti's gone. I don't have it in me to reprimand her.

We light more diyas in the backyard after dinner. Alina and Nikhil pose by the flower beds with their candleholders held out in front of them, and I snap pictures before the November wind can blow out the flame.

Unfortunately, Rakhi Aunty notices my photography. "Dekho, Arya is having a photo shoot!" she announces to the whole party. Heads turn to my direction, and Rakhi Aunty beams at me. "Arya, beti, you must take pictures of us all in our saris."

I am stuck taking pictures for the next half hour. I'm relieved from my post only when Rakhi Aunty offers to take a photo of the five of us. As the baby of the group, I stand between Alina and Nikhil, Mamma and Papa flanking.

"Now one with just ladies?" Rakhi Aunty suggests. "Each looking so pretty tonight."

"Looking like three sisters," Papa says generously. Everyone joins in with their assent, and Mamma waves the compliments away, airy and disbelieving, ever the modest hostess.

"You truly are all so similar in appearance," Rakhi Aunty marvels between takes. "I had forgotten just how similar when Alina was away. But you are mirror images."

Mamma stills beside me. She slips back into a camera smile a moment later.

I forget sometimes too, but we do look very alike. Mamma

and Alina, especially. While all three of us have the same dark eyes and sloping cheekbones, they share the same posture, head tilts, manner of speaking. I guess I don't see them side by side enough to always remember.

When we are done, Deepti Aunty requests her own mother-daughter photos with Shruti. They giggle and pose a dozen different ways, and I feel grateful to Nikhil for taking on the photographer role this time. Mamma looks on pensively before turning to face her guests.

"I will use the restroom, then we will have ladoos and sweets when I return, yes?" Mamma says. "Everyone, stay hungry."

Guests laugh and agree and move closer to the firepit. The weather has been nice for November today, but it's dark now and starting to get chilly. Nikhil goes to relight the walkway diyas that blew out while we were busy taking photos.

I use the break to check my messages. I have two new ones from Dean, sent fifteen minutes ago.

Are we supposed to like Darcy

Then, two minutes after the first: Do you like Darcy?

I smile at my phone before I notice Deepti Aunty walking toward me and grimace instead.

"Arya, rani, go inside and bring out ladoos, will you? It is high time for sweets; everyone is wanting. Manav has put them on kitchen counter."

I know she's asking while Mamma is away because she wants her dish to be passed around first, and she's asking *me* because even Deepti Aunty has enough propriety not to personally go against the hostess's wishes. Either Alina or I must be the means to her end, and I have always been much more agreeable than my sister.

The whole aunty social politics of the situation is messy and exhausting, and while I don't plan on aiding Deepti Aunty, I also don't have the energy to put up a fight.

"Sure," I say. I slip past her to the back door, but instead of heading to the kitchen, I go to the stairs. I'll hide out for the next few minutes. I'm nearing my room when I notice the master bedroom light is on.

I wonder what's been taking Mamma so long. I tiptoe over and peer through the door.

She is leaning over her vanity, head down so I can see the gray roots she missed on her last dye job peeking out from the crown of her head. Half a dozen jewelry boxes lay open and discarded on the dresser top, and unzipped garment bags with silk sari material spilling out are strewn over the armchair beside her.

The mess must be from her getting ready process. I didn't know Mamma was so indecisive.

I'm about to enter and let her know what Deepti Aunty requested when her shoulders begin to tremble. She looks up to the mirror and I see she is silent and crying.

I snap away from the door before she can catch me watching in the reflection. I stand still in the hallway, too stunned for further movement.

The last time I saw Mamma cry was on the anniversary of Naniji's death. I can't make sense of her tears this time. Diwali is a day she plans for, a day she awaits. It is the most important event of her social calendar. But maybe it's just that: the need to perform and make merry and lie all night. Alina's presence can't help in that regard, either.

My stomach feels heavy as I walk back to my room. Just then, a loud thump sounds from downstairs, followed by a gasp and a woman's shriek.

I listen from the railing. Alina is apologizing; Deepti Aunty is in hysterics.

"Spoiled, all spoiled," she cries, and Alina issues another, shorter apology. "Oh, what will we do now?"

More voices sound from below; guests must be entering from the backyard. I gather from the comments that there has been a little accident with Deepti Aunty's prized ladoos.

"It's so lucky that we have already prepared dessert," Alina says over the commotion.

Deepti Aunty moans. Somehow her reaction doesn't bring much satisfaction. I enter my room, shut the door behind me, and spend the rest of Diwali alone.

Twenty-Five
This Is Not Zombie *Pride and Prejudice*

Sunday evening, I spend my Belle's shift checking my phone beneath the register. I'm waiting for a reply from Andy. I asked him to come with me to the Merri Berry Sweets anniversary celebration tonight. It begins in a half hour, and I still haven't told Dean if I can make it.

Andy is my last shot to attend the event. I'm not sure I feel comfortable showing up alone, and Emilia is busy babysitting her brothers for the whole day.

It's one of those moments—that have been all too common lately—where I feel the impact of my rift with Lisa so acutely. Lisa has been my automatic plus-one for as long as I can re-member. I hate not having her around, but I also don't have it in me to reach out again, not when she's been so decisive about cutting me out.

Andy texts as I am checking out eight copies of *Erotic Stories for Punjabi Widows* to the leader of a local women's book club. I add a few of our yellow Belle's bookmarks to go along with the order before sliding the bag across the counter.

"Enjoy!" I say. She waves goodbye, and I pull my phone out to check the notification the moment she exits.

My heart twinges. Andy is at a study session for the upcoming Science Bowl and won't be able to make it. I try not to feel too disappointed. Hanging out with Dean was never meant to be on tonight's agenda.

"What's going on, Arya?" Mindy asks. I didn't notice her approach, but she's by the register, flipping through printed photos from past Belle's events. We'll hang the best of the lot on our community board for customers to admire.

I put my phone down. "Oh, nothing," I say. She tilts her head at the lie, so I add, "I was thinking about going to this party tonight? But it's not going to happen. Neither Andy nor Emilia can make it."

She frowns. "How come Andy and Emilia need to go for you to go?"

"I didn't mean it like that." I twist an earring. "It's just—" I stumble. My cheeks feel warm. "It's just that they make me feel more insulated, I guess."

Maybe it's a little pathetic of me, but I worry about how well I'll fit in with Dean's friends. I would hate for them to find me awkward or boring. I would hate for Dean to regret having asked me.

She nods, thoughtful. "And this party—Dean will be there?"

My head snaps up. Mindy is smiling. "You should go, Arya. Sometimes it's good not to be insulated. To be vulnerable instead." She pauses, voice teasing now. "I won't even give you shit for trying to leave early."

"I wasn't trying to leave early," I say quickly.

She gives me a sharp look, and I sit back, caught. "Okay, I was trying to leave early." She rolls her eyes, and I give her a small smile. I know she's not too upset, especially since I picked up an extra shift yesterday. More out of my desire to be away from home post-Diwali instead of my devotion to Belle's, but she doesn't need to know that. "I'll think about it. Thanks, Mindy."

She smiles too, then returns to her stack of photos. "Look at this," she tells me. She lifts a picture of two young customers in Dragon Witch costumes at the Vicky Lane reading. She sighs. "God, this day was lovely. The kids were so cute, it was almost enough to make me wish Cleo and I were parents." She pauses, then grins. "Almost."

I laugh. Mindy has never entertained thoughts of motherhood for very long. Being mom of Belle's Bookshop is all she desires.

We slide the photos away to make room for a new customer, and Mindy tacks her favorites to the board beside me.

Twenty minutes later, I'm walking to Merri Berry Sweets, arms crossed against the cold. I'm wearing a coat over my jumpsuit, but the night is dark and frosty, and goose bumps cover my legs by the time I reach the entrance. I'm inside before I remember that I neglected to rehearse a hello or even tell Dean I was on my way.

Merri Berry Sweets is cozy, toasty, and busy as can be. I feel my legs begin to defrost. Relaxing into my coat, I take a moment to survey my surroundings.

The decor is as welcoming as I remember from Lisa's grade-school birthdays here. Festive lights glitter from the windows, floral centerpieces sit on the dining tables (all of which are occupied), and a painted banner above the pastry counter spells out: CELEBRATING 12 YEARS IN CHANDLER. Jazz music plays over customer chatter, and pictures cover every inch of open wall. It feels more like a home than a business.

I pause at a framed portrait by the side door. It's of a young Dean, front teeth still missing, and an even younger Georgia, likely not yet in kindergarten. They are both in soccer uniforms and have their arms slung around each other.

Someone speaks from behind me. "God, I *hate* that picture."

I jump. I twist around to see Georgia before me, dressed in burgundy overalls for the occasion. Her signature choppy bangs are clipped behind her ears. I wonder if Ms. Merriweather insisted on the hairstyle.

Her brows rise in recognition when she sees it's me. "Oh, hi, Arya. Dean didn't mention you were coming tonight."

There's nothing unkind in her tone, but my stomach twists at the comment. Maybe I shouldn't have come. Maybe it was an offhand, obligatory invitation and I'm foolish for taking it seriously.

I try for a smile. "Bit of a last-minute decision." I pick at the sleeves of my coat. "What's wrong with the picture?"

She shudders. "I'm a *baby*. My mom only hangs up pictures of us from when we were little. Like a shrine to our childhood or something. Have you noticed there's no photos of either of us above the age of ten?"

I take a quick glance around and see she's right. There are newborn photos and first-day-of-school photos, but nothing recent. I make a mental note to document the pics later (future blackmail material) before turning back to Georgia.

"I think it's kind of sweet," I say.

"It's embarrassing. I begged my mom to replace at least one of the diaper pictures with me in my Dragon Witch cosplay, but no luck."

I love the logic that a baby picture is more embarrassing than a picture in costume as a fantasy creature, but before I can tell Georgia so, the side door clangs open. Dean emerges, balancing an empty platter and two pitchers in his hands. He stills when he sees me.

"Hi," he says, something like wonderment in his voice. "You made it."

My lips press into a smile. "Hi." I nod at the dishes in his hands. "Are you on duty?"

He seems to realize he is still carrying tableware and blinks. He rests the items clumsily on the nearby counter. "No, Kevin just eats like a pig." He tilts his head at Georgia. "But *you're* supposed to be on duty. Don't make me tell Mom that you're off task."

Georgia glares at her brother. "I was literally *just* about to go back." She glares again over her shoulder as she hurries to the opposite end of the shop, where customers are crowding around a sample booth. Ms. Merriweather greets patrons a few feet away.

Dean rolls his eyes, moving behind the counter to restock treats, and I take the time to admire the pastry display. There are rows and rows of hand-decorated pies, cookies, and other sweets. A tier of frosted confetti cupcakes sits in the center, and I spot the famous pumpkin tarts from Fall Festival beside a blueberry crumble. The whole space smells of sugar and vanilla and warmth.

"Sorry I'm late," I tell him. I fidget in my coat. It feels too lumpy and big. "And that I forgot to text. I wasn't sure I could make it till just now."

"It's no problem." He uses a pair of tongs to lift a few cupcakes onto the platter. "You haven't missed much. My mom had me helping out until a little while ago. Georgia only took over when the others arrived. But we're nearing closing, so the event room is ours for the night."

I nod even as some of my initial nervousness begins to return.

I twist my necklace and clear my throat. "Twelve years," I say next. "That's so long. You've really grown up in this place."

"Basically," Dean says. Done with the pastries, he shifts to the blackberry iced tea station beside him. "My mom opened the bakery a couple months after my dad left." He must see me start to do the mental math, because his lips twist into a half smile. "I was about five, and my mom was still pregnant with Georgia."

My brows rise. "Wow," I say. I consider the childhood pictures Georgia pointed out earlier, and the decision makes so much more sense given the context. This shop has been the Merriweather family home for twelve years now. "That must have been really challenging for your mom."

"Probably," Dean says. "She never made it seem that way, though. So I try not to be too much of a bother when she asks me to pick up shifts." The snacks are finally ready, so he rests against the counter and looks at me. "Did you get your Northeastern app in?"

It's not the smoothest subject change, but I don't mind. "Not yet. I have another essay to polish. Did you get your BU app in?"

I still have a week left to make my Northeastern deadline, but Boston University's early period closes tomorrow.

"Last night," he says. He seems to relax with the words. He sends me an accusatory look, but his eyes are bright. "It's your fault I almost didn't."

"Well, you're welcome," I say. Dean finished reading *Pride and Prejudice* yesterday and decided to start watching the BBC miniseries adaptation immediately. More live-texting updates followed.

"You know, I suggested we watch the movie tonight," he says. I perk at the information. "Really?" The 2005 Keira

Knightley adaptation is pretty much my favorite English film of all time.

"The zombie version, of course," he clarifies. "But *Iron Man* won out in the end, since Katie's never seen a Marvel movie before."

I should have expected as much. I bite back a smile and try not to feel too disappointed.

"Speaking of," he says. "They're probably waiting on us. Can you grab one of the pitchers?"

I take a pitcher, and Dean takes the other as well as the dessert platter. I follow him to the event room, but he stops when we are at the door, so suddenly, I almost run into his back. Iced tea sloshes in the pitcher. I feel lucky nothing spills over.

"Something I should probably tell you," he says, twisting to look at me. His expression is odd, like he's not sure how to continue.

I furrow my brow. "What?"

"I didn't realize," he starts. The words are hurried. "And once I did, I wasn't even sure you were going to make it." Now he sounds almost defensive. He hesitates again.

My brows draw closer still. "Dean, what?"

The door opens from the inside. My mouth drops. It's Clara Armstrong.

"*There* you are!" Clara exclaims. She must not have seen me yet, because she rushes on. "I wanted to press play without you, but Katie wouldn't let me, so I was coming to find you. You are so slow, God."

She says all of this very fast. Then her eyes narrow on me. "Arya," she says. "I had no idea you were coming."

This seems to be the theme of the night. "Hi, Clara," I say. I try for a convincing smile. "It's been so long."

Her lips thin. "*So* long." She crosses and uncrosses her legs. "I love the jumpsuit. Purple is so your color."

I choose to believe she's being sincere. "Thank you."

We lapse into silence. Clara twists at a curl. I tug on the hem of my sleeve.

Dean coughs. "Shall we?" he asks. He nods awkwardly at the door. "The tea's going to get cold," he adds.

"It's iced," I say.

His ears redden. "Oh," he says. "Yes." He clears his throat and doesn't speak again.

Clara stares at us before rolling her eyes and opening the door. I kick Dean's ankle as we follow her in.

"I was trying to tell you," he whispers. He flattens his hair and grimaces helplessly. "There's more."

I don't have to ask what he means because I see her the moment I enter. Lisa's sitting on a corner couch, feet curled beneath her. She's wearing a basketball hoodie and athletic braids, and she startles the second she sees me.

"Arya," she says. She straightens on the couch. "You're here."

Dread sinks in my chest. Lisa and I have been careful to avoid each other since our parking-lot fight, and this now, with Clara and the others, when I am anxious enough, is hardly an ideal setting for our next interaction. The irony of my longing for Lisa just hours ago and feeling only panic at actually seeing her doesn't escape me. I swallow. "Hey, Lisa."

"What a surprise, right?" Clara says. She's regained some of her composure from the hallway and is settling into the seat beside Lisa. She pushes a curl out of her eyes and looks at me, curious. "But so good to have you. Should we be expecting Andy too?"

There's nothing obvious in her tone, but heat rushes to

my face anyway. Lisa blinks away. I notice Dean still in my periphery.

I draw my coat tighter. "He's at Science Bowl prep tonight," I say. "I'll let him know you say hi, though."

Clara smiles. I set the pitcher on the center table and wish to God I'd listened to my reservations and stayed at Belle's.

Katie Nguyen interrupts the quiet. "Arya, be sure to try the cupcakes. The frosting is *so* good." Then she looks around the room. "Are we good to press play?"

Everyone murmurs their assent, and the lights switch off as the movie begins. I take a paper plate, load it with snacks from the center table, and try to relax. I probably should have anticipated this. Emilia had mentioned Clara and Katie are friends, and Lisa and Dean have known each other since childhood. It's not at all an unexpected guest list.

When I have enough treats on my plate to guarantee a sugar coma, I walk to the seating area. The event space has an almost living room–style setup tonight, with cozy couches bordering the food table and a portable projector presenting the movie onto the blank wall facing us. Katie and Kevin are on one sofa, Lisa and Clara on another. I take the one farthest from Lisa and try to get comfortable for what is certain to be a long night.

Dean sinks down on the cushion next to me a few moments later. There are four pumpkin tarts on his plate. "Hi," he says.

It makes me gladder than I'd ever admit that he decided to sit next to me. "Hi," I say.

"Tony Stark just made it out of the cave," he tells me. He takes a giant bite of tart and whipped cream smears his cupid's bow. He chews before speaking. "In case you're wondering where we are."

"I'm sorry we aren't watching zombie *Pride and Prejudice*," I say, and he ducks his head to hide a smile.

"Night off to a good start?" There's enough care and hesitation mixed in his voice that I guess he has probably been kept very well informed of the status of my and Lisa's relationship. I'd wondered before if he had heard the gossip, beyond what I've told him myself.

I decide to get confirmation. "Do you know?" I ask. I shift in my seat to see him better. "What have people been saying about Lisa and me?"

He picks at a piece of tart. "I've heard—" he starts. His cheeks flush. He clears his throat. "I've heard some things."

I blush at what he left unsaid. I don't think Dean is one to give much credence to Clara's rumors, but it makes me uncomfortable knowing he has heard them at all. I try not to dwell on it.

"Katie invited Clara," Dean adds. "And Clara showed up with Lisa. It wasn't the most planned thing."

I nod. I'd guessed as much. He's quiet, probably waiting for me to speak.

"I hate that we're angry with each other," I say honestly. "She's my best friend and we're not talking. Over something so stupid."

I'm probably oversimplifying; I can't shake the feeling that something deeper than Clara's gossip has caused this rift between me and Lisa, but I don't know how to explain that to Dean. And it feels so silly and juvenile all the same.

He twists a hoodie string. "Right," he says. He clears his throat again. "Stupid."

I smile. I'm glad he isn't pressing the subject more because I really don't want to spend the night talking about Lisa. I take a bite of confetti cupcake and turn back to the screen. The frosting is as delicious as Katie said, sweet and tangy on my tongue.

Dean interrupts the quiet as we near the halfway mark of

the movie. "Something that confused me," he says. "When I finished reading *Pride and Prejudice*."

The topic makes my chest warm. I'm clearly not the only one just half watching the movie. Dean should have campaigned harder for an Austen movie night.

He frowns in thought, searching for the right words. "I guess," he says, "I don't quite understand how Elizabeth goes from hating Darcy to really loving him."

I look up at Dean, surprised but eager at the question. I could talk about this forever. "I think it's the most natural thing, actually."

He raises his eyebrows. "Really?"

I nod. "Yeah," I say, animated. "It's like this: In their first interaction, Darcy makes Lizzy feel insecure. So from there on out, she's predisposed to dislike him. It becomes so much easier to hate him than to get to know him, to risk developing feelings for him."

I stop, worried I'm going further than his interest. But he's watching me with a focused curiosity, so I continue.

"Anyway, since so much of that hate is manufactured, it falls away pretty quickly as she learns more about him." For some reason, my face grows warm as I speak. I clear my throat and pluck at my coat sleeve. "And Darcy does grow a lot in the novel, of course," I add. "Plus, it helps that he's so rich."

It's dark enough that I can't be sure, but I think Dean is smiling. "Okay," he says after a pause. "That was clarifying."

We return to the movie. I finish my first cupcake and start on the second. A few minutes later, there's a shuffle and the screen freezes mid–fight scene.

As the lights flicker on, I look around the room, startled. Lisa and Clara are getting to their feet, zipping purses and retying shoes.

"Sorry, guys," Lisa says, pushing a braid over her shoulder. "Clara and I have morning practice tomorrow, so we're going to get going."

Katie frowns. "Are you sure? There's only fifteen minutes left in the movie."

Lisa purses her lips. "We really should get some rest. Practice has been brutal lately. But this was really fun, guys."

"So fun," Clara agrees.

There's a bit of a bustle to get them out the door. Lisa and Clara wave goodbye to the room, and Lisa doesn't look at me once.

My heart twists. Her excuse was perfectly logical, but I can't help but wonder if the reason Lisa was so intent on leaving early is so she wouldn't have to talk to me again. I lean back in my seat and tell myself I'm just being paranoid.

Dean nudges me. "Hey," he says. The lights are still on, so I can see him clearly, see how little space there is between us. His eyes are dark as he looks down at me. "I'm really glad you came."

Something inside me relaxes at the admission. "I am too," I say, and as the words leave my lips, I realize I mean it.

Twenty-Six
Blame Game

I push my batata vada around on my plate. Batada vada is Nikhil's favorite Marathi snack, and I decided to take him up on the recommendation today. The crispy potato fritters are delicious, everything at Chai & Chaat always is, but I don't have much appetite somehow.

Alina and I are taking care of a few smaller shaadi tasks this afternoon. The wedding is only a month away, and the Khanna household has been working around the clock to get everything prepared. We had a minor scare last week when the florist sent us an invoice for the wrong-color flower garlands, but a single phone call resolved the issue. Everything has been going smoothly otherwise. Alina has even invited Mamma to all the major planning sessions.

Too smoothly, maybe. I frown as I take a sip of masala chai. I instantly regret it. The drink is still scalding hot.

"How's your chai?" Alina asks. She's halfway through a plate of dahi papdi chaat, the same order Andy and I got the last time we were here. She sucks some green chutney off the tip of her thumb.

"Great," I say. I take a bite of cold yogurt to soothe my tongue. "Yours?"

She stares, a frown starting on her lips too. "Great," she says. She sits straighter in her seat. "This decor is beautiful, right?"

I have to nod. We're in a window seat, so we have a clear view of both the café and street decorations. Chai & Chaat still has diyas and rose petals up from Diwali, and as it's mid-November, Chandler's downtown has begun holiday setup as well. Gold lights spiral up lamp posts and holly-ribbon wreaths glimmer from storefronts. The most beautiful time of year.

"Truly," I say.

For some reason, Alina sets her cup down on the table with a clang. "What is going *on* with you?"

I draw back, surprised. "What do you mean?" I ask, brows furrowed.

She huffs. "I mean we've been here twenty minutes and you've barely spoken a word even when prompted." Her frown deepens. "This whole week, really, we've barely spoken a word."

I pick at my batata vada because I can't play dumb to the second charge she's laid against me. I haven't been right around Alina since Diwali. I can't explain it, exactly, but something about seeing Mamma in that state resurfaced my resentment for Alina. I've been avoiding her for days to prevent a fight. If not for maid of honor duties, I would have skipped our chai date too.

I take a deep breath and opt for honesty. "I've been thinking a lot about Mamma," I say finally.

Alina's eyes widen. This is clearly not the response she anticipated. "Oh," she says. She takes a sip of her chai.

"I think she's been really unhappy lately. More so than usual." I hesitate. I don't want to tell Alina specifics about Diwali night because that would be sharing something I wasn't even meant to witness. I pluck at a loose thread on my sweater sleeve. "I guess that's just been weighing on me."

Her face crinkles in understanding. "Oh, Arya." She reaches across the table to squeeze my hand. "You know it's not your responsibility, right? To make her better?"

"It's not about responsibility." For some reason, her sympathy is so frustrating. "And it's not like I'm blaming *myself.*"

I don't mean to emphasize the last word, but I must, because Alina jerks her hand away. She looks wounded, but I'm too tired to be sorry.

She twists her ring. "Got it," she says. Her voice is icy.

"I just mean . . ." I say. I lick my lips. "You were gone for three years. That had consequences."

I'm probably being unfair, and I'm definitely oversimplifying, but this is a conversation I've put off with Alina for far too long. Diwali was just more evidence.

Her eyes flash. "I was gone for three years because Mamma all but kicked me out for leaving school."

There's bite to her words, but they still fall flat, and we both know it. Mamma feels and speaks in extremes, but Alina could have returned anytime she wanted. Pride, self-regard, love of independence all worked to keep her away.

"And I don't regret it," she continues. She looks at the window. "Leaving was best for me, for my career, and for my mental health."

I can't help the scoff that escapes my throat. "It's really not the girlboss, self-care move you think it is to be that selfish. It's good to be conscious of how your actions affect others, actually."

Her expression grows righteous and angry. "Get off my back, Arya. Mamma has always been like this. Nothing is new."

"She's been sadder in the last few years," I say. Alina opens her mouth to reply, so I add, "And I would know."

Alina presses her lips closed, falling silent. Finally, she says, with an air of forced calm, "It's really wrong of you to put all this on me. But I don't want to argue with you. Let's please talk about something else."

I sink back in my chair. I think I have been unreasonable, because the harder truth is that there is no obvious reason for Mamma's sadness. And it's so much easier for me to be angry at Alina on Mamma's behalf than on my own. I let out a long breath, but some tightness remains in my belly. "Fine," I say.

Relief crosses her face. She wraps her hands around her mug for warmth. "So, how are things with Lisa?" she asks. "She still hasn't RSVP'd, and the deadline was last week."

The tightness in my stomach grows as I remember movie night. I feel certain Alina chose this topic of conversation on purpose. I roll my shoulders back and hope I appear composed. "Put her down as a yes. I'm sure she's just been busy with the tournament season starting."

Alina tilts her head curiously. Before she can ask a follow-up question, I say quickly, "How's the painting coming? Your deadline's in two weeks, right?"

It's payback for the Lisa question, and Alina scrunches her nose in irritation. The truth is Alina has spent the last week demanding quiet from the whole family as she locks herself in the garage to work. Then she retweets baking videos for the next hour before abruptly leaving the house for one of her "creativity walks." I have never seen her return from these without a Starbucks and at least two shopping bags in hand.

"Really good," she says. "I've made a lot of really good progress." She suddenly pushes her plate aside. "Are we good to start shaadi things? I'm mostly done eating."

I stuff a piece of batata vada in my mouth before setting my plate to the side as well. "Works for me."

"Great," she says. She ducks down to fiddle in her bag and resurfaces with a heavily sticky-tabbed bridal magazine and two dark pink lipsticks. "First things first," she says, flipping through the magazine to find the page she's looking for. "We need to pick my lip color for Haldi."

The Haldi ceremony is the portion of Hindu weddings where family and friends coat the bride and groom in yellow powder from head to toe. Alina's makeup will barely be visible for this event, but I don't have the heart to remind her.

"I know, I know, I can't believe I'm finalizing this so last-minute," she continues, still searching for the page. "But I've been swamped." She sighs with satisfaction as she finds what she's looking for. She angles the magazine toward me so I can see the two lipstick shades as worn on Desi models. She quickly swatches the colors on her wrist as well. "Which?"

They are identical, but I deliver my opinion with conviction anyway. "Definitely the left."

She beams. "Good answer."

I click submit on my Northeastern app later that evening. It's been finished in my drafts for two days, but I hadn't had the courage to turn it in. It's dark out, and everyone is already done eating by the time I decide I have proofread my final essay (a two-hundred-word piece on my time at Belle's) as much as humanly possible. Digital confetti fills my screen once the application is on its way.

Smiling, I take a screenshot of my submission confirmation and text it to Andy, Emilia, and Dean. They respond within seconds with varying numbers of exclamation marks.

Then I slip out of my seat and walk down the hallway to Mamma's room. My stomach is growling, but I want to see her before I go to eat.

"Hi," I say when I'm in the doorway. She looks up from her

bed, where she's lying on her stomach, watching a Pakistani serial on her laptop. "I applied to college," I announce.

She pauses her episode. "Very good," she says.

"I sent in an early application." I shrug like it's no big deal. "Most people are still drafting essays."

I can tell this impresses her. She raises her eyebrows and nods. "Very good, Arya," she says again.

I take two steps forward, then stop. "Can I—" I falter. I clear my throat and try again. "What's happened so far?" I nod to her open laptop.

Mamma looks surprised at the question, but she answers after a short pause. "Fawad is about to get married," she says. "But he does not know Zara is in love with him, as Fawad's mother has torn Zara's letter."

I bite back a smile at the predictable storyline. I've only seen one episode of this show, weeks ago when Nikhil forced me and Alina, but it's all going like I expected.

I step forward again. "Can I watch with you?" The question comes out tentative.

Mamma moves the duvet to make room for me. I climb in, sitting up on my elbows to see the screen better.

It's not my responsibility to make Mamma better; Alina was right in that regard. And whatever my own messy feelings toward Alina, I know it's not hers either. But beyond taking care of Mamma, I do still want to be closer to her. Just for myself. Diwali brought me that much clarity.

Mamma tilts an open bag of dried mango slices toward me. "We have not watched like this in a very long time," she says.

It's just an observation; there's no bitterness in her tone. But my eyes feel hot all of a sudden because I know it's largely my fault.

"Too long," I say after a beat, and Mamma smiles. We munch on the treats as we watch.

Twenty-Seven
Popcorn and Poetry

My music cuts abruptly. I lift a hand to touch my left ear and realize it is bare. I turn to see Dean holding one of my wireless headphones in his hand.

"Did you know Antonin Scalia wanted the government to kill kids?" he says.

It's Sunday afternoon, and Dean and I are supposed to be working on formal tasks at Mellie's. The dance is officially less than a week away, and we have some last-minute items to check off our to-do list. For my part, I've been online shopping for the perfect heels to match the red velvet dress I picked out weeks ago. I'll have to expedite shipping, but it's an important cause.

I tilt my head. "I thought you were working on patron thank-you notes." Our dance decor and refreshments are generously sponsored by local Chandler businesses, and Dean is responsible for lavishing our gratitude so that they feel inclined to support us again next year.

"I finished most of them," he says. "So I started studying for our Civics exam. Then I fell down a Wikipedia rabbit hole."

I smile. I'm in no position to judge; I've been distracted all afternoon. Alina texted me a while ago about having a movie night since we'll have the house to ourselves this evening— Papa's working late, Mamma's having dinner with Preeti Aunty, and Nikhil's meeting college friends in Boston. Normally, I would be down, but a sister movie night really interferes with my commitment to steer clear of Alina until I can sort out my thoughts toward her.

There's only so long I can avoid her. She's been trying to make plans since our Chai & Chaat date a few days ago. I keep blowing her off, but I'm terrible at excuses. Last night, I told her I couldn't grab dinner because I needed to work on college apps about two minutes before Papa congratulated me on turning Northeastern in. I had to invent two new schools I'm applying early to in order to leave the conversation unscathed.

"Hey," Dean says. I startle and look up. He frowns, forehead creasing. "You good?"

"Sorry," I say. I clear my throat. "Spaced for a minute. What was that about Scalia killing kids?"

Dean turns back to his laptop, reading from the screen. "*Stanford v. Kentucky,*" he says. "1989. Scalia thought the death penalty should be allowed on minors."

"That tracks," I say. My Civics class readings have brought me more insight into the late justice as well, all of it ugly.

Dean nods, and then, like it's the most natural thing in the world, he pushes my headphone into his ear and presses play.

Thomas Rhett's deep, sweet voice fills my right ear. Dean smiles at the music choice. I can't keep a blush from starting. I turn back to my laptop and try to focus on shoe shopping.

Sharing headphones isn't a big deal; friends do so all the

time. But it's just more proof of how comfortable Dean and I have grown around each other in the past few weeks.

Mellie's with Dean is now an expected part of my routine. Usually with the object of getting Leadership work done, but sometimes for no real purpose at all. On Thursday, Chandler had its rainiest day of the season yet, and I mentioned to Dean how soothing Mellie's peppermint teas are in wet weather. So we went over after class and split a slice of pumpkin cake before Dean drove me home.

Dean drives me home again today. It's only drizzling, but his windshield wipers are on the highest setting. I try not to stress about alone time with Alina on the ride over.

It takes less than ten minutes to reach my house. He pulls into the driveway, then looks at me. "I'll see you tomorrow?"

I tighten my raincoat around me. "See you." I'm turning to go, but my fingers linger on the door handle. I think of Alina waiting for me and look back at Dean. "Actually," I say. I lick my lips. "Do you want to come inside?"

We open the door to a mess. Cardboard boxes and packing paper covers every inch of carpet; Alina appears to have unloaded the entire storage closet onto the living room floor.

I pause in the doorway and frown, fingers still clutching my keys. "Are we moving?"

Alina peeks out from behind a box in the corner. What looks like a piece of tinsel clings to her neck. She pushes a sweaty lock of hair out of her eyes with the back of her hand. "Hey," she says. "You're home."

I lift my eyebrows at the scene. "What's all this?" I ask.

"Oh," she says happily. "Just taking out the holiday decorations." Then her eyes slide over to Dean. "You've brought a friend."

"I thought Dean could join us for the movie," I say casually. I slip off my shoes and coat by the door, and Dean follows suit. "That cool?"

Alina looks a little too glad at the arrangement for my comfort. "Of course," she says. "It's so nice to finally meet you, Dean."

I hope Alina's emphasis on "finally" escapes Dean's notice. I pull at the hem of my sweater, concern rising. I invited Dean as a buffer and I'm hoping the decision doesn't backfire.

"Thanks for having me," Dean says. He has his class-president charmer voice on. I smile at the thought of meeting Alina warranting the tone switch. "I've heard so much about you."

Alina glows. "Likewise," she says.

I jump in before either can ask a follow up. "Why the holiday decor?" I ask Alina. "I thought you were spending the day painting."

She sniffs and plucks off the tinsel stuck to her neck. "Well," she says, "I figured this was more time-sensitive. It's mid-November, and we still haven't put anything up."

I bite back a smile. The clutter makes a lot more sense now.

She jumps up from her seat on the floor. "But that can wait now that you guys are here. Dean, have you ever seen a Bollywood movie?"

"Never," he says. "I'd like to, though," he adds.

"You're in for a treat, then," Alina says. She stirs at the word. "Speaking of," she says, tightening her ponytail, "let's go get snacks ready. I've been dreaming about the wedding cake leftovers from our sampling session all afternoon."

I glance at the cardboard boxes still strewn across the floor, some half-opened with ornaments and tangled lights spilling out. "What about the mess?"

She gives a half-hearted shrug. "Nikhil will be home soon enough," she says, disappearing into the kitchen.

Dean starts on some stovetop hot cocoa (using a Merri Berry Sweets secret recipe) while Alina and I get the microwave popcorn ready. I'm emptying a freshly popped bag into a large porcelain bowl when Alina nudges me.

"He really is cute," she says. Her voice is not quite a whisper. "Just like you said."

Heat climbs in my cheeks. Dean is bent over the stove, so I can't be positive, but I think a smile is pushing at his mouth.

"Alina," I hiss. "Will you not. He can hear every word."

She grins wickedly. "That," she says, pulling the bowl of popcorn toward her. A few kernels drop to the floor, and she doesn't bother to pick them up. "Is the whole point."

We decide on *Kabhi Khushi Kabhie Gham,* a three-and-a-half-hour-long romantic saga with questionable takes on filial duty and a woman's role in marriage. But we pulled Alina's Sangeet song from the film's unmatched soundtrack, so it's pretty much required pre-shaadi viewing.

I pause the movie every ten minutes to make sure Dean is following along. Alina swats my shoulder the next time I do so.

"I'm pretty sure he can read," she says.

"It's true," Dean confirms. He's sitting lazily on the opposite couch, feet reclined on an ottoman, so he has to lean back to make eye contact. "I can."

"The subtitles don't quite carry the same poetry," I huff, but I sink back into my pillows anyway.

Alina's mouth twitches. "Poetry?"

Onscreen, in one of the most loved and recurrent Bollywood tropes, the heroine's cheeks flush as she tries to untangle her jewelry from where it caught in the hero's dupatta while dancing.

"This is literally as poetic as it gets," I say. I straighten in surprise when Dean and Alina laugh together in an unexpected and, frankly, upsetting display of kinship. "Don't get too comfortable," I say. "We're watching a sobfest of a movie."

Dean looks stricken at my announcement. "What do you mean?" He glances between me and Alina. "I've been having a good time."

I take a bite of raspberry-chocolate wedding cake. It's a few days old, and Alina and Nikhil rejected it, but it's still rich and sweet on my tongue. "Well," I say, "keep watching."

Alina rolls her eyes. "It's not that bad," she says. "Arya's being dramatic."

Dean seems to relax. "That would be consistent," he says.

I shoot him a dark look. He hides a smile behind his mug of cocoa.

Everyone is crying by the time the credits roll. Dean and I are more delicate about it, turning our cheeks and swiping tears as they fall, but Alina is beyond composure.

She blows her nose loudly on some Kleenex. "So," she says. Her eyes are puffy and wet. "Karan Johar needs to pay for my therapy."

I have too much empathy to tell her *I told you so.* "And mine," I say. It's maybe my twentieth time watching this film and it's never gotten any easier.

Dean shakes his head. "I don't understand," he says. His face is dry now, but his nose is still red. "Why did it take the grandma dying for the dad to finally tell his son he loves him?"

"Because the dad sucks," Alina says fiercely. "Evil personified." Strength returns to her with the statement. She wipes her cheeks and clears her throat. "If you'll excuse me, I need some more cocoa after this," she says. Picking up her mug, she heads for the kitchen.

Dean and I are alone. I turn to him, but he's typing something on his phone, brow creased in a frown.

"Hey," I say, and he looks up. "Everything okay?"

He tries for a smile, but his features don't quite relax. "Yeah," he says. "Totally." He clears his throat and stretches a long leg out. "I should probably get going, though. It's getting a little late."

I glance at the clock and notice with some wonder that it's already half past seven. Dean and I have accidentally spent the whole day together.

"Sure," I say. "I'll see you out."

We head for the door, Dean typing away on his phone while he walks. Alina's holiday decor is still strewn about the carpet, and we are careful to maneuver around the sharp ornaments and tangled string lights. My chest warms when I realize that my buffer plan was successful—because of Dean's presence, I avoided solo interaction (and by extension, further conflict) with Alina. I even had *fun* with my sister for the first time since Diwali.

Dean slides his phone into his pocket when we reach the entrance, but his expression is still troubled, so I pause. "Are you sure everything's all right?"

He starts to nod, but I must look concerned, because he sighs and relents. "I was kind of supposed to go to a soccer thing today," he admits. "A pasta feed. My absence caused a little fuss in the group chat."

"Oh," I say, struck by the information. "You should have said something. We could have postponed."

He shakes his head. "No," he says. "It's okay. Really. I don't even like pasta."

"Everyone likes pasta," I say.

He laughs. He scratches his cheek. "No," he says again. "I wanted to be here." He pauses, and his voice is gentle when he speaks next. "You asked me to be here."

I blink twice. And then, before I can overthink it, I stand on tiptoes to wrap my arms around him. He goes still with surprise for a moment, but then his arms come around to rest at the small of my back. His neck smells impossibly good, like rain and bakery sugar.

I draw away a second later, almost embarrassed by how affected I am. My cheeks are growing warm, so I fold my hands together and take a step back for good measure. "I hope you liked the movie," I say finally, like nothing about that was out of the ordinary.

He swallows, and I follow the movement in his throat. "Yeah," he says after a beat. "I did." He runs a hand through his dark hair. "Tell Alina it was great to meet her," he adds, and then he's reaching for the handle and is out the door.

Twenty-Eight
'Will You Dance with Me?

O n formal morning, Nikhil makes waffles for brunch. He can't help much in the beauty department, so this is his way of making the day special.

I slice strawberries and spread Nutella over my dish, and Alina dunks each bite in melted butter and nothing else.

"You eat like a caveman." I watch, horrified and yet unable to look away as Alina dips a forkful of waffle into the butter.

She speaks through a full mouth, waving her fork in the air. "It's called taste."

"Caveman," Nikhil agrees.

Upstairs, Alina spreads her makeup and brushes out on the counter. I sit on the bathtub edge, like I did before the Roka, as she gets products prepared. She volunteered to do my glam today, and it was easy enough to accept. Whatever my feelings toward her, Alina is far more talented with makeup than I am, and nothing is more important than my vanity.

"Tell me what you want," Alina says.

It's only noon, but I have to be at Emilia's by three, and I'm picking up Andy on the way over. Besides, getting ready is my favorite part of formal day. I always like to extend the process.

"Glowy and bronzy," I say, and she gets to work.

An hour later, I study my reflection in the mirror. My eye makeup is shimmery and just the right amount of smoky, and my cheeks are a dewy bronzed pink.

"I love it," I say, turning my face to see the look from all angles. "It's perfect."

Alina looks pleased. I spritz my face with some all-nighter setting spray to lock the product in since I've still got hours until the dance.

After I've curled my hair, slipped into my dress, and accessorized, Alina beams at me.

"You look radiant," she says. "I can't believe I'm sending my baby sister off to formal."

I laugh, but something tightens in my chest. Alina hasn't been home for any of my formals; the last time she helped me get ready for a school dance was in eighth grade. It feels odd to have her with me today.

Papa takes pictures of me in our backyard before I leave to pick up Andy. He never changed the default settings on his phone, so the camera shutter sounds off each time he clicks a photo.

"My movie star beti," he says between takes. "Makeup is looking so nice."

"I did it!" Alina chimes in, never one to miss out on credit.

When I've been posing for ten minutes, I remind Papa, "I'll be taking a million more pictures at Emilia's." My cheeks are starting to hurt. "Are you almost done?"

"Take some with me now," he says. "I will upload to Facebook."

I hide a smile at this. Papa passes his phone to Alina and comes to stand with me by his flower bed.

"You spoke with your mamma?" he asks me.

I stopped by the living room where she was watching her favorite serial on the TV to show her my outfit before heading to the backyard. "Dress is too revealing," she said, meaning that the neckline exposed my collarbone. It was as kind of a response as I could have expected.

"I did," I say. "I think she liked the dress."

"Good," he says.

"I want some photos too," Alina says when Papa and I are finished.

"Alina!" I groan, stomping my foot. I'm acting like a child, but I'm beginning to get frustrated. Somehow, despite getting ready so early, I am about to be late to Emilia's.

"You're pretty today because of me," she says. "Be more grateful."

Twenty minutes pass before I'm able to leave the house. Nikhil and Mamma come out to take pictures too. Mamma applied lipstick and draped a shawl just for the occasion, so I don't dare complain.

I promise to text updates and wave goodbye through the car window as I drive away.

Andy and I arrive at Emilia's at a quarter after three. I park across the street, and we head straight to her backyard, the way she instructed.

I've been to the Lopez home for a few of Emilia's birthday parties before, and the backyard is as spacious and gorgeous as I remember. Today, balloon bunches mark the photo area, string lights line the fence, and paper lanterns glimmer from fruit trees. Self-serve food tables are set up along the back porch too.

My mouth waters at the smell; we all pitched in to get catering from a local Italian restaurant.

Emilia clicks over to us in strappy heels moments after we enter. "You're here!" she exclaims.

"Hi, Em," I say, pulling her in for a quick hug. I am careful not to mess up our hair. "Everything looks so beautiful." I stare. "*You* look so beautiful."

Lighting in the pictures she sent must have been off, because the dress is not as outrageously bright as I had been led to believe. Instead, it's a more muted orange that complements her brown skin. She's wearing simple jewelry and cherry-red lipstick that somehow really works with the look.

Her mouth drops. "Was that *surprise?*"

Andy winces. I scrunch my face, apologetic. "You prepared me for surprise!"

She deflates. "Yeah, well, I didn't try it on till today. I might not change into the replacement dress after all."

"Your boobs look really good in that one, though." The replacement dress is a slinky gold piece that I definitely want to borrow one day.

She purses her lips, thinking. "That's true. I'll consider." She beams. "Anyway, help yourselves to the food and drinks. We'll do group pictures in a half hour. I'm going to go say hello to the other guests." She does an excited clap and smiles deeper. "I love playing hostess."

Emilia hurries off to greet Lacey and Meena, who arrived right after Andy and me. About a dozen people are invited today, and I know most of them only distantly.

We head to the food table. "Is Emilia going to formal with anyone?" Andy asks as we begin to load pasta and salad onto our paper trays.

I glance at Andy, but he's focused on unsticking two pieces of garlic bread. "No," I say. "Just the group, I think."

It's not unusual to go to formal stag; the majority do. The last time I had a date was freshman year. Siddharth Choudhoury, a boy from my English class, asked me two nights before the dance by replying to one of my Instagram stories with: Hey u free 4 formal. I said yes because I once saw him use the compost bin. Most people threw their banana peels into the garbage.

I hadn't known how to reply, so Lisa typed a response for me. It was something simple but flirty that I could never have come up with on my own. My heart tightens at the memory. I have never taken formal pictures without Lisa, and I want her here with us. But I haven't seen her since the night at Merri Berry Sweets. I wish we could have a do-over reunion. I wish we could have a do-over, period.

Andy doesn't ask a follow-up question, and I don't continue the subject. After filling our plates, we sit on the chairs set up on the grass and fall into conversation with Candace Lee and Nick Casey, who are sitting nearby. I pull out my phone to check social media when the talk turns to *Game of Thrones* conspiracy theories.

Katie Nguyen just posted a picture to her story of her manicure and corsage against Dean's suit. My stomach twists. I click on the tag and scroll through Dean's profile.

"What are you doing?" Andy asks, leaning over to check my phone. He sees the screen before I can click away. He raises his eyebrows, and embarrassment churns in my stomach. "You guys get in another fight?"

"No," I say quickly. "Actually, um. There was kind of a moment."

His brows go higher. "A moment?"

"I think so." Our goodbye after the movie has been in the back of my mind all week. It's probably just the Bollywood fangirl in me—sensual hugs are the romantic climax of so many of my favorite films, after all. But I can't help but think it meant something deeper all the same.

I push the thought away. I shouldn't make myself even more nervous before I see Dean at formal tonight. "I'll tell you the story later."

"Later," he agrees.

We arrive at the venue just before seven. Familiar anticipation grows in my stomach as we show our tickets and enter the hall. But it's mixed with some melancholy too. Autumn formal has always been one of my favorite days of each school year. It's hard to believe this is my final formal.

Colorful lights dance around the otherwise dark room, illuminating the lovely decor job our team did, and throwback music blasts from the speakers. The first songs of the night are always the biggest hits from the current senior class's freshman year at AAHS. It's one of my favorite traditions. Right now, a Taylor Swift anthem that Emilia clearly loves is playing.

"Let's go!" she shouts over the music. She pulls me with one arm, Candace with another, toward the dance floor.

I look over my shoulder for Andy, but he and Nick are already by the dessert bar. We just ate, but I guess it's a smart move to grab the best treats before everyone else gets to them.

The center of the dance floor is so hot, sweaty, and packed with bodies that it is the place I usually spend all night avoiding. But Emilia is excited, and it's my last school formal. A few songs can't hurt.

Twenty minutes later, my dress is rumpled, the curls I spent so long perfecting are a flattened, tangled mess, and I'm pretty sure a sophomore grabbed my ass at some point during Panic! at the Disco's "High Hopes."

Worst of all: "My boobs are sweating," I mumble to Emilia.

"What?" she yells over the music. We're inches apart and somehow she still can't hear me.

"My boobs are sweating!" I yell right as the song begins to fade. A few junior boys hear and glance my way. I'm too disgruntled to feel embarrassed. "I'm going to head to the bathroom!" I point in the direction of the ladies' in case she misses my words again, and she nods.

I pass Dean on my way to the restroom. I haven't seen him all night, and I'm glad to have a quiet, unnoticed moment to survey him. He's by the dining tables, laughing at something Kevin Chang is saying. He looks particularly handsome tonight. His dark hair is styled in his signature messy-on-purpose way, and he's dressed in a black suit with a red boutonniere that matches Katie's dress.

And mine, I realize belatedly. I shake the thought off and slip away before he sees me; I probably look like a sweaty mess.

A group of freshman girls are exiting the bathroom as I enter. Looking in the mirror, I smooth down my skirt, adjust the pins in my hair, and touch up my makeup. Then I go pee.

Lisa is at a sink when I exit my stall. She must have come in while I was inside. Our eyes meet in the mirror, surprise registering on both our faces. Of all the girls here tonight, we had to be the only ones in the bathroom at the same time.

She speaks first. "Hi, Arya." Her mouth pulls into something resembling a smile. Or maybe a grimace.

"Hey, Lisa." I swallow, walking to the sink farthest from her. I rest my clutch on the counter and wash my hands. It's silent but for the running water, and I can't stand it. I take a deep breath. "You look really pretty. That dress is your color."

It is. She's wearing a teal slip dress I don't recognize, meaning she must have bought it for this year's formal. This might be the first time Lisa's bought an outfit for a dance without consulting me. Even in middle school, when she went shopping with her mother, Lisa would call me from changing rooms to get my opinion.

"Thank you," she says. Her smile is more genuine this time, if still a bit stiff. "You look really nice too."

"Thanks." We fall quiet. I dry my hands, something nervous building in my chest. Maybe it's the silence, maybe it's that we're meeting at formal, the very cause of our conflict, but something makes me blurt out: "I need you to know. There was never anything between me and Andy."

Lisa stares for a second, then scoffs, the sound sticking in her throat. "Arya," she says, and her voice is the verbal equivalent of an eye roll. "*Obviously.*"

My brows knit together. This is so not the reaction I anticipated. If not for the rumors—"Then why—?"

"If we're doing this now," she draws out, "it was never about that for me. It was about how you chose Andy even when you knew how much he hurt me. Even when you knew that I needed you more."

Struck, I pull back. "I didn't *choose* Andy," I say weakly, but I'm trying to play it back, and it all feels so much messier in rearview.

"I'm over it now," she continues, though her eyes look shiny. "It just sucked in the moment." She sniffs and raises her chin higher. "Have a good night, okay?" she says, and then she's brushing past me.

The door swings shut. My throat is thick. There's so much more I want to say to Lisa, so much we have to talk through, and it's hitting me now it'll all have to start with another, larger apology. I was so concerned with trying to ensure the breakup didn't derail my senior year that I glossed over how severely Lisa was still going through it. How hurt she truly was.

There's nothing I can do at the moment, so I take a deep breath and smooth down a crinkle in my dress. I'll reach out to Lisa again after formal, and we'll set things right. We have to.

Assurance growing, I exit the bathroom. A country song is ending. I'm still shaken, but the slightest smile touches my lips. Dean must have gotten his way after all.

I make it to Emilia right as Meena Mukerji and Kevin Chang are announced as this year's formal royalty. Cheers fill the hall, and then a throwback pop hit begins to blare, overpowering the applause.

"Come on!" Emilia beams, looping her arm through mine.

I hesitate before giving in and joining her. Lisa isn't with me now, but it's like the night of the Roka once more. I have a lot to sort through tomorrow. For now, we shout familiar lyrics and dance, loose and carefree, to song after song.

Half an hour later, I sink into a chair in the dining area, exhausted but not in a bad way. Emilia is still on the dance floor, somehow not out of energy. I can see her from my seat; she stuck with the bright orange dress. But my feet are killing me; these heels, though worth every cent, are too delicate for excessive dancing.

"I'm going to get something to eat," I tell Andy and Nick, who came off the floor with me. They nod, and I head over to the dessert bar. Most of the good choices are gone, but I manage to get a lemon cupcake, a fancy chocolate pudding cup, and the last can of cherry cola.

I'm grabbing a napkin when I notice Dean sitting alone at a table by the dance floor. He must have just gotten there. I didn't see him earlier.

After the night I've had, Dean might be a pleasant distraction. Another moment of hesitation, and then I'm walking over. "Hi," I say.

"Hi," he says. His eyes linger on the skirt of my dress. He reaches a hand over to slide a chair out for me, and I take the seat.

"Pudding?" he says, nodding to my plate. It's clear he doesn't think very highly of my dessert choice.

"It's all that was left," I say.

He reaches across the table to pluck the cherry from the top of my cup. He smiles when I don't stop him. "There were brownies earlier," he says after he's done chewing.

"How were they?"

"I've had better."

I pick at the cupcake wrapper because I'm pretty sure I'm blushing. I swipe some buttercream frosting off with my index finger to taste. It's sweet and tangy on my tongue.

"We did great with formal," I say. "All those Mellie's trips really paid off."

I mean to sound glib, but the corner of his mouth quirks up. "Truly," he says. "We should have worked together all along."

"We could have, if you'd been nice all along."

He rolls his eyes, but he's smiling. "All I ever did was return your energy, Khanna."

This is a downright lie, but I let it slide.

The music changes. It takes only seconds for me to recognize a slow song is starting. I wish the night would last longer; slow songs typically are the last songs played at formal. The crowd on the dance floor starts to split into couples, with some larger groups dawdling together on the edges of the space.

"Will you dance with me, Arya?" Dean asks. When I am too stunned to respond right away, he adds, "We made formal possible. It's only right."

"Where's Katie?" I ask. The words are out before I can remember to sound casual.

His brow draws together. "With Kevin, I think," he says, and sure enough, I see Katie leading Kevin to the floor a few feet away.

"Oh," I say. I hadn't expected that. I am positive I'm blushing now.

There's a pause. "Were you jealous?" He seems ridiculously amused at the prospect.

"Please. Hardly." I remember to be casual this time. I tuck a curl behind my ear and push my plate away. "Yes, I'll dance with you."

I follow him to an emptier part of the hall. Then his arms slide around my waist, and my arms drift up, kind of hovering around his neck. My heart is going fast. The last time I slow danced with a boy was with Siddharth at freshman-year formal, and we did an awkward step-forward, step-back pattern until the song ended.

Dancing with Dean is smoother, but scarier too. I have so many tangled, confusing feelings for this boy. Our relationship for the past four years was built on the simple truth of our mutual dislike, and only recently did that begin to change. This, dancing with him now, so close I can feel his every inhale, is very uncharted territory.

I lower my arms so they are resting fully on his shoulders. He is so much taller that even in heels, the top of my head just reaches his chin. He smells sweet and intoxicating, just like he did on my doorstep last weekend. I tell my nose to stop.

"You look spectacular tonight," he says. His words are in my

219

ear. I wish he wouldn't compliment me when he is near enough to feel my heart respond.

"Thank you," I say, grateful my voice does not waver.

"Are you going to tell me I look spectacular too?"

"Are you fishing?" I don't have to see him to know he's smiling. "You look handsome, Dean."

He laughs softly. Warmth glows in my chest. He draws back just so, and now we are looking at each other, his dark eyes inches from mine. He blinks, and that's when the strangest thought enters my mind: *Dean Merriweather looks like he wants to kiss me.*

And stranger still: *If he tried, I think I would let him.*

But then the song ends and the lights flicker on and we step hastily away from each other, and I bury those inconvenient thoughts deep in my chest, left to be examined another day.

Twenty-Nine
The Khanna Women

When I get home, I head straight to the garage. I waver, hand poised to knock. I let it drop. Alina is in another one of her Do-Not-Disturb art sessions. But I need to tell my sister about formal, need to have her analyze every detail of my dance with Dean. I'll be up all night replaying it in my head otherwise.

I think of all the times Alina has bothered me with boy drama over the years, and my hesitation gives way. I knock twice before I can change my mind.

When there's no answer, I twist the doorknob and enter. "Alina?"

The garage is dark, so Alina must have left already, but I fumble for the light switch and glance around. Both Papa's car and Alina's car are gone. The little alcove in the back where Alina sits to paint is empty as well.

I pull my phone out to open Twitter. As expected, there's a string of *Great British Bake Off* tweets on Alina's profile, the last one timestamped forty minutes ago. I click over to her Instagram

221

story and see she's posted pictures of a Mellie's drink with the captions: late night Mellie's stop and coffee is an artist's fuel.

She won't be home for at least an hour. I have to smile at the unsurprising scene. Alina's creative process is very much characterized by distraction and procrastination until the last possible minute.

Since she's not here, I should probably go. But curiosity climbs in my chest. I slip off my strappy formal heels at the door before walking up the steps to Alina's workspace.

When she was in high school, Alina got Papa's permission to turn the back of the garage into her home studio. Previous owners had built some kind of toolshed structure into the space, complete with an island, wooden shelves, and a corkboard wall. Mamma and Papa had used the area for storage until Alina requested it for herself. She spent so much of her adolescence down here, breathing life to canvas. And online shopping during frequent creative blocks.

After she dropped out of college, the space stayed mostly dormant. Sometimes Papa used one of the emptier shelves to house his garden supplies. Sometimes Mamma took a mug of chai and watched her serials here, perhaps imagining when her elder daughter sat and watched beside her. But I avoided it at all costs. I couldn't be in a place so Alina without missing her terribly, painfully.

Now her studio is almost exactly as it was during her teen years. Papers and brushes strewn over the island, doodles and sloppier artwork tacked to the corkboard, a stool and an easel beside the window. The only noticeable difference is a white sheet set over the canvas. Before, Alina left her art out in the open. As I waited for her to drive me to school in the mornings, I would sit on her stool and admire the previous night's progress.

I know it is the biggest violation even as I reach for a corner

222

of the white sheet. But I have the strangest need to see what lies beneath. I tug the sheet off.

And I gasp. It's a portrait of two Desi women, both draped in finery. They sit before a mirror, close but not quite touching, admiring their reflections. The woman on the right is dressed in regalia fit for a queen. Fit for a bride. She caresses the jewels at her throat.

My throat tightens when I realize the woman on the left is not looking at herself. Her eyes are melancholy as she gazes at something—someone—in the distance. I peer closer and see pencil marks on one end of the canvas. See what Alina has left unfinished. See that this will be a portrait of three women, not two.

Tears prick my eyes. Because the painting is us, so clearly. And it feels ugly somehow. Like Alina has mined our family hurt for artistic profit.

I can't look at it any longer. Swallowing hard, I hurry to sweep the sheet back over the painting. But my movements are clumsy, and papers and supplies from the island beside me tumble to the ground. I drop to my knees, vision blurry as I gather up the spilled pens and brushes and scrap paper.

My fingers freeze on a piece of cardstock with a sketch of the Golden Gate on the front. I flip it over and see it is dated early November, the weekend Alina was visiting her gallery in New York.

A—

Cheers to your next venture. We have loved sharing these last years with you. SF isn't ready for your magic.

Best Wishes,

Colleague signatures fill the rest of the page.
Ice floods my veins. It can't be true. It can't. And yet, I

know it is. Rupa Aunty's words play in my head, and I think I must have been the worst kind of foolish to ever expect a scenario where Alina wouldn't leave like she always does. I sink to the floor, the red velvet of my dress rumpling below me, too stunned for further thought.

In my daze, my eyes catch on a Post-it note stuck to the leg of the easel, so low I didn't notice while standing. It's a title, penned in Alina's loopy handwriting: *Something Blue, Alina Joshi.*

I pluck the note from the easel. Ink is bleeding through the back. I trace over the *J* in "Joshi." And then I let the tears spill.

Act IV
The Bollywood Moment

Thirty
Resolved in Act One

Mindy is calling my name. Even in my weary state, I know it's not the first time. My head snaps up.

She's by the display window, arms knotted in yards of string lights, expression cross. "Have you been listening to a word I've said?"

I can't blame her for the tone. My shift began forty minutes ago, and I've been lost in thought the whole time—something probably made more frustrating since I requested the extra hours. It's the Monday after formal and the first day of Thanksgiving break, so schoolwork is no longer a viable excuse to be away from home. Belle's is all I've got.

"Sorry," I say. I hug my arms to my chest. The heater is on full blast, but I'm still cold. "Really, I am. What did you need?"

"Thumbtacks," she says. She gives me a look, but her features are softer now. "And colored lights, not white lights."

I squeeze my eyes shut. Mindy had texted me in the morning to see if she could borrow lights for the holiday season.

Nikhil never actually ended up putting Alina's holiday decor boxes away, so I picked up the first pack of string lights I could find about two minutes before leaving for work. I didn't bother to check the colors.

"I'm sorry about that too," I say. "I can bring colored lights in tomorrow. We have both rainbow and red-gold lying around somewhere."

She shakes her head. "It's okay," she says. "I'm kind of liking these. It's giving a very 'white Christmas' theme to the shop." She starts to untangle the wires from her hands before narrowing her eyes at me. "Did you say tomorrow? You're not scheduled again till Wednesday."

I busy myself at the register, searching for thumbtacks. "About that," I say. I lick my lips. "I was thinking I could work every day this week. I don't even need compensation for the extra hours." I find the box of thumbtacks in the second drawer and start walking it over to Mindy. "Thanksgiving morning too, if you need."

Concern creases her forehead. "We're never open on Thanksgiving. You know that."

"I could do inventory," I suggest. I know how pathetic I must sound even as the words leave my mouth. I place the box on the counter near her. "Or something. It was just a thought."

She's still studying me, so much care in her gaze that I have to glance away. "Okay," she says after a pause. "Belle's is always open for you."

My eyes grow hot. "Thank you."

Mindy reaches a hand out to squeeze my shoulder. "Honey, is something going on?" She raises her eyebrows. "Is it Dean-related?"

"No," I say. "Nothing like that." I twist a strand of hair behind my ear. "Dean is something that's been going right, actually," I say. The words tumble from my lips, accidental.

This makes her smile. "Well," she says, "that's good." She starts to frown. "So it's about Lisa?" Realization clicks. "Alina," she says.

I look down so she can't read the confirmation on my face. I'm not ready to discuss Alina. Speaking it aloud makes it real, and I can't handle that just yet.

She understands. "You don't need to talk to me about it." Her voice is gentle. "But you should talk to Alina," she says. "If it's about Alina," she adds.

"I don't know if that will help," I say. If Alina really is leaving, a conversation isn't going to stop that. I pick at my nails. "In this particular case."

"Talking about hard things is always valuable," she says. She gestures around the shop, at the rows and rows of packed bookshelves. "Do you know how many of these stories would have been resolved in Act One if the characters had just had an honest conversation with each other?"

I smile in spite of myself. "Okay," I say. "Point taken."

Her eyes sparkle. "Communication is better than avoidance," she says. "That's all I'm saying."

I nod. I might not be in the right mental space to listen to Mindy at the moment, but I know she's right. "Thanks, Mindy. You always give good advice." I lift my eyebrows at her. "Do you ever take it yourself?"

Mindy laughs weakly. She hasn't said too much, but Cleo's work schedule seems to have been weighing on her lately. She raises her shoulders in shrug. "Do as I say, not as I do?"

I laugh too. She lets the moment pass before reaching for the thumbtack box.

"All right, let's get these lights up before rush hour," she says. Belle's has been empty for most of the last hour, but business always picks up later in the afternoon. "I don't need too many customers seeing our behind-the-scenes."

We listen to holiday music while stringing lights around the display windows.

Thursday night, I arrive at Andy's just before seven. I've spent Thanksgiving with the Millers every year since eighth grade. Mamma and Papa have never minded, since we don't do much for the holiday as a family. One year, Rakhi Aunty held a potluck, but there was nothing too festive about it. We ate turkey kebabs instead of the real thing and falooda instead of pie. Probably a better menu than a traditional American Thanksgiving, in all honesty.

After exchanging pleasantries with Andy's very large and very boisterous extended family, we escape to his room. He releases a theatrical sigh after closing the door. "Finally, some peace."

I smile, but it makes me wistful to see Andy's house so full of life and togetherness. Even if it's the chaotic kind of togetherness. I can't remember a time I ever had anything similar at home.

I sink down onto the cushion beside the bookshelf, my usual spot in Andy's bedroom, and he takes the desk chair. "How has your week been?" I ask. I haven't seen Andy since formal, he's been so busy prepping for the upcoming Science Bowl event.

"Nineteen days till UChicago decisions come out," he recites, and I laugh.

"I should have known better than to ask," I say. Nearly every text Andy has sent me in the last two weeks has been related to his anxiety about release day. It would be the truest act of friendship to block the College Confidential page from his internet browser.

230

He grins. Then his features soften. "I did run into Lisa," he says casually. My brows go up, and he adds, "Nick Casey and I were studying for Science Bowl at Mellie's yesterday. She was there too."

"Oh," I say. I've been trying not to think about Lisa. Even in my crisis about Alina, I sent Lisa a text the day after formal, apologizing and asking to meet, and in an all-too-familiar move, she left me on read. I pick at a loose thread on my dress. "Did you talk to her?"

"Yeah," he says. "It was good, actually. We had a really good conversation." He pauses before hurrying to clarify. "I mean, I don't think we'll be best friends anytime soon. But it was nice to know we could still speak to each other like that. Natural, no tension."

"That *is* nice," I say, but it comes out a little warbled. Because why can Lisa talk sweet with Andy but still hold a grudge against me? It stings more than I want to admit. Lisa's comment about how I *chose* Andy in the breakup comes to my mind, and I clear my throat. "Really."

He nods. "She's seeing someone new," he adds. "She mentioned it when we spoke. In case you didn't know."

My brows rise higher. Then my throat tightens. I've heard the lowdown of every single crush Lisa has had since age nine. And now I'm learning of a new relationship secondhand. I want to ask Andy for details, *who-when-how,* but mostly I just want Lisa to tell me herself, so I swallow hard and try to smile.

"I heard. Yeah. She told me, I mean. Last week." I stop talking before the lie gets even more tangled and Andy catches me in it. I clear my throat again. "Are you going to Emilia's party tomorrow?"

It's a sudden subject change, and from Andy's frown, that doesn't escape him. But he goes along anyway.

"I'm planning to," he says. "Nick and I might be a little late, though. Science Bowl's the next day."

Emilia's annual Friendsgiving dinner is tomorrow. She's hosted the event every year since ninth grade, and this time, it's the day before her birthday, so it's double the celebration.

"Dean's going to be there too," Andy says. There is absolutely nothing subtle about his tone.

"Just like he is every year," I say.

"Some things are a little different this year, though," he says.

I tilt my head, daring him to be straight with me. "Like what?"

He ducks his head to hide a smile. "I only mean," he says, "you guys have been spending a lot of time together lately. Slow dancing together, even."

My cheeks flush. "We were spending time together for Leadership," I say, ignoring the second charge. I know I'm being false even as the words leave my tongue.

He gives me a look. "I have never met two people more passionate about student government, if that's the case."

I fall quiet. He's right, and if I'm being honest, I should probably be applying Mindy's advice from earlier this week to my relationship with Dean too. There are some things I could do with more clarity on. Like what he meant when he said he's always wanted to be my friend. And why it took so long for us to finally get here. And what would have happened if that last song at autumn formal had lasted just a little longer.

"I didn't mean to press," Andy says when I don't speak for a few minutes. "It's just that we haven't talked about your romantic life since probably Siddharth freshman year. I guess I've always wondered if Dean was a reason."

It's no secret that I haven't led a very exciting love life, but hearing it phrased like that is particularly depressing. "Thanks," I say dryly, and Andy laughs.

"All I'm trying to say is that I want good things for you. And maybe Dean could be a good thing for you."

The care in his voice makes me warm. Right then, Mrs. Miller's voice sounds from the living room. "Dinner!" she calls. A moment later, she adds, "You better have on some slacks for pictures, Andy!"

We make eye contact and grin. "I didn't hear the second thing," he tells me.

The next evening, I stand in front of my bedroom mirror, hold different outfits up to my body, and wonder why everything I own is ugly and shapeless.

In the back of my head, I know I am just being fussy. Because I have plenty of cute clothes. I have spent lots of money collecting plenty of cute clothes. But somehow, nothing feels right for tonight.

I toss yet another dress onto the ever-growing pile of discarded options on my bed. I close my eyes and groan. And then I pull out my phone and call Emilia. Andy's at a study session, and Emilia is better suited for this particular dilemma as it is.

She picks up on the second ring. "Hello?"

"Hi," I say. "Do you have a minute?"

"Sure. What's up?"

"So," I say. My heart starts to thrum faster. I twist a lock of hair around a finger. "As it turns out, I do actually have a bit of a Jess Bhamra thing going on."

I can hear her confusion through the phone. "Who?"

"*Bend It Like Beckham?*"

A surprised sound escapes her lips. She's stunned silent for a minute. Then: "How soon can you get here?"

Thirty-One
Friendsgiving

I tug at the hem of the dress. The material is smooth and shiny and short, so short. "It's gorgeous," I say, and I mean it. Emilia's lent me the delicate gold slip dress she originally intended to wear at autumn formal. It is very much an Instagram-model selection. "But," I start.

She raises her eyebrows. "But?"

"It's so tiny," I blurt. "Like, so tiny."

"That's kind of the point," she says.

"My shoulders are so bare," I add. I pull on a spaghetti strap to demonstrate.

Her lips twitch. "No one's here to give you a dress cut, if that's what you're worried about."

I ignore the dig. "Maybe I'll wear a coat over it."

She closes her eyes. "Arya."

"Or a cardigan. A long, woolen cardigan. Do you have one I can borrow?"

She pinches the bridge of her nose. "This cannot be a real conversation." She takes a deep breath and opens her eyes.

"Don't wear anything you're not comfortable with. But please never talk to me about pairing that dress with a grandma cardigan."

I deflate. "I was just trying to be weather-conscious. It is late November," I say, even though we will be indoors with the heater blasting the whole night. I turn to face the full-length mirror on the back of Emilia's bedroom door.

The dress really is fabulous. Maybe a little daring for something as wholesome as Friendsgiving, but I look pretty, and that's what counts. I've also never been one to shy away from the more daring options. Why should tonight be any different? Gaining confidence, I smooth down the skirt and take a deep breath.

"Okay," I say. "I'm going to wear it."

She raises her eyebrows at me in the mirror. "Sans cardigan?"

"Sans cardigan."

Emilia beams. "Perfect. We can get started on makeup, then."

We listen to Kelly Clarkson's holiday album while we get ready. Emilia pulls the most ridiculous faces as she begins to apply mascara. I'm untwisting a tube of stick blush when she turns to look at me.

"So," she says. Her lashes look full and fluttery. I make a mental note to ask for her mascara brand later. "What's the plan?"

I frown, fingers paused over the blush. "Plan?"

"How are you going about talking to Dean?"

I can't help it; a laugh escapes me. "Oh," I say. "I am definitely very much not talking to Dean."

Her mouth drops. "Arya!"

I rush to clarify. "I mean, I'll *talk* to him. About Leadership, country music, Jane Austen." I begin to apply blush and meet her eyes in the mirror. "I'm thinking of recommending *Persuasion* next."

She swats my shoulder with the back of her hand. "I thought you talking to him was the whole point of us playing dress-up."

"The whole point was more that playing dress-up is fun," I say, glib. She's not buying it, so I sigh, feeling like I owe her some honesty. "And that I feel nervous about seeing him now."

But that's not exactly right. I twist at an earring. "I think maybe I've always been nervous around him," I say. "Or at least just very aware of myself when I'm around him. And maybe the reasons for that are becoming clearer."

It's the most I've ever said aloud about what I feel for Dean, but that's because I still have so much left to understand and figure out. Emilia doesn't push.

"Okay," she says. "I guess that makes sense. You don't need to do anything rash tonight."

I smile. And because I'm ready to move on from the topic and because Emilia has been such a comfort today, I lean over to grab her birthday present from the floor.

"Do you want to open your gift early?" I ask.

Excitement leaps to her eyes. She tries to downplay it. "Oh," she says, waving a hand. "You totally didn't have to. I mean, my real birthday isn't even until tomorrow."

I give her a look. She wavers and drops the act.

"Fuck it," she says. "Hand it over."

She tears through the tissue paper very ungracefully, squealing when she discovers signed Taylor Swift merch.

I split a plate of sweet potato casserole with Andy after dinner. We sit on the living room sofa by the fireplace. Andy curls his feet up beneath him. I cross my legs with care to make sure I'm not accidentally flashing anyone.

Emilia's family is one to start decorating for Christmas the second the clock strikes midnight on Halloween, so her whole home is already decked with tinsel and festive lights and holly-ribbon bows. The effect is cozy and magical.

Someone taps my shoulder right as I scoop the last bite of casserole from our plate and into my mouth. I look up to see Candace Lee beside me. "Hey," she says. "Where's Em?"

I pause to swallow before responding. "She was with Meena last, I think?"

Sure enough, I glance around the room and spot her with Meena by the back door. Emilia's hands are to her heart, which means she's just been bestowed another gift. Every guest who has entered so far has brought Emilia a birthday present, and each time, Emilia gives a surprised "For me?!" before lavishing her thanks.

"Okay, sweet," Candace says. Her voice drops to a conspiratorial whisper. "Nick put the cake in the fridge. We'll unveil after everyone's eaten?"

Candace and I coordinated to surprise Emilia with a birthday cake at the end of the night. We enlisted the help of Candace's boyfriend, Nick Casey, to be our delivery man. He and Emilia have really only ever interacted through Candace, so he's the least likely to be suspected of any birthday mischief.

"That sounds great," I say. The cake is chocolate with strawberry filling, so I'm planning to make room even if it means risking a food coma.

"Perfect," she says. "I'll text you with updates." Candace beams and slips away. I watch her join Nick, Lacey, and Dean at the bay windows with an odd feeling in my stomach.

I haven't spoken to Dean all night. He only arrived a little while ago, and he waved when he walked in, but he's been surrounded by other people ever since. As have I, I guess, and it's not like I've tried to seek him out. But my stomach still knots at the thought. This is the first we've seen each other since formal, and I want everything to go smoothly.

Dean and Nick start for the drinks table, not far from where I'm sitting. I look away before my gaze can draw his attention and take a sip of apple cider to calm my nerves.

"Hey," Andy says. I turn to see him frowning at an empty casserole plate. "You finished the sweet potato?"

"You were occupied," I say, defensive, but it's true. Andy has been flipping through Science Bowl Quizlet cards on his phone for the last fifteen minutes, totally removed from his surroundings. "Don't worry. There'll be cake later."

This grabs his attention. "What kind?" he says.

Emilia sinks down on the seat across from us before I can reply. I shoot Andy a warning glance, hoping he understands not to mention the cake, and he goes quiet.

"Hey, Em," I say. "You having a good night?"

She sighs dreamily. "The best," she says. "I've gotten so many presents." Her forehead furrows when she catches sight of something behind me. "Though, it would be nice if my brothers decided to stop stealing our food."

I turn to see Anthony, Emilia's youngest brother, piling a plate high with potatoes and stuffing. This is the third time tonight one of Emilia's siblings has violated her demand for family members to stay upstairs for the night.

"Let him," Andy says. "In the holiday spirit."

Emilia smiles in spite of herself. "Holiday spirit," she repeats. She smooths the skirt of her dress down. "How have you guys been doing?"

My eyes slip involuntarily back to Dean. He's laughing at something Nick said, dimples splitting his cheeks. His sweater is the same blue as his eyes, and his dark hair is floppy as ever.

I wish he would come over and talk to me. I wish it didn't bother me that he hasn't. I take another gulp of cider.

Emilia follows my line of vision and giggles. "You know, it's not the fifties. Women can make the first move. You don't have to sit here and pine all night."

I gasp. "Emilia," I say, horrified. "I am not pining. And no one is making any moves."

"The last part is certainly true," she says.

My head is starting to throb. I sip my cider again. I think better of it and drain the whole glass.

Andy looks like he's struggling not to laugh. "That's not doing what you think it's doing."

I give him a dark look before swallowing and resting my empty cup on the coffee table. Then I push up from the couch. "I'm going to go on a walk," I say.

Emilia raises her eyebrows. "A walk?" she repeats.

I nod. My belly feels warm from cider. "To get some fresh air." I adjust the straps of my dress, and then I'm off for the back door, leaving Emilia and Andy bemused behind me.

The icy air is a shock to my skin. Goose bumps cover my legs within moments. Maybe I should have worn the grandma cardigan after all.

I wrap my arms around my chest as I wander through Emilia's backyard. I stop when I reach the edge of the property line, right by the small pond the Lopezes share with their neighbors. We took pictures here before formal, and the water is even more beautiful, dark and glittering in the night.

I'm not sure what's gotten into me, to be this anxious and wanting for Dean's company. At last year's Friendsgiving, Dean and I weren't even on speaking terms, and I preferred it that way. He had just announced his bid for student body president and kicked off the campaign season with some particularly vicious (though admittedly clever) attack ads.

A twig snaps behind me. Then another. And another. Startled, I turn around. Night obscures my vision, but I can just make out Dean's outline.

My heart jumps to my throat. "Dean," I say. "You scared me."

He pauses when there are just a few feet between us, and the rest of him comes slowly into focus. He cocks his head. "Going for a swim?" he asks.

"Only after you."

He smiles, just barely. His nose is already red from cold. "I saw you leave the house," he tells me.

"You followed me?"

"Not followed," he says quickly, and I'm reminded immediately of our interaction behind the history building so many weeks ago. Maybe he is too because he clears his throat. He crosses his arms against the chill. "What are you doing out here? It's freezing."

"I'm fine," I say, even though my fingertips have gone numb and I can see my breath in the air. "This outfit is pretty warm."

I am speaking nonsense. His eyes drop to my dress, lingering a little too long on my décolleté, and color rises in his cheeks. I think of our night at formal, of how it felt when he told me I looked spectacular, and now I'm blushing too.

"You didn't say hi," I say next. I want it to sound like I'm just making an observation, but it comes out wistful. "Inside, I mean."

His forehead furrows. "You looked busy," he says, puzzled, and it's not exactly wrong. I've been beside Andy or Emilia the whole night.

I kick at a pebble with the toe of my boot. "You didn't say

hi at last year's party either," I say. "You didn't speak to me at all then, really."

He raises his eyebrows. "You remember what I was doing this time last year?"

"Oh," I say. I duck my head, heat crawling up my neck. "I have a good memory."

His lips push up. "Right."

"Really good memory," I say. "Elephant-like."

"Sure," he says. He is fully smiling now, the same crooked way I have grown so used to. "For the record," he says, "you didn't exactly make it easy for me to talk to you. I'm pretty sure you've spent each day of the last four years frustrated with me for something."

"You are very frustrating," I say, but I don't dispute his claim further. I've always been quick to spar with Dean, quick to hold a grudge when resolution was on the table.

He rolls his eyes. He carefully plucks a piece of lint from his sweater. "But things are different now," he says after a beat. He tilts his head to meet my gaze. "Better."

There's a gentleness in his tone, like he wants to confirm we're on the same page, and it makes my body feel warm. The knot in my stomach starts to loosen. "Better," I agree.

He stands taller and turns to face the pond so that our shoulders are almost touching. "The water's really pretty," he says, and I nod my concurrence. "I had my first kiss at a lake," he adds.

I'm not sure why he's telling me this. I toe another pebble. "This is a pond," I say.

He ignores me. "Joanna Dagai. At Hebrew Camp the summer before freshman year. When we went rafting together one afternoon."

The last thing I want to do is think about Dean and another

girl. "I mean, it's barely even a pond," I continue. "More of a ditch during the summer."

He ignores this too. "She got seasick and threw up after." He smiles a little and looks sideways at me. "What was your first kiss like, Arya?"

I hug my arms tighter around me. I've never been that embarrassed about my inexperience, but there's something about speaking the words aloud, to Dean, that feels too vulnerable. Especially after our dance together. I decide to say it quick, like ripping off a Band-Aid.

"Actually, I've never kissed anyone before."

He seems surprised by the information. "Not even Andy?"

My brow furrows. "Andy?" I repeat. I consider my conversation with Dean at his mother's bakery, when he said he was familiar with the rumors going around. I realize I never asked Dean if he believed them.

It's too dark to be certain, but his cheeks look pink again. "I just meant—" he says. He stops and rubs his neck. "I've wondered—" He breaks off once more.

"It's not like that with Andy," I say. "He's my best friend. Like you and Katie."

Dean nods. There's a beat. "Okay. I mean, Katie and I did go out for a bit, so—"

"Oh. Right." I clear my throat. I wonder if seeing me with Andy tonight is a reason Dean didn't approach me. "Bad example. But Andy's like a brother to me. That's all. Really."

His face is still flushed, but his voice is steady when he speaks. "Okay," Dean says again. His breath curls white in the air between us, and some of the tension seems to leave his body. "I'm glad."

There's silence. A smile pushes at my lips. I tilt my head so our eyes lock. "Why?"

"Hm?"

"Why does that make you glad?"

He looks so caught in that moment, lips parted just so, eyes blue and wide in the moonlight, that something reckless stirs in my stomach and I feel bold enough to push on.

"Dean," I say. "Do you have feelings for me?"

He stills. He opens and closes his mouth. He tries again. "Do you have feelings for me?"

The way he's repeating my question back at me should sound childish, but instead it's tender, hesitant, hopeful. I know the answer must be all over my face, so I turn back to the pond, nerves extinguishing my moment of courage.

"You didn't answer my question," I say. My cheeks are hot enough to permanently guard against the chilly night.

He angles back to the pond too, and our shoulders bump. I can hear the smile soft in his voice. "You didn't answer mine."

We stand there together, silent and watching the water, until Candace comes out to usher us in for cake.

Thirty-Two
Minor Update

My leg won't stop bouncing. It's Monday morning, and I'm in the Leadership room waiting for Dean to arrive so we can film this week's news show. The digital clock on the wall reads two minutes past the hour, which means Dean is officially late.

I can't help but wonder if his tardiness is because of what passed between us at Emilia's a few nights ago. We haven't spoken since, not unless the Jane Austen meme Dean tagged me in on Instagram Saturday counts. But we've also been on Thanksgiving break, so I haven't had much opportunity to see him. Plus, last night's shameful venture into social media sleuthing informed me that the soccer team had another preseason tournament this past weekend, which is a perfectly valid reason for Dean not asking to meet at Mellie's the way he often does.

Perhaps exhaustion from the tournament caused Dean to oversleep. I glance at the clock again and see it now reads 8:04.

Emilia appears unbothered, twirling a lock of hair as she scrolls on a laptop with the film team. I decide not to panic as long as Emilia is calm. She manages production, and if she's not worried about Dean's lateness, there's no need for me to be.

He walks in a few minutes later, a coffee tray balanced in his hand. He's wearing an Abigail Adams High half zip, and his hair is smoothed back for filming. Our eyes meet and my chest tightens.

"Hi," Dean says. He rests the coffee tray down before me. "Right one is for you," he says, though there's no need to specify. Dean gets plain black coffee, while my drinks contain such absurd amounts of whipped cream that dome-shaped lids are always required.

I reach for the sugary concoction, gratitude loosening the knot in my stomach. Dean bringing me coffee unprompted must mean nothing major has shifted between us since the night at Emilia's. He's picked up coffee for the two of us before filming several times now.

"Thank you," I say. "You really didn't need to."

"It was no problem." His voice is pleasant, professional.

He takes his seat beside me. We are just inches apart. My leg starts to bounce again. This time my knee hits the underside of the news desk with a thunk, sending pain up my leg. I try not to wince.

Dean twists in his chair to face me. His eyes are dark under the fluorescents. "Arya," he says. The same pleasantness is back in his tone. "I—"

For some reason, I'm terrified of whatever he is going to say next. "You were late," I blurt.

He stops. He frowns. "What?"

"You arrived late to production." I glance at the clock. "Seven minutes late. Or six minutes. At least six minutes late."

His frown deepens. "The line was long at Mellie's," he says. "Where I was buying you coffee."

"Oh," I say. I swallow the panic in my throat. "Right. Thanks for that again."

His eyes narrow slightly, like he's trying to decipher my expression. Then he shakes his head, impatient. "Okay," he says. "Let's try that again." He opens his mouth to speak, but this time Emilia interrupts.

"We're ready!" Emilia announces. She beams at us. "Sorry for the delay. Some last-minute script editing. But we can start if you guys are good?"

"So good!" I say. My voice is too loud. "Let's start."

Dean is still staring at me. Emilia raises her eyebrows but doesn't say anything further.

With a huff, Dean sinks back into his seat. He uses a pinky to rub his eye. "What Arya said."

Emilia pulls up our lines on the teleprompter. The junior officer playing cameraman today signals action.

"Good morning, Eagles," Dean begins, and we are off. I recite the sports schedule, Dean gives information about our upcoming Diversity Day, and then we introduce the Leadership students who are set to perform a skit about tomorrow's blood drive.

It is the work of ten minutes. When we're done, I sit at a table in the back, sipping my coffee, waiting for Emilia to finish filming. I mean to avoid walking to class with Dean, but it proves pointless when he plops into the desk in front of me. He sits backward on the chair so we are facing each other.

"Hey," he says. His elbows are on my desk. "You're being elusive today."

"Am I?"

He nods. It was much easier to look at him in the dark. I go for over his shoulder instead, at the production area. One of the underclassmen alternately raises a banana and a candy bar in demonstration of which snacks are appropriate and which are taboo before having blood drawn.

"Unintentional," I maintain.

He studies me. Then he sucks in a breath. "So," he says, "I wanted to ask. Are you free Saturday evening?" His voice is calm and conversational, but his knuckles are striped pink and white.

For the first time today, I meet his eyes on purpose. "For Leadership?"

"No," he says. He runs a rough hand through his hair. He clears his throat. "For dinner."

My brows fly up. "Like a date?" I want to snatch the words back the second they leave my lips, because maybe I am totally misjudging and he's inviting me to another bakery-like event with Katie and Lisa and Clara. Maybe now I've made him horribly uncomfortable.

He *does* look uncomfortable. A flush is crawling up his neck, but he doesn't look away. "That's the idea."

My brows merge with my hairline. "Oh," I say. I am nodding too much. I must look like a bobblehead. "Yes. Okay. Yes." I force myself to be still. "I mean, yeah, I think I can pencil it in." I shut my eyes and shake my head. "I don't know why I said that. I'm not a secretary."

My nervousness appears to elicit the opposite effect from him. His features are softening with amusement, no longer formal or tense as he was throughout the morning.

"Nor an assistant," he says helpfully. "Not mine, at least."

My nostrils flare. "No," I say. "Very much not." I sit taller in my chair. "Yes, Saturday works for me. I'll see you then."

He cocks his head. "I mean, we're going to see each other before Saturday," he says. "We're going to see each other in two periods."

"Right," I say. My face is hot. I twist a lock of hair behind my ear. "See you in two periods."

He smiles, full and dazzling. "See you, Arya."

If I was a Bollywood heroine, this would be the moment I turned over and over in my mind before bed. Preferably while nestled in silk sheets and having a monologue with myself in moonlight. In any case, I know I'll be up late tonight playing it all back.

Emilia arrives as Dean leaves. She watches him go, then turns to me. "Something up?" she says.

I am too dazed to respond right away. I look up at her. "Kind of," I say finally, and she raises her brows, expectant. "I have a minor update."

Thirty-Three
Maharani

J ust a little higher," Alina says, and Veena adjusts the chunni accordingly. "And more to the left, I think," Alina adds. She gives a satisfied nod when the positioning is correct, and Veena smooths the scarlet pleats down with a manicured hand before pinning it to Alina's blouse.

"There," Alina says. She plays with the loose end of her chunni, pausing at the handwoven golden deer lining the edge. The embroidery is so masterful that the deer appear to be running across the fabric. Alina catches me watching in the mirror and beams.

Immediately, I look away. I might have been roped into attending Alina's final pre-shaadi fitting at Maharani Bridal, but I don't have to pretend to be enjoying myself.

It's Saturday morning, and Alina's last jewelry pieces arrived with Rupa Aunty last night. The wedding is only two weeks away now, and in true Desi joint family fashion, the Joshis are staying in our guest room until the big days. We ate dinner together for their first night. Papa came home early from work, and Mamma, presenting as a dedicated homemaker for the evening, even decided to cook the meal.

Alina seized her opportunity at the dining table. Rupa Aunty had just asked me my plans for the weekend, and since I couldn't exactly divulge my dinner date with Dean, I told her my day was empty.

"Perfect," Alina jumped in. "Then you're free to come with me to Maharani tomorrow. I want to try on my ceremony dress with Rupa Aunty's gorgeous jewelry. And I know you must be dying to see the look together too."

She smiled at Rupa Aunty, who glowed right back.

And that was that. Mamma and Rupa Aunty already had breakfast plans at Chai & Chaat, so the morning was reserved for just us, as I'm sure she intended. I've been avoiding alone time with her since the day in her studio, and she's grown suspicious.

So far, today has been an exercise in caution for Alina and in passive-aggression for me. I have always been terrible at confrontation, and as fiery as Alina is, I can tell she's trying to tread carefully. She even let me have the aux on the car ride over. I chose Thomas Rhett's latest album because Alina despises country music, but spending time with Dean has made the genre surprisingly bearable for me.

I pick at a loose thread on my seat cushion. At the mirror, Alina begins trying on Rupa Aunty's jewelry. It's a set of rubies and gold that Joshi women have worn for generations. Rupa Aunty brought the pieces to the Roka for Alina to view, so they are familiar, just sparklier from a fresh cleaning.

The choker looks so heavy, I have to admire Alina's ability to keep her head straight. She strokes the ruby at the hollow of her throat, and I am instantly reminded of the woman from her painting. My stomach knots.

"What do you think?" Alina asks, curling a lock of hair behind her ear so the matching jhumke are also visible.

She's looking at me, but it's Veena who answers. "So beautiful," she says. "You are truly looking like a maharani."

Alina smiles. "Thank you," she says. She sneaks another glance at me, expression turning prickly, and asks Veena, "Would I be able to try on my other lehengas while I'm here? I want to take full advantage of my time today."

Veena looks a bit surprised. Alina booked a session specifically for her ceremony gown, since it was the only dress she hadn't yet worn with finalized jewelry selections. It's possible the other pieces are away in storage. She's tried them all dozens of times as it is. But Veena is amenable.

"Certainly," she says. "I will bring them. Though it may take some time, as a few clothes will require pressing."

"That's no problem at all," Alina says. "Take all the time. Thanks so much."

Veena exits, and then Alina and I are alone in the dressing room.

I take out my phone so I appear busy. Emilia just texted me outfit inspo for tonight, and I have a few unread messages from Andy. One is about Dean but the other three look to be links to College Confidential threads. I say a prayer for Andy. His academic anxiety has been at an all-time high as decisions approach.

Alina sits delicately on a dressing stool near my cushion, careful not to muss her skirt. She clears her throat. When I don't look up, she breaks the silence.

"Sheila's home for the weekend," she says. "I almost asked her along today. But I'm glad it's just the two of us. It's so special to share this time with you." Her lips stretch into a soft smile.

I don't understand how Alina can wax poetic about sisterly

bonding when she's been keeping such a giant secret from me for weeks. Months, maybe. Irritation scratches at my throat. "You should have invited Sheila," I say.

Her smile sours. She stands from the stool as abruptly as she sat down. She retreats to a corner, and I think she's finally going to leave me alone, but then she returns, a small red box in hand. I didn't notice it in the car, so she must have kept it in her purse.

Alina thrusts the box into my hands. "Open it," she orders.

I consider refusing. But curiosity wins. I slip my phone back in my pocket and open the box.

Pearl-gold jhumke glitter up at me. I lift one earring and suck in a breath. The stone work is exquisite. But there's something more. A familiarity I can't immediately place.

Alina answers for me. "I wore them at my Roka," she says. "But they were Mamma's before that, and Naniji's even before that." She squeezes my hand. "It would mean so much to me if you wore these for the ceremony."

Everything in me wants to say yes. The jhumke are beautiful, royal. They will go perfectly with my ceremony lehenga. But I see the expectancy in Alina's eyes and know she sees this gesture as her way of smoothing out whatever rift has grown between us. I think of how she still hasn't told me about San Francisco. I think of how she might be the most selfish person I know. And I drop the earring back in the box and close the lid.

"No, thank you."

She blinks. "What?"

"I already have my earrings picked out for the ceremony."

Her brow furrows. "So wear these for the reception."

"I have my reception jewelry picked out too."

Indignation twists her lips. "Haldi, then." I open my mouth to reply, but she cuts me off. "Or the Sangeet. Or the Vidai.

We're Hindu, Arya; I promise there are more events than you have jewelry for."

I push the earring box away. I make my words forceful. "I don't want them."

She stares. She pulls back. Then, voice thin and biting, she says, "What is wrong with you?"

My fingernails press crescent moons into my palms. "I don't like the jhumke, Alina."

She stands and steps away from me. Hurt as she is, angry as I am, there is something striking about seeing my sister in all her bridal regalia, more beautiful than I have ever known her. Once again I am reminded of Alina's painting, and my anger only grows roots.

"You are being so cold to me," she says. She's pacing the length of the dressing room now. "You've *been* so cold to me. For so long now, I can't remember when you weren't."

She's being hyperbolic, but there's some truth to the claim. I haven't been right around Alina for almost as long as she's been back. Too much shifted between us in her absence.

"I just don't like gold jewelry as much as you do."

"Being cold to me has become your static state," she continues, ignoring me. "And I'm still here trying to do something nice for you."

Is this how she sees herself—charitable, enduring? I raise my voice to match hers. Or drown hers. "Gold earrings are *far* too heavy."

Her voice rises too. "It's like I've always done something wrong."

My fingers curl to fists at my side, knuckles white. "The weight would literally rip my ears off."

She stops pacing to glare at me. "I don't care about the fucking earrings, Arya!" Her eyes are blazing. And shiny. "I care that

253

I came back home for you and you don't even speak to me anymore."

"Please," I say. I stumble to my feet. My throat is so thick, I have to choke the words out. "Don't act like you've done me a favor. Don't act like you've ever thought about anyone but yourself."

Her breath catches, furious. Her hands settle on the silk pleats at her waist. "Are you talking about Mamma again? Is it blame-Alina-for-her-mother's-mental-illness time?"

"I'm talking about San Francisco!" I shout, and Alina draws back, stunned. "That's right," I say softly. Awful confirmation is sinking in my stomach at her expression. I hadn't known I still retained hope for her move to be a hoax until this moment. "I know."

She shakes her head fast. "How?" she says. "How do you know?"

"Never mind how I know," I say. But the words are pushing at my lips, spilling out. "Rupa Aunty told me. In September. Then I saw a note in your studio. I saw your painting there too." I mean to clamp my mouth shut, but it comes out anyway: "Is your creativity so dry that you can't think up anything but family drama to paint?"

Pink spots bloom on her cheeks. After a long silence, she takes in a shaky breath. "I get it," she says. Her voice is clipped. Her hands are quivering, so she clasps them together, and the bangles on her wrist clatter. "You resent me."

My jaw tightens. "Yes," I say hotly. "I do."

She continues. "Because you're jealous of me."

My mouth snaps open. "What?"

"Because I have my art, I have Nikhil, I have a way out, and you have none of that."

"Alina," I say, horrified. Pressure is building behind my

eyes. Her words are cruel and dismissive and, if I am being totally, mortifyingly honest, true. But it's not as shallow as that,
and anger overpowers sense. "Are you really so self-absorbed
that you think everyone wants your miserable life?"

Her lips curl into an angry frown. "That's not what I—"

"You are everything I don't want to be," I say. I watch with
a kind of vicious satisfaction as her mouth shuts and she starts
to blink rapidly. "You're unkind and selfish and don't know the
first thing about maintaining relationships, not with Mamma,
and not with me."

Bitterness swells in my chest as I push on. "Did you ever
think about what my life was like?" I say. A single tear slips
down my cheek, and I am quick to wipe it away. "Alone in the
mess you left? Mamma sadder than ever, Papa always working
so he wouldn't have to be around her, my sister, not even home
for the holidays." I shake my head, breathing labored, chin
wobbly. "And now you're all set to do that again."

I stop because I am moments away from fully dissolving into
tears, and I have just enough dignity not to break down in a
public place. Finally, I have said everything that has been pressing on me all these months Alina has been home. But I feel
more hollow and spent than relieved.

During the summer, I thought the hardest part about my
sister's return would be mediating Mamma's relationship with
her. I never thought to consider how damaged my relationship
with Alina had become.

Before me, Alina hugs her arms to her stomach, eyes large
and wet and sorry. "Arya," she begins, and I worry she might
apologize. I don't want to hear it, don't want to forgive, so I cut
her off.

"Keep the earrings, Alina," I say. "And leave me alone."

She swallows her words. She smooths down the wrinkle

forming in her skirt, hands shaky above the sparkling fabric. Somehow, still, she is a glorious bride. I whirl away from her and sink back onto my cushion.

Veena chooses that moment to enter the fitting room, wheeling inside a clothing rack lined with garment bags. It's hard not to wonder if she's been listening at the door, waiting for a pause in argument to make her entrance.

"Beautiful gowns all ready for trial," she says, singsong, and Alina and I mold our expressions into pictures of composure.

Thirty-Four
'Will They, Won't They (They Will)

My fingertips are frozen stiff. I sit on my hands for warmth, but the cold porch tile is no comfort to my skin either. I fold my arms across my chest and scan the street for Dean, hoping his car's seat warmers are operating at full capacity.

He can't be far. He texted ten minutes ago saying he was on his way, and I slipped out of the house the moment my phone buzzed. Papa was trying to organize a Khanna-Joshi game night, and I had never been more grateful to have plans. I explained my absence by saying Emilia and I would be studying for Bio together. (Proper Indian girls never so much as think about boys until they graduate college, after which, of course, marriage must become the primary item on our agendas.)

Papa praised my academic dedication for scheduling school-work on a Saturday night, but Mamma definitely didn't buy that I was wearing a full face of makeup and my favorite dark green turtleneck for a study session. She raised Alina, after all. But Mamma didn't stop me, and I'm grateful for it. I need space from home after this morning.

I haven't spoken to Alina once since our terrible fight at Maharani Bridal. In the car home, I blasted music and put on my darkest sunglasses despite the overcast day so she couldn't see the tears still threatening to spill on my lashes. Every so often, Alina looked over from the steering wheel, lips apart like she was preparing to speak, and I pressed the volume button higher.

I locked myself in my bedroom after we got home and watched reruns of *Gossip Girl*—my go-to show for whenever I want to turn my brain off—till evening. It helped, but it also meant I went without lunch. My stomach growls now, and I hope the restaurant Dean chose for us has generous portions.

Dean has told me basically nothing about tonight's agenda. In Civics on Friday, he said he would pick me up at seven. He became deeply absorbed in our *Shelby County v. Holder* reading the moment I asked him what the evening's plan was.

Headlights glow in the corner of our otherwise empty street. My heart gives an anxious lurch in my chest as Dean's car rolls into our driveway. I was too angry with Alina to feel much of anything else today, but now Dean is near and the nerves are returning to full intensity.

I smile when I see SENIOR SEASON is back on Dean's rear windshield in fresh red-and-blue paint. November sleet faded the original lettering job. He must have repainted sometime this week.

The driver's door opens with a click, and Dean steps out. In the streetlight, I see he is wearing a navy button-down, and his dark hair is styled in his classic, intentionally messy look. My throat tightens, and I remind myself that I look very nice too.

He stops a few feet before me. "Hi," he says.

"Hi, Dean."

There's a pause. Then: "You look great," we say at once.

I blink. He blinks. "Thank you," we say together.

Amusement pushes at his lips. We're both so nervous.

I walk toward the car. He hurries to open the door for me. "Very gentleman-like," I say.

"Yes," he says. "I am."

"Modest, too," I say, and he shuts the door in my face.

In the car, my fingers pluck anxiously at my necklace. Dean starts to pull out the driveway, and I realize I've never been in Dean's car at night before. Somehow, the energy is totally different. It is so much more personal to share this space with him in the dark. I cross my legs in my seat as though trying to take up less room.

He's nearing the edge of my neighborhood when I glance at him. "Are you going to tell me where we're going?"

His smile deepens, dimples appearing. "You'll see," he says. "Soon enough."

My foot taps fast against the car floor. For some reason, panic is growing in my lungs. Maybe it's the day's events, still mostly unprocessed in my head, or maybe that I'm on the first date of my life, and it's with Dean, my rival of four years, my friend for maybe four weeks. Maybe it is just our proximity.

"This is strange," I say. I pick at my necklace again. "So strange."

"Because you don't know where we're headed?"

"That too," I say. I twist to look at him. "But also all of it," I add, and his smile falters. "You don't think this is strange? The two of us going out?"

He isn't smiling anymore. His hands tighten on the steering wheel. "Not really, no."

I know that I'm ruining it, but I can't stop speaking all my worst thoughts aloud. "Maybe this was a terrible mistake," I blurt. "I mean, not too long ago, you hated me."

He blinks twice. "I never hated you," he says.

"Disliked me, then," I say. My heart is going fast. My mouth is going faster. It's got to be some kind of a record, to make a mess of the night in such little time. I grasp around for reason. "Strongly disliked me. How do you even go from that to—"

He takes a sharp left turn at the light.

I snap back against my seat. My brows knit. "Dean?"

He doesn't reply, just keeps driving, eyes on the street ahead. For a sinking moment, I think he's about to drop me back. But we're moving farther away from my house on a road I don't recognize.

"If this has all been your very elaborate plan to get me alone, kill me, and hide my body in a ditch, consider me impressed."

More silence. I open my mouth, then clamp it shut. My words haven't exactly had the best track record tonight.

He pulls into an empty corner of a grocery-store parking lot a minute later. He puts the car into park, unclicks his seat belt, and releases a long breath.

I swallow. The car feels even smaller stopped. "Dean, why are we here?"

Finally, he turns to face me. His eyes are so blue. "Because," he says, expression lazy and knowing. "You're in your pick-a-fight mood."

I draw back, indignant. "I don't have a pick-a-fight mood."

He scoffs. "You do. You so do." He snaps his fingers, recalling. "Like, the morning behind the history building. That was you in your pick-a-fight mood to the max."

"Oh," I say. "You mean the morning you told me you've always wanted to be my friend."

He makes a noise in the back of his throat. "You have *got* to stop phrasing it like that."

"Well," I say, "you phrased it like that."

"Yeah, but you make it sound like I'd been *yearning*."

I don't say anything. He gives me a dark look. "I had *not* been yearning," he says. He sinks in his seat, silly with embarrassment. He runs a rough hand over his eyes. "Not really."

I laugh in spite of myself. He takes it, good-natured. "That's not the point," he says. "The point is something's up with you. What is it?"

I take a deep breath. Ruefully, I realize how the last time Dean asked me a similar question, at Fall Festival, my answer was the same. "I got in a fight with Alina," I say. I'm surprised at how easy the words roll off my tongue. Dean doesn't say anything, just tilts his head at me, attentive. "She's moving."

This admission too comes easy. I take another deep breath, and then I'm telling him about the argument at Maharani. I skip over the parts about Mamma, the parts that don't feel like mine to share, but I tell him the rest. How much it hurt when Alina left the first time. How much it hurts that she's leaving again. How much I hate that we've grown so far apart, I had to find out such monumental news by accident.

"There was a point when we told each other everything," I say. I press a finger to the corner of my eye to catch a tear before it falls. I spent far too long on my mascara today to let it end up smudged. "But that's gone now."

He's quiet for so long, I worry I've freaked him out with my rambling. But then he speaks. "I'm sorry, Arya," he says. "Really. That sucks."

I nod, in total agreement. "It sucks."

"But maybe," he starts, "and I'm not trying to excuse her," he rushes to clarify. "But maybe she kept the news from you because she knew it would be painful to hear. And she wanted to spare you that." He hesitates, then adds, "It's something I would do with Georgia. When she asked questions about our

Dad. Conceal the bad, highlight the good. Maybe it's an older-sibling thing."

My heart softens in my chest. "You're a good older brother, Dean," I say, and I mean it—though someday Georgia should probably be told the unfiltered truth, whatever that may be. "But I don't know if Alina's intentions matter much. She should have respected me enough to give me the truth and trust I could take it."

Because it all feels too similar to three years ago. When Alina dropped out of college and just never came home. I didn't think I'd have to go through that kind of blindsiding again.

Dean doesn't have a rebuttal to this. I don't mind. I already feel so much lighter having told him. I've never even talked to Lisa or Andy like this before.

"Thank you," I say. I reach across the car to squeeze his hand. "For listening to me."

It's not quite a dream-sequence getaway, but I can't help but think that Dean has been such an escape for me these past few weeks. Whether it be the movie nights or the Mellie's coffee runs, our moments together have brought comfort when everything else has felt wrong.

He squeezes back. His hand is large and warm. "Thanks for telling me."

I release him, then lean back in my seat. I make a sound that's a cross between a sigh and a laugh. "I know this has been pretty messy first-date behavior."

He shrugs, a smile starting on his lips. "Messy is kind of fitting for us." He corrects himself. "For you."

I laugh, fully this time. I pick at the sleeve of my top. "I hope I didn't make us miss a reservation."

He twists the car key. The engine sputters on. "No," he says.

We lock eyes as he pulls the car out of park, and his smile deepends with mischief. "But we're not going to a restaurant."

Ten minutes later, we arrive at Chandler Community Center, the much-loved venue of autumn formal. I recognized the route as Dean was driving, though I had assumed he was just taking us somewhere in the vicinity. But he parks at the back entrance of the center's ballroom, leaving no room for doubt.

My brow furrows. "What are we doing here?"

He takes off his seat belt. "We're having dinner," he says. He drops his keys into his pocket and steps out the door.

I follow suit, bemused. He's at the trunk, pulling out a picnic basket. I smile at the sight. When we reach the door, Dean rummages in his pocket, a challenge while balancing the basket, and comes up with a silver key.

"That can't be—" I break off. He jiggles the key into the lock. "How did you—?"

The door clicks open. Dean's smile is quicksilver. "Being student body president comes with a few privileges," he says. "I wouldn't expect you to understand."

I hit his shoulder as we stumble inside. He laughs, the sound loud and echoey in the wide, empty ballroom.

I hesitate a few feet in. "If we get caught . . ." I begin, and he raises his eyebrows, waiting for the end of the threat. I deflate. "I'll do absolutely nothing. But let's not get caught."

"Relax, Khanna," he says. "I asked my contact here for a favor. We're not going to get in trouble. I would never jeopardize the whole Annabeth Chase thing you've got going on."

I remember how effective Dean was with negotiating a venue discount all those weeks ago and take him at his word. He obviously has better connections with the Community Center than I do.

263

"Just so you know, I'm taking the Annabeth comparison as a compliment."

"That's how I meant it."

It's not too dark in the ballroom, but I fumble for a light switch on the wall. Dean stops me, nodding at the windowed ceiling. I look up.

"Oh," I breathe. Because the expansive skylight is letting in a glow from the stars and the moon and probably nearby businesses. I've only been here during school dances, when the floor is packed with bodies and colorful lights pulse overhead, so I've never noticed how serene the space is in its natural state. "It's lovely."

We set up our indoor picnic in the center of the ballroom. Dean came prepared with a blanket, plastic utensils, and takeout from the same Italian eatery Lisa and I have our annual dinners at. There was clearly so much effort put into planning that I'm struck with a wave of guilt over having almost wrecked the evening earlier.

"This is really nice," I say after swallowing a bite of penne pomodoro. The pasta is a little cold, but that's mostly on me, and it's still pretty delicious. "Dinner, the view, everything. Something out of a *Bachelor* hometown, basically."

"Bachelor what?"

"Never mind." First dates are maybe not the time to reveal I've never missed an episode of the hit reality show. I clear my throat. "Just that this is nice. And I'm glad to be here."

He smiles, the warmth reaching his eyes. He rests his fork down on his plate. "You know," he says slowly. He runs a thumb along the edge of his sleeve. "There's a reason I wanted to come here tonight."

"Yeah?"

"Yeah," he says. "I feel like this place is an origin for us. Autumn formal, I mean."

I think of the night I danced with Dean, inside this very room, how it felt to be so near him, and I have to agree. And earlier than formal itself—planning for the dance, despite the many initial road bumps, is what ultimately brought us closer.

"I don't mean this year's formal," he rushes to clarify, and I furrow my brow, no longer comprehending. "I mean freshman year. We'd only known each other a few weeks. We were already in an argument. But I remember thinking you looked so pretty. And I remember thinking I liked you already."

I'm flushing at his first words, but I call his bluff on the last part. "You so did not already like me."

He laughs. "Okay," he says. Dimples crinkle his cheeks. "Maybe not yet. But I was on my way."

The corners of my lips push up. I think of Ms. Merriweather's words from Fall Festival, about Dean's admiration of me at the very start of our acquaintance, and I have to admit that I probably bear the bulk of the responsibility for our past rivalry. Dean adjusts his position on the blanket, expression growing a little more serious, a little more hesitant.

"I remember you brought a date," he continues. "And I remember how you smiled at him. You never smiled at me like that, not then."

There's no draft in the ballroom, but I shiver a little. "Because you made me nervous," I say. "Even then, you made me nervous."

He lifts his eyebrows. His eyes are dark under the moonlight. "And now?"

"You still make me nervous." My words are a confession. I

draw my arms closer around me for warmth. "But maybe that's not such a bad thing."

This makes him smile. "No," he says. "Maybe not."

We split a slice of blueberry cheesecake for dessert. When we finish, we pack away our takeout boxes and lay down on the picnic blanket, looking up through the skylight, indoor stargazing.

"That one's Cassiopeia," Dean says. He points to a collection of tiny bright dots.

I squint to see clearer, but all the stars look the same to me. "Really?"

"Maybe," he says. "Probably not. I don't know. Cassiopeia is the only constellation I've heard of."

"There's also Taurus," I say, unbothered by the deception. "Orion, too." I stop because I can't think of any others.

We lapse into silence, still gazing up at the night. I can hear the rhythm of his breath. Our every exhale is synced.

"Dean?"

"Hm?"

"I don't truly think tonight was a terrible idea."

I can hear the smile in his voice. "No?"

"No," I confirm. "I think it was a really good idea, actually."

I've said all of this to the sky, but now I turn on my shoulder so I can see him. "Don't you?"

He mirrors my shift in position, then stills because our noses are almost touching. He blinks. He nods.

There's a lock of hair behind his ear that's askew. I reach to smooth it down without thinking. He freezes at the contact.

His hair is so soft. I should ask him about his conditioner. I pull my hand away.

Dean blinks again. "Is it—" He swallows, and I follow the

266

movement in his throat. He is so close, I could count the freckles on his nose if I wanted. "I'd like to—" He breaks off once more.

I understand. I lean up, and then we are kissing.

I have imagined kissing Dean before, more often than I would ever admit to him, but the reality is so much better than anything I could construct. Our mouths fit together just right. His lips are soft and warm and honey sweet. His fingers are gentle in my hair, at my neck, above my waist, pausing for permission each time they slip lower. He pulls away too soon.

His eyes are more pupil than iris. He inhales, and the action is shaky. "I wanted to do that the last time we were in this room," he admits.

"I know," I say. The corner of my lips twist up. "I wanted you to."

He draws another long breath. "I really like you, Arya Khanna."

My voice is a whisper. My heart thrums in my chest. "I really like you."

Dean Merriweather smiles. He kisses me again.

Thirty-Five
A Longhand Letter

There's a letter for me in the mailbox the following afternoon. No stamp or return address, just my name in familiar slanted penmanship.

Arya,

This is my first time writing a longhand letter. It might not be very long, probably more of a note. I admit, I don't totally understand the point when I could just text you this. But you've got your thing about letters, pen pressed to paper, all of that, so here goes.

Last night was one of the best nights I've ever had. It didn't start out great—but our beginnings have never been very great. I don't mind how long it took for us to get here. It feels right now that we are.

I want you to know that I think you are so beautiful and so frustrating. I would watch four-hour Bollywood movies with you any day. I'm so glad to have you as my second-in-command, as my assistant. And maybe longhand letters do have a point, because you can't get angry with me through paper.

You make me nervous too. I couldn't say it at the pond, but obviously. I'll see you tomorrow, and the day after that.

Yours,

Dean

Act V
Shaadi Season,

Thirty-Six
Decision Day

Chandler's first snowfall of the season arrives the day Northeastern releases their early decisions. I sit on the floor by the Belle's display window, laptop open to my application portal, nails bitten to stubs. Mindy was gracious enough to give me time during my shift to check my decision, though she might regret that when I begin weeping openly in her place of business, something I am likely to do regardless of what happens.

Outside, Dean is making Emilia take pictures of him by a bare branch tree. Snow flurries to the ground around him. He gestures at Emilia to demonstrate the angle he wants the photo at, and I smile because my boyfriend is such a snob.

He'll probably caption the photo with a wintry pun like "snow place I'd rather be" or an equally embarrassing alternative, and I will like and comment anyway.

Dean catches me watching through the window, and he stops in the middle of the photo shoot to wave at me with a mittened hand. I wave back.

It's been over a week since my first date with Dean, and things have been going really well. I've spent pretty much every day since with him, and I have yet to self-sabotage (again), which alone is quite an accomplishment. We've hung out with Georgia at the bakery, and he's brought me more coffee and I have recommended more books, so pretty perfect, all in all.

And now he and Emilia are here to show some moral support for decision day. Yesterday, they both earned very well-deserved acceptances to Boston University and Tufts University, respectively, so the pressure is off for them. My stomach twists with anxious hope when I realize that in just a few minutes, I could join their number.

A low moan emits from a few feet away. I jerk my head up to see that Andy is now curled in fetal position, head between his knees. He's directly across from me, by one of the least popular bookshelves (Western Horror), so at least he isn't disturbing any customers.

"You okay?" I ask.

"I am going to throw up," he replies to the ground. UChicago decisions come out today too.

"Aim for a trash bin," I say. "Mindy won't forgive vomit on her new carpet."

He sits up straight suddenly. He *does* look like he's going to be sick. I use my foot to surreptitiously scoot a trash bin closer to him.

"Maybe if I check College Confidential again—"

"Say 'College Confidential' one more time." My voice is a warning.

He blinks. "College Confi—"

I kick his shins. He yelps.

The door jingles open before Andy can retaliate. Cold air swooshes through the room. Dean and Emilia enter, snow sticking to their shoulders. Dean looks glad, Emilia looks grumpy, so I imagine the photo shoot was successful.

"Hey," Emilia says. "How much longer?"

"Three minutes," I say. I check my phone. My heart starts to race. "Make that two."

Andy moans again. I hit refresh on my portal tab.

"Just remember," Dean says. He brushes some snow off his jacket, and it melts onto the carpet. "Decisions don't mean a thing. Don't stress at—"

Andy and I speak at the same time. "Shut. Up."

Dean closes his mouth.

"Sorry," I say, almost meaning it. "But people who have gotten into college aren't allowed to soliloquize at those who haven't."

"I wasn't soliloquizing," Dean says, but he doesn't push it. He takes off a mitten and rummages around in his coat pocket, then passes me a slightly smushed brown bag. "Here," he says. "Maybe a latke will make you feel better."

I push the bag back at him, laughing. "I can't believe you actually bought them."

Today is the fifth day of Hanukkah, and it was also Diversity Day in school, so our cafeteria chose to serve the most inedible latkes possible in celebration. They cost three dollars each and are somehow gray.

He cracks a smile. "I thought my mom would find it amusing," he says.

I don't get to reply because Andy is screaming. "Ohmygodohmygodohmygod!"

Panicked, I whirl to face him. Several customers look over. I'm going to have to apologize so hard to Mindy later tonight.

"Andy?"

His hands are to his face, fingers splayed so his eyes are only half visible. "Ohmygodohmy*god*." He spins his laptop around for our viewing. His arms are shaking. "I got in."

We all gasp in unison, and then there are squeals and cheers.

"Congratulations!" Emilia beams, reaching down to give him a hug.

"That's my man!" Dean says, though I wasn't sure he and Andy were even friends.

I lean forward to squeeze Andy's hand. "I'm so happy for you," I say. "You deserve this so much."

"Thank you. Yes. Wow. Wow." He shakes his head, drunk from joy and relief.

Emilia turns to me. "Um, Arya?" she says tentatively. "Your decision is probably ready now too."

"Oh," I say. There are stones in my stomach. "Right."

"You got it, Khanna," Dean says. He massages my shoulder. His fingers are still icy from snow.

"Take it easy," Andy says kindly. "College results don't—"

I glare at my hypocrite of a best friend. He stumbles silent, chagrined.

My cursor hovers above the "view update" button. My heart is pounding in my throat. I remind myself that getting rejected is not the end of the world. I'll just have to write a few more applications for the regular round, which will only take about ten years off my life.

I click the button. For an agonizing moment, the page struggles to load. Then confetti fills the screen.

I let out a shout almost as obnoxious as Andy's. My hand flies to my mouth. "I'm in!" The sound is muffled. I pull my hand away. "I got in!"

Emilia lets out a whoop. "Hell yes!"

"Thank God," Andy says. "I would have felt so bad to be the only one celebrating."

"I knew you would," Dean says. He wraps an arm around me from behind. I reach up to kiss his cheek. He kisses my mouth.

"Get a room," Emilia groans. "Or at least get me a boyfriend too."

"Tufts men, Emilia," I say. "They're waiting for you."

She laughs. Dean brings us victory hot cocoas from Mellie's to enjoy as I finish out the rest of my shift.

Nikhil picks up some mithai in honor of my first college acceptance, a gesture that must be his way of reaching out to me. Our relationship has staggered over the last two weeks, collateral damage in the wake of my and Alina's fight—most of the time we spent together before, Alina was there too. Since I'm steering clear of her, I'm steering clear of him by extension.

We eat mithai in the living room after dinner, a Pakistani drama playing in the background at Mamma and Rupa Aunty's request. It's the same serial I watched with Mamma a while back. The characters are now in the thick of wedding planning, which feels particularly apt.

"This is amazing," I say after taking a big bite of barfi, even though it's pistachio-flavored and my preference is mango. "Really, so delicious. Thanks, Nikhil."

I'm laying it on thick because I feel sorry for the distance that's grown between us. I don't blame him for keeping the move a secret. The idea was certainly Alina's, and she's the one who had an obligation to tell me.

"Of course," he says. "We're so proud of you, Arya."

"So proud," Papa echoes. "Now I have one daughter all ready for college, the other daughter all ready for marriage."

Alina, flipping through her planner at the coffee table, smiles at his words. She glances up at me, and I look away.

Alina and I have barely spoken since the morning at

Maharani Bridal. It hasn't been too hard to avoid conversation. With the Joshis staying with us, home is always loud and busy. When I can, I slip out of rooms she enters as an extra precaution. Alina hasn't forced interaction either. I don't think she's interested in another blowup right before her shaadi.

Today is Monday, which means the first wedding festivities are only four days away. The Khannas and Joshis have spent the last couple weeks dotting our i's and crossing our t's. We've finalized seating charts, confirmed orders with various vendors, and followed up with out-of-town guests on their arrival plans. My main contribution has been assembling gift packages, one of the shaadi tasks that involves minimal contact with Alina.

"I spoke with Aaji and Ajoba today," Nikhil says, referring to his grandparents. "They are set to arrive Thursday evening."

Both sets of Nikhil's grandparents live in Pune, Maharashtra. They are actually neighbors, which is how Rupa Aunty and Yash Uncle met. The wedding will be the first time Alina sees them in person.

"Yes," Rupa Aunty says. "Your baba and I will stop at airport to pick up on our way to the resort."

Our working plan is to drive up to the shaadi venue Thursday night so that we are situated for Friday's mehndi ceremony and welcome dinner. It's convenient timing, since my last exam of the year is Thursday morning. I have a shift at Belle's afterward, and then I'll drive to the Chatham resort with everyone else.

Nikhil and Rupa Aunty go back and forth, still discussing airport logistics, so I finish my mithai and let my attention wander. I'm scrolling through Instagram when I come across a picture of Lisa, smiling with her dog beside a half-lit menorah. It's the post she re-creates annually, and I'm struck with a wave of nostalgia because every year prior she sent me the picture for approval and caption advice before posting. I waver, and then before I can talk myself out of it, I've clicked on Lisa's contact and typed Happy Hanukkah.

I've just hit send when Alina sinks down on the sofa beside me. "Hey," she says. Her hands are tense in her lap. "Congrats on Northeastern."

I narrow my eyes. She knows better than to approach me, but it's not as though I can up and leave with the Joshis here. Which is how she planned it, probably.

"Thanks," I say.

She tries for a smile but falters when she sees my stony expression. She takes in and releases a slow breath. "Sheila and I want to run through the Sangeet routine on Friday. In our mehndi clothes, but before the ceremony. You'll be there?"

We haven't practiced the dance together since our fight. I feel pretty confident about my steps, but at least one rehearsal in lehengas and heavy jewelry is imperative for a smooth performance.

"I'll be there," I confirm, and she nods, satisfied. But she doesn't leave, not yet, and something prickly and restless scratches at my belly. I don't like being around Alina for longer than I have to anymore. "Was there something else?"

She draws back, wounded. She shakes her head after a moment and leaves, and I try to push down the immediate guilt.

A few hours later, I'm Netflix-partying a new Jane Austen movie with Dean when someone knocks on my bedroom door.

I hit pause and type an apology in the chat before calling, "It's open!"

Mamma enters, her nighttime shawl draped around her. "Hello," she says.

"Hi," I say, surprised. Mamma rarely ventures to my corner of the house.

"Good job with college results," she says, and I smile.

"Thank you," I say.

She nods, then sits delicately on the edge of my bed. "You are fighting with Alina," she says. It is not a question. Before I can dispute the claim, she adds, "Because she is moving."

My mouth drops open. "You know?" The words are shocked, hurt.

"I have known for long time," she says. "Nikhil and Alina told Papa and me before they arrived here."

My lips flatten. I hate knowing that this plan has been in the works for as long as Alina has been home. I hate knowing that I'm the absolute last person to hear of the plan's existence. When Alina said she came home for me, I wonder if this is what she meant, if the only reason she came back is because she knew she would be leaving again.

Mamma must guess what's going through my mind, because she squeezes my leg. "She did not wish to tell when so much was still undecided. She did not wish to hurt you with such news."

"Then she shouldn't leave," I blurt. I blink rapidly, the tears close. I clamp my mouth shut to keep from saying anything further.

"She is not leaving to hurt you," Mamma says gently. "She is getting married. Women begin new chapters after marriage. Your papa and I moved countries after marriage."

I don't know what to say to this. I swallow down the lump in my throat.

Mamma looks me in the eyes, expression fierce, not at all unlike Alina's resting face. "You should forgive her."

I pull back, incredulous. "*You're* telling me to forgive her?" I say. Mamma is the last person I would ever expect to advocate on Alina's behalf.

"Yes," Mamma says. "Alina makes many mistakes. She will make more. But she is your sister." Mamma goes silent, as though sisterhood is reason enough to warrant forgiveness.

And maybe it is. Being angry with Alina has never been a very sustainable practice for me. I need her too much, I love her too much, to ever be able to do without her.

Which is why her leaving is so painful.

I wipe my cheek. A tear slipped without my noticing. "I'll think about it," I say to Mamma. And then, suddenly, mostly to change the subject but also because I want her to know, I add, "I'm seeing a boy."

She frowns. "Seeing?"

"Dating," I correct. I am speaking fast, ripping off the Band-Aid. I clear my throat. "I have a boyfriend."

Her dark eyes widen. "Oh," she says. She is quiet, and my heart starts to race. I wonder if I've made a big mistake. Mamma and I don't really talk like this. But I'm trying to build a better relationship with her, and honesty is a part of that equation.

She raises her eyebrows. "He is nice to you?"

Something in me relaxes at the question. "Yes," I say. The answer is mostly true, anyway. "He is very nice to me."

"Good," she says. She squeezes my leg once more, and I can tell she's exhausted her capacity for conversation tonight. I squeeze her hand, and then she stands and leaves.

I let out a sigh and settle back in my bed, pulling the covers around me like a cocoon until only my head is visible. I tell Dean I'm ready to resume the movie. We've just pressed play when my phone buzzes. I swipe to see the notification, and my breath catches.

It's a text from Lisa: Are you free for coffee tomorrow after school?

Thirty-Seven
Reunited

On Tuesday afternoon, I drive over to Mellie's right after finishing my Bio exam.

I order my drink and secure a table as I wait for Lisa, and she sinks down onto the chair across from me a moment later. Her red hair is pulled back into her usual high pony with a scrunchie.

"Hi," she says. She sips her cold brew, and I almost smile because it is so like her. Even in the dead of winter, Lisa will order iced drinks.

"Hi," I say. We fall silent. This is at once achingly familiar and terribly foreign. We have had Mellie's coffee dates dozens of times in the past, but none in recent weeks.

I sip my coffee for something to do. It burns my tongue.

"Congrats on Northeastern," Lisa says, breaking the silence. "I saw on Emilia's Instagram story," she adds.

Emilia is very big on documenting everyone's college decisions on social media. She has an entire highlight dedicated to the subject on her Instagram.

"Thank you," I say. I realize I don't even know for sure where Lisa's applied, so I ask, "Have you heard back from anywhere yet?"

She shakes her head. "I didn't apply anywhere early. The UCs don't even have that option."

I nod, remembering. Lisa has always wanted to go to college in California. She made me listen to "UCLA" by RL Grime on repeat freshman year.

Before I can make a joke—albeit a bad one—about the song, Lisa blurts out, "I'm not coming to Alina's wedding."

There's a beat. "Oh," I say, more stung than I expected to be. I shouldn't be surprised; she never RSVP'd, after all. But I didn't want to believe that whatever drama has developed between us would actually cause Lisa to skip such an important moment in my life.

"Not because I don't want to," she hurries to add. "But because our first tournament of the season is this weekend too. I'm really sorry," she says, and she looks it.

"Okay," I say after a beat. This is at least a better scenario than her not making it because she's angry with me. "I understand." It's not as though the captain of varsity basketball can miss the season opener for her friend's sister's wedding. But—

"I wish you had talked to me about it sooner." I can't keep the next words in. "I wish you had talked to me, period."

She draws back. "Yeah," she says finally. "I think I spent a lot of time feeling too hurt to talk it all through." She picks at her nails. Her polish is chipping. "But I'm ready now, and I'm glad you texted."

Lisa pauses, and I take the opportunity. "I didn't choose Andy," I begin. "I didn't mean to, at least. I was trying to make the most of formal given the circumstances, but I should have prioritized your feelings more. I'm sorry I didn't."

"You should have," she agrees, but she softens. "I know I played a role. I responded to the breakup by pushing you away along with Andy. It was just so fresh and painful, and I reacted poorly."

"Still, I should have considered how formal must've looked to you," I continue. Some of the tension is starting to leave my shoulders. We are finally having it out, the way we have needed to for weeks and weeks. "But it was never like that. Truly."

"Well, I'm glad. And Clara's little hypothesis seems even more silly in retrospect." She allows a small smile. "Dean, right?"

"Kind of," I say. For some reason, I'm blushing. "Yes."

She laughs. "I've missed so much," she says. Her eyes are shiny. "I know it's mostly my fault. The breakup was really tough on me. And then I convinced myself that you going to the dance with Andy meant you didn't care about me." She ducks her head, pulling at her ponytail. "Which was pretty dramatic."

I give a wobbly smile. "So dramatic," I agree.

She laughs again, reaching her hand out to squeeze mine. "I missed you, Arya," she says.

I squeeze back. "I missed you too," I say, and she smiles. But something is still weighing on me, twisting at my stomach. I release her hand.

"Andy says you guys spoke," I say. "Over Thanksgiving break." I pick at the sleeve of my sweater. I wonder if there's a way to say what I want to without sounding childish or needy. I can't come up with one. "Why could you make up with him but not me?"

Her cheeks go pink. She looks like she's chewing on her words. "It was bigger with you," she says eventually. "Because I'd messed up too. And I was embarrassed of how I'd acted after our fight. Like at Merri Berry Sweets."

284

I think of that evening, how Lisa had barely looked my way, how she left early almost certainly because of me, and my cheeks flush too.

"And even when we spoke at the dance, I could have handled it better," she continues. "So while I had mostly moved on by Thanksgiving, gotten over Andy, gotten over formal, the memory of how I behaved was still there." She is speaking to her hands. "I never thought I would be this messy about a relationship, you know? But I was, and that was embarrassing."

She looks up. Her eyes are shinier. "Besides," she says, "you seemed like you were fine." Her tone is light, but I know Lisa well enough to know it's forced. "You and Andy were still close, you had Emilia, you had Dean. It's not as though you needed me."

"Lisa Greenfield," I say. I swat her arm. "I will always need you."

I mean the words. Some things have changed, but this much is still true. Lisa, Andy, and I may no longer be the trio we once were, and it might take some time to restore the strength of my and Lisa's friendship, but she has been a constant in my life forever. I don't intend to lose her.

She gives a shaky laugh. "I will always need you too."

My body warms at the statement. I take a sip of my mocha, which has reached a drinkable temperature, and realize that patching things up with Lisa means I get to ask after what I've been curious about for a while.

"Andy mentioned you've started seeing someone new," I say conversationally.

Lisa blushes again, but she doesn't hold back. "I have," she says. "Honestly, that's probably part of why I was comfortable talking to Andy during Thanksgiving. It's always nice to establish you've won the breakup."

I bite back a laugh on Andy's behalf, even though it's not as if he's been searching for a new relationship. I tilt my head at Lisa. "Who is it?"

Lisa swirls her drink. "Her name is Quinn," she says. "We met at Mellie's. She's a barista here, actually."

Immediately, I glance to the counter, scanning for a worker with the name tag QUINN. Lisa kicks me under the table.

"Stop that," she says, but she looks amused. "Quinn's not working today."

"Shame," I say. I reach back in my memory, trying to put a face to the name. I'm at Mellie's often enough to be familiar with most of the staff. I look at Lisa. "Is she blond?"

"Yes," Lisa says. "With some pink streaks."

My eyes brighten with recognition. "I think I've ordered from her. She's very talented with latte art." Lisa nods, confirming, and I push on. "How did it happen?"

"Mostly how you'd expect," Lisa says. "We met early November, she made me coffee, I fell in love."

"Wow," I say. "That easy?"

Lisa sighs dreamily. "You know me," she says. "I always fall in love with my baristas."

I nod, solemn. "This is true," I say. "Not that I'll ever understand it."

Freshman year, Lisa was besotted with a Mellie's barista who wore a beanie to work every day no matter the weather. Lisa swore the look gave him character, but I was sure it was just a cover for really bad dandruff.

"Baristas provide me coffee," Lisa explains. "It's an addictive stimulant."

"So, like a dealer."

Lisa frowns. "Well, much more romantic than that." She sits up straighter. "It's like this," she says. "I get to thinking about how they probably work at a coffeehouse as a day job. But then they go home, and, like, work on their poetry."

I am very lost, and Lisa must be able to tell from my expression, because she adds, "Obviously that's just conjecture. But it's all about the vibes. And I get major poet vibes from so many baristas."

"And poetry is hot?"

"In a vague, theoretical sense," Lisa clarifies. "Like, the *idea* of a poet is hot. Making me read the poetry is not hot." She shudders. "Dear God, don't make me read it."

I laugh. I've missed Lisa's nonsense. "Is Quinn a poet?"

"Even hotter. She's a songwriter. She studies music composition at CC."

"Well, I'm really happy for you, Lisa."

She warms at the words. "Thank you," she says. She rests her chin in her palm. "I'm very happy for you too," she says. "I want to hear all about Dean, all about how it happened."

"That would take much longer than a single coffee date," I say.

She shrugs, corners of her lips pushing up. "I have time."

Later, when I'm back in my car and waiting for the heater to kick in so I can drive home, I take out my phone and click the third speed dial. As disappointing as it is that Lisa can't make the wedding, it also means one of the three invites I was given (the other two being for Andy and Emilia) is suddenly open.

Dean picks up on the second ring. There's a blender working in the background; he must be at the bake shop. "Hey, Khanna."

"Hi," I say. "What are you doing this weekend?"

Thirty-Eight
Found Family

Thursday evening, as I'm getting ready to leave for the day, Mindy pushes a gift box toward me. It's small and gray with an extravagant red bow.

"For you," she says when I look at her questioningly. "Holiday gift and college congratulations in one."

I put a hand to my chest, struck by the gesture. "Oh, Mindy," I say. "You really didn't have to."

Her lips stretch up. "I know," she says. "Now hush and open."

"I feel bad," I say, even as my fingers work to undo the bow. "I didn't get you anything."

"My birthday is coming up soon," Mindy reminds me. She leans against the register and tucks a midnight blue lock of hair behind her ear. "You can make up for your neglect then."

I laugh. I pull the lid of the box and suck in a breath. Nestled in white tissue paper is a framed portrait of me and Mindy. It's a photo of us from Halloween, me dressed as Belle, Mindy dressed as Mrs. Potts. I pick up the frame and see there's more to the gift: two beautiful bookmarks, one with Dragon Witch art and the other with a Jane Austen quote.

"I love it," I say, turning to Mindy. Tears are sparkling in my eyes. I have been crying so easily this past week. "The bookmarks are such a perfect summary of my reading preferences."

Children's literature and romantic classics—I could never do without them.

"I thought it was fitting," Mindy says. Then she tilts her head, and I see something wistful in her expression. "I am going to miss you so much, Arya."

"It's only two weeks!" I say, a little bemused. Mindy and Cleo always close shop around this time to go on a holiday trip. The dates coincide with Alina's shaadi this year, which is convenient for me. "We'll see each other in the New Year."

She shakes her head. "No," she says. "I mean I'm going to miss you when you head to college." She tries for a quick smile. "But that's why you have the picture. You won't forget me so easy."

"I could never forget you," I say. The tears are back, fresh and hot behind my lids, and I blink them away. I have been trying hard not to think about all the change ahead of me. I don't want to imagine not having Belle's in my life. "Anyway," I say, "Northeastern isn't that far."

Mindy nods at this. "Yeah," she says. "Just forty-two minutes from here."

My heart warms hearing the exact amount of time. Mindy must have consulted Google Maps. "Probably even less without traffic," I say. I pick at the ribbon on one of the bookmarks. "So, you know," I say lightly, "if you ever get tired of my replacement, I can just drive over to keep you company."

She takes a deep breath. "Actually," she says, "I'm not hiring a replacement."

I raise my eyebrows. "You're not?"

"No," she says. She starts fiddling with the register computer, looking both pleased and bashful. "Cleo just took an editor role at the paper. She won't be traveling for assignment anymore, so she'll be around to help me run Belle's."

I gasp. "Mindy," I say. I squeeze her hand on the countertop. "That's amazing. Both for you and for me." I have not been looking forward to getting replaced.

She laughs. "I'm pretty happy with the arrangement." She looks at me, eyes large and caring. "I want you to know there will always be a place for you here," she says. "Okay? Belle's will always be home for you."

I blink fast, then I reach up to hug Mindy. "Thank you," I say softly. A tear slips past, and I wipe at my cheek.

She hugs me tight. "Of course, Arya."

We pull away, still teary. Mindy presses her sleeve to the corner of her eye, and I busy myself with the gift box, plucking at the tissue paper.

"I wrote my Northeastern essay about this," I tell her after a beat. "About Belle's; about you."

I glance sideways at her, and I see a smile start. "Yeah?"

"Yeah," I say. I turn toward her, and I spend the rest of my shift telling her about the essay and Northeastern and how scared but excited I am for starting college. Mindy listens, attentive as always, my mentor and friend all in one.

Nikhil is in the driveway when I return home, loading garment bags into the trunk of his car.

I stop by him on my way to the porch, keys still in hand, puzzled by his presence. "Hi," I say. "I thought you would've already left."

We're all driving up to Chatham today, getting settled in the resort before shaadi festivities begin tomorrow. Rupa Aunty and Yash Uncle left in the morning to pick up the Joshi grandparents at the airport, and I'm leaving with Mamma and Papa later tonight. The plan was for Nikhil and Alina to leave at some point in between.

Nikhil shakes his head. "Alina's nail appointment ran late," he says. "We're heading out in about twenty minutes."

"Okay," I say. It makes sense. Alina always picks at her fingernails, so she must have scheduled her manicure at the last possible moment. I twist at a lock of hair, restless. It feels odd to be alone with Nikhil when I'm in a fight with his fiancée. "Well, I'll see you."

I start for the door, but he stops me.

"Arya," he says. He hesitates when he's a few feet away from me. He scratches his neck. He looks handsome in the lamplight, stubble freshly shaven and hair freshly trimmed for the wedding. "I've been meaning to talk to you."

He hesitates again, and I hug my arms to my chest. It's too chilly to have conversations outside. "What's up?"

"I wanted to tell you I'm sorry," he says at last. "For keeping the move from you. I shouldn't have done that."

I blink. "Oh," I say. I'm surprised at his use of the first-person singular. "Okay. It was Alina's fault, mostly."

He shakes his head. "It's on me too. I messed up. I should have told you." He pauses, and his voice is impossibly gentle when he speaks next. "Because you're my family now, Arya."

I blink faster. I am constantly on the edge of tears lately. "Nikhil," I say, and my voice is wobbly.

He steps forward, and we embrace. His hold is warm and tight.

"I've always wanted a brother," I say to his shoulder.

He laughs in my ear. "I've always wanted a sister," he says.

"Especially one who shares my love for Bollywood," he adds, and I laugh.

Nikhil steps away and studies me, expression tentative, analytical. "Will you and Alina be okay?" he asks finally.

I shift on my feet, nervous at the question, though I should have expected it. He's about to become her husband, after all. "I don't know," I say.

He nods. "She didn't want to hurt you," he says.

"I wish everyone would stop saying that," I say. "Because she did."

"Okay," he says, nodding. "That's fair."

I reach forward to squeeze his hand. Nikhil really is such a good man. I wouldn't want anyone else as my jijaji. He squeezes back. "I'll see you tomorrow," I tell him, and then I turn away to walk up the stairs and inside.

Thirty-Nine
Mehndi Laga Ke Rakhna

I dress for the mehndi ceremony in my resort suite. Sheila Jawani and I have to share, but I don't mind, because our balcony offers a breathtaking view of the sea. When we arrived last night, I sat at the railing for an hour despite the biting cold, just watching the water glitter under moonlight.

Sheila was gone by the time I woke, so I have the space to myself as I get ready. My lehenga for today is marigold-colored with a whisper-soft chunni and a jeweled blouse, and my skirt is the kind of flowy that makes me want to spin and spin and spin. Which is good for today, I guess, because we have dance rehearsal for an hour prior to the ceremony.

When I finish getting dressed, I head to the bridal suite, where we're practicing our Sangeet routine. It will be the first time all three of us have rehearsed together in person. Sheila's had to FaceTime into our other practices.

"You want to, um, try *not* to move like that," Sheila is saying when I open the door.

I knock to signal my arrival, cutting off Alina's retort. They turn to look at me.

"Hey," Sheila says. She's wearing a lavender lehenga with silver detailing, and her dark hair is curled to perfection. "You're here."

"Hi," I say. My mouth feels dry suddenly. What kind of maid of honor am I, to not even be on speaking terms with the bride? I clear my throat. "I'm ready to run through the routine whenever you guys are."

Alina steps forward. She is dazzling in the blush-and-champagne ensemble that took my breath away during her first fitting at Maharani Bridal. I wonder if Veena and Mamma helped her dress. I think about how I shouldn't have to wonder. I should have been here, with my sister on mehndi morning.

"Arya," Alina says. She is looking everywhere but my face. "You look so beautiful."

I wonder how she can tell when she still hasn't looked straight at me yet. "Thank you," I say. The words are warbled. Pressure is already starting in my eyes. I am basically more waterworks than human at this point. "*You* look so beautiful."

We lock eyes for the first time since I stepped inside. We burst into tears.

Sheila stands suddenly. "I have to make a phone call," she announces mechanically. She presses a few buttons and raises the phone to her ear. "Hi, my name is Sheila," she says as she hurries from the room. "Sheila Jawani."

We are alone. Alina sinks onto a dressing stool, careful not to crease her skirt. I plop onto a nearby cushion, skirt bunching beneath me.

"I'm sorry," she blurts. Tears are spilling down her cheeks, but her makeup remains unsmudged. Her waterproof products are clearly worth their price tag. "I'm so sorry. I should have told you about San Francisco."

"You should have," I agree. I know my tears are leaving mascara tracks down my face; I didn't think to go waterproof. I feel so thankful we hired a makeup artist for the evening. "I deserved to know, and I deserved to hear it from you."

She sniffles. "I know," she says. "I was so worried you would get angry with me. And then I made you even more angry by keeping it secret."

"I *am* angry," I say. I wipe at my nose. "But it's about more than the move. I think I've been angry with you for years now. I've been angry with you since you first left."

She blinks. There's a tear clinging to her eyelashes. I continue. "I was all alone without you. I was all alone with Papa and Mamma, and it was too much responsibility."

She cuts in. "It's not your responsibility—"

"But it felt like it," I say. "And it felt like I was failing."

She stands up from the stool and sits back down beside me on the cushion. Her skirt creases this time. We'll need to press our lehengas again before mehndi.

"I'm sorry," she whispers. She clasps my hand in hers. "I didn't think about how leaving would affect you. I was just doing what was best for me. And leaving was best for me. But it hurt you, and for that, I'm sorry."

Another tear slips down my cheek. She goes on. "That's why I wanted to come home before the shaadi. So I could be with you, spend time with you the way we didn't for so long." She swipes away a tear. "It hasn't gone as planned, clearly."

I take a shaky breath. I can understand that any harm Alina caused me was a side effect, not the intention. Alina has never been malicious toward me. But the impact is still there, too deep to move past with ease.

"I don't want to be angry with you anymore," I say.

"Especially not now. I want to celebrate you. It's your big day, after all."

A wavering smile starts on her lips. "My big week," she corrects, and I almost laugh.

"You told Mamma before you told me," I say now. I don't mean for my tone to be accusatory, but it is.

She twists at her ring. "Yeah," she says. "I know that Mamma is sensitive about these things, about not hearing of milestones firsthand." She stumbles. "Not that you aren't sensitive." She shakes her head. "I didn't want to mess up again this big with Mamma."

I think of Mamma's hurt three years back, when she learned Alina dropped out of school through the aunty rumor mill, and I get Alina's logic.

Alina continues. "I also felt like this was something she would understand. My moving, I mean."

"I guess," I say. I'm reminded of Mamma's words from a few nights ago, about moving to Boston with Papa after their marriage. "Maybe, yeah."

We fall quiet. Alina nudges me. "I meant what I said earlier," she says gently. "It isn't your job to make Mamma better. Or to make Papa a better husband. Or even to hold that pain at all. That isn't your burden to carry."

I pluck at a gem on my choker. "I know," I say, and I mean it. It's a lesson I've been learning slowly. "Though I'm still trying to be closer with Mamma. For myself." I look up at Alina. "That's something you can try too, by the way."

She makes an unintelligible sound that certainly isn't agreement. I don't push her. It isn't my job to mend Alina and Mamma's relationship, either.

"There's something else," Alina says. She bites her lip. "About my art," she continues. "I don't expect you to understand, but

I have to paint about these things. It's how I make sense of it all."

I don't understand, but I know it's how Alina's mind operates, how it always has. "Okay," I say. I remember how cruel I was about the painting at the dress shop, so I rush to add, "I was trying to wound at Maharani. I was thrown off; that's all. It's a good painting. Everything you paint is good, always."

She smiles at this. "I'm glad you think so. Because I have a lot of plans for my career in the SF art scene." Her smile deepens, but more tears fill her eyes. "There's so much I want to fill you in on."

"I want to hear it," I say. "All of it, and soon."

I lean my head on Alina's shoulder. She leans back against me. There's still a lot for us to sort through, more hurt left to unpack, but this is a beginning. We have always found our way to each other in the past, and we can do it again.

Sheila enters the room, just as abruptly as she exited. She looks between us, studying, then says, "I finished my phone call."

"Took you long enough," Alina says, and Sheila laughs.

Finally, we start rehearsal. We need to perfect the performance to make sure Alina gets her desired honeymoon location. Sheila connects her phone to a speaker, and the first instrumentals of "You Are My Soniya" begin to play, bouncy and familiar.

"Hey," Alina says, and I look up at her. Her nose is still red from crying, but her eyes are bright and playful. "Don't forget. You are my soniya, Arya."

I smile at the line. She laughs and plants a lipsticked kiss on my cheek.

Alina writes Nikhil's name in mehndi on her left hand all by herself, and the henna artist works around her lettering.

The final design is an intricate portrait of a bride and a groom who appear to be embracing each other when Alina's palms are adjacent.

I ask for paisleys and peacocks so my mehndi matches my wedding ceremony lehenga. Sheila gets a simple lotus design, and when all our arms and feet are stiff with drying henna, we sit at the side windows and watch the sun set over the water. In the background, the classic shaadi song "Mehndi Laga Ke Rakhna" sounds on the speaker.

We are in one of the resort's spacious seaside halls tonight. Somewhere upstairs, Nikhil is getting ready with his grooms-men. We'll assemble together for dinner later, but mehndi time is reserved for the women.

"You know," Alina says. Her arms must have gotten tired on the crimson resting pillow, because she's stretching them above her head in a very unladylike fashion. "I always loved the idea of a mehndi ceremony. I thought it was so superior to the usual Western bachelorette parties."

"Except . . ." she continues. Her nostrils flare, and I can guess exactly where she's going. "Now it's like I have Deepti Aunty at my bachelorette."

I giggle. Some twenty feet away, Deepti Aunty is chattering animatedly to a weary-looking henna artist, likely issuing very specific demands about her desired mehndi pattern.

"That is a drawback," Sheila agrees. "But don't think of her. Just think about how beautiful your mehndi pictures are going to be."

Alina sighs dreamily, and I share her response. We took some classic hands-to-camera photos on the bridal love seat af-ter getting our mehndi done. My favorite is the one Alina and I took with Mamma, looking regal as ever in a deep maroon sari, seated between us and smiling true.

She didn't say it, but I know she's glad her daughters made up before this momentous occasion.

"Arya," Alina begins. I glance at her to see her eyes are narrowed and curious. "I've wanted to ask. What's this I hear from Nikhil about your big new romance?"

My cheeks go warm. "I never told Nikhil about Dean," I say, defensive.

Her mouth drops at the confirmation. "So it is true!" she says, and my cheeks glow hotter. "He heard from Rupa Aunty," she explains.

I tilt my head. "I never told Rupa Aunty, either." Alina's eyes furrow in confusion, and I fill in the blank. Desi families are as gossipy as they come. "She must have heard from Mamma," I conclude.

Alina shakes her head. "I can't believe you told Mamma first."

I let out a sound that's a cross between a gasp and a laugh. "Do you hear yourself?" I say, and she sits back, chagrined. Sheila watches the exchange with amusement.

I look at my hands. "He'll be at the Sangeet tomorrow," I tell Alina. My mehndi is beginning to crack, which means I should be clear to scrape it off soon. "You guys can reconnect then."

"I'd like that," Alina says.

I look at my sister, and we smile.

Forty
Shaadi

My leg twitches beneath the table. In ten minutes, we'll be dancing before almost two hundred guests, and the performance will be recorded, so it will live on forever. I am running through the routine in my mind, trying to recall all my steps, when Alina nudges me.

"What?" I whisper. Two seats away, Nikhil's brother and best man, Neil, is rising to his feet, preparing to give a toast.

"Let's go over the plan again," Alina says.

Beside me, Sheila barely stifles an eye roll, and I share her sentiment. "We've been through it a million times," I hiss. "Before, during, and after Haldi. Now hush and listen to your brother-in-law."

It is so improper for the bride to be otherwise occupied during the best man's speech. Nikhil has already tossed Alina a questioning glance, and guests are likely to notice too if Alina continues talking.

Alina glares. "It's the most important night of my life, Arya."

"Then pay attention," I retort, and she huffs, sinking back in her seat.

It's Saturday evening, and we're in the resort's ballroom for the Sangeet. The space is lovely, with high ceilings and golden chandeliers and windowed walls that overlook the glittering sea. Lilac bunches sit in the center of each dining table, the perfect color match to Alina's gown of the day.

My lehenga complements Alina's, dandelion yellow with silver embellishments. If we trip and fall during the dance, we will at least look beautiful doing so.

"—can always count on my elderly brother," Neil is saying, champagne glass raised.

"Elder brother," Nikhil interjects.

"I said what I said."

Light laughter echoes, and I use the time to glance around the ballroom. We arranged seating so the head table—soon-to-be newlyweds and their wedding party—borders the dance floor, and the neighboring few tables are composed of family members. Seating continues down in order of importance to the couple, which means Dean, Andy, and Emilia have been grouped with old college acquaintances Nikhil and Alina felt obligated to invite.

Dean is massaging his temple, looking thoroughly bored, which I take to mean that the blue-haired philosophy major beside him is just as dry as I remember from a former trip to visit Alina.

He catches me looking, and a smile starts to form. My lips push up too. He looks so handsome tonight, a yellow tie paired with his dress shirt to match my lehenga.

People are clapping. I join the applause as I turn back to Neil, who is beaming and taking it in. Amid the noise, Alina pokes my arm.

"It can't hurt to go over it one final time," she tries, and I sigh, exasperated but appeasing.

"Fine," I say. There's enough clamor to mask her words. "But quickly."

She nods, satisfied. "So Sheila will start her toast," Alina says with a meaningful look at her best friend. Sheila gives a mock salute, but Alina continues, unbothered. "And when she gets to the anecdote about the first time I told Nikhil I loved him, instrumentals begin. Then you two—"

Alina stops abruptly. She tilts her head, listening. She frowns. "Is that—?"

It is. "You Are My Soniya," our beloved Sangeet song, is beginning to play in the background.

I smile, utterly bemused. We're not meant to be on for another few minutes. "Did the deejay make a mistake?"

But I know there hasn't been a mistake when I see that Neil and his boyfriend, Rishabh, are both standing now. Nikhil is pushing back his seat. All around us, guests are quieting in anticipation.

Sheila's mouth drops. "Why do the boys look like they're getting ready to dance?"

Dread sinks in my stomach. "Because they are," I whisper. My heart is going fast. I chose Alina's Sangeet song, and: "Nikhil and I have the same taste in Bollywood."

A gasp escapes Alina. "No," she says. "No, this cannot be happening."

Nikhil is walking to the dance floor, Neil and Rishabh flanking him on either side.

"This is why," Alina says fiercely. "This is why I wanted to go over the plan. I knew—"

I snort. "You knew this would happen?" I say, and I receive an elbow to the ribs.

302

Now center stage, Nikhil grins at his fiancée. He blows her a kiss, and Alina catches it in spite of herself, putting a hand to her heart. Everyone *awh*s collectively at the sweetness.

"I'm in love with him," Alina declares. "I am so in love with him. And I am so mad."

"What should we do?" Sheila asks.

The music is getting louder; the boys are seconds from the start of their dance. Alina and I look at each other. She raises her eyebrows, a question.

"It's not like we can perform a routine to the same song," Sheila continues. "I mean I guess we could, but it would be so underwhelming." She frowns when she sees our expressions. "What?"

Guests are clapping and whooping, some rising to their feet to get a full view of the dance. Nikhil and his groomsmen have officially begun.

Alina and I hesitate for another few moments. Then we rush the stage.

Sheila follows a second later, lifting her skirt and kicking off her heels in the process.

It is pure chaos. There's the initial confusion, the boys startling when they realize we're joining them, and elbows bump and feet are stepped on as we try to perform wildly different dances to the same song. But it is also pure joy. I am laughing so hard, I can barely remember half my steps.

At some point, guests filter onto the stage too, inspired by the bridal party's crashing of the dance floor. Everyone from Emilia and Dean to Papa and Yash Uncle joins in, and it's the messiest, happiest five and a half minutes I have spent in a long time.

When the music ends, Alina and Nikhil cling to each other, and people cheer in celebration.

In the mayhem, Alina's eyes find mine. She reaches for me, grasps my hand, and squeezes tight.

TWO hours later, after dinner and a few more toasts, I dance to a Hindi ballad with Dean Merriweather.

His hands rest at my waist, and my hands are around his neck. It's the same way we danced at formal, but we are so much more comfortable with each other now. I push a lock of hair from his eyes, and he smiles.

"Tonight has been intense," he says, and I nod. "You guys really know how to throw a wedding."

I lift my brows. "You guys?" I repeat.

He opens and closes his mouth. "I meant—" He stops. He shakes his head. "I won't continue."

I laugh. He pulls me closer, tugging on my chunni. Over his shoulder, I see Emilia and Andy dancing together, and farther away are Alina and Nikhil, holding each other close, so terribly in love.

"Dean," I say. Something has been stirring in my mind for a while now. I lick my lips. "So this is new and everything," I begin, gesturing between us. "And it's been going well so far," I continue.

He leans forward to kiss me. I smile against his mouth. It's been weeks and his kiss still makes my body turn fluid. "Really well," he agrees when he pulls away.

"What if—" I hesitate. "What if we have another fight?"

My words are hushed. It's not so outrageous a worry; for years, the structure of our relationship was fight follows fight, after all. But Dean doesn't look concerned.

"Oh," he says. "Well, of course we'll have another fight."

I draw back, flushed. "That is *so* not the reassurance I was looking for."

He laughs. "I just mean," he begins, curling a strand of hair behind my ear. His fingers play with one of my earrings. His touch is gentle. "One day, we'll fight with each other again. But you'll apologize, I'll forgive, and we'll move on."

I frown. "Why am I the one who'll apologize?" My frown deepens. "Why am I the one who *always* apologizes?" I give Dean a pointed look. "That's revealing."

"Yeah," he says. "It reveals that you're the problematic one."

I swat his shoulder. "The conciliatory one," I correct. "Besides, you've definitely done a lot over the years that you should apologize for."

"You want me to apologize?" Dean says, eyebrows raised, and I shrug, because I definitely wouldn't mind. "Okay," he says. "I'll apologize. I'm sorry it took me so long to ask you out."

I roll my eyes, but I'm smiling, probably a little too big. "Ugh," I say.

He continues. "I'm sorry it's taken me so long," he says. He hesitates, swallows. "To tell you I love you."

I stop and stare. "You love me?"

He hesitates again, then he nods. My smile deepens, and I go on tiptoe so we are at eye level. "Dean Merriweather," I say. "I love you too."

He kisses me. He tastes of wedding cake. I pull away quickly because we are surrounded by my family, and we settle for blushing at each other in the dark.

This moment is temporary, and there is still so much that is uncharted ahead of us. Ahead of me. But for now, time is still, I am happy, and that is more than enough.

In the morning, before her shaadi, I stand with my sister in the bridal dressing room. We are alone; the tailor has left, and our Mamma is waiting for us outside the door.

Alina is radiant in her ceremony red. I am wearing the navy lehenga with embroidered peacocks that she gifted me all those months ago. The pearl-gold jhumke that were once Naniji's, Mamma's, Alina's glitter from my ears.

I watch in the mirror as Alina caresses the ruby pendant at her throat. She catches my eye and glows.

I lean forward to take my sister's hand. Her fingers close around mine, warm and firm. "Ready?" I ask.

She squeezes my hand. "Ready," she says, and we step forward together.

Closing Credits

ARYA:

"Bole Chudiyan"—*Kabhi Khushi Kabhie Gham*, 2001

ALINA:

"Mere Khwabon Mein"—*Dilwale Dulhania Le Jayenge*, 1995

DEAN:

"Deewana Hai Dekho"—*Kabhi Khushi Kabhie Gham*, 2001

ANDY:

"Ilahi"—*Yeh Jawaani Hai Deewani*, 2013

LISA:

"Kabira"—*Yeh Jawaani Hai Deewani*, 2013

EMILIA:

"Senorita"—*Zindagi Na Milegi Dobara*, 2011

NIKHIL:

"Tujhe Dekha To"—*Dilwale Dulhania Le Jayenge*, 1995

Closing Credits

MAMMA:

"Kabhi Khushi Kabhie Gham"—*Kabhi Khushi Kabhie Gham,*
2001

PAPA:

"Dilbaro"—*Raazi,* 2018

SHEILA:

"Sheila Ki Jawani"—*Tees Maar Khan,* 2010

Acknowledgments

This book is a dream come true. I am indebted to so many incredible people for making all my 11:11s, eyelash wishes, and birthday candle blows from age twelve onward a reality.

Thank you to my lovely agents, Rebecca Rodd and Kerry Sparks. I knew from our first phone call that you both understood the vision I had for Arya's story. I totally cried on my dorm room floor after I got your offer. Thank you for helping this book reach its full cinematic potential and for being such dependable advocates for my career. I feel so lucky to have you in my corner, and I can't wait to keep working together in the years to come.

Thank you to my spectacular editor, Vicki Lame, for taking a chance on me and Arya. All my gratitude to Vanessa Aguirre as well. Thank you both for sharing my joy for this project and for knowing exactly what I meant when I said I wanted to write a Bollywood drama in young adult novel form! With every step of the publishing process, we've worked toward that goal. It has been a gift to bring this book into the world with you.

Acknowledgments

I am deeply appreciative of the rest of my wonderful team at Wednesday Books: Eileen Rothschild, Sara Goodman, Olga Grlic, Soleil Paz, Jonathan Bennett, Lauren Riebs, Marinda Valenti, Diane Dilluvio, Eric Meyer, Rivka Holler, Brant Janeway, and Austin Adams. Thank you for the care and enthusiasm you brought to *Arya*. Thank you also to Petra Braun for the magnificent cover design. Seeing Arya in her "Bole Chudiyan"–inspired lehenga immediately made me teary.

Thank you to Lillie Vale, Nisha Sharma, Racquel Marie, Aamna Qureshi, and Jesmeen Kaur Deo for taking the time to read and support my debut. Thank you also to Brittany Cavallaro for all the guidance and for telling a fifteen-year-old Arushi you saw promise in her work. It meant the world to me then, and it means the world to me now.

My career is a possibility because of the many remarkable South Asian women who came before me and created space for themselves in publishing. Thank you in particular to Sanjena Sathian (and to my lovely friend Anisha Menath for connecting us!) for your wisdom and encouragement. I've never taken so many notes so fast on a phone call before. Thank you also to Roshani Chokshi, who is the first Indian author in YA fantasy that I ever read. Your advice during my submission process was so invaluable. If teenage Arushi knew she had your number, she'd probably cry. Thank you also to Sabaa Tahir, my fellow UCLA and *Daily Bruin* alum, for your guidance and generosity of spirit. It is impossible to put into words what *All My Rage* means to me, and it was the highlight of my student journalism career to interview you. I admire you all immensely.

Thank you so much to Tashie Bhuiyan for shepherding me through my very first revision process. You were one of the first people to read *Arya* in her earliest entirety, and your faith in this story was so meaningful to me. Thank you for being my mentor, and thank you to the entire Author Mentor Match community for your commitment to supporting emerging authors. I am so grateful!

Meeting other young writers has been such a highlight of my debut experience. Thank you to Kalie Holford for being in my corner from day one. You made querying feel far less overwhelming. Thank you also to Ann Zhao, Victoria Wlosok, and Ananya Devarajan for the advice during my publishing journey. I am so thankful, and I hope you know I'm always cheering you on!

Thank you to my Mamma, who has sacrificed more for me than I can ever know or repay. Thank you for indulging all my shaadi questions and for letting me borrow your maiden name. You once told me you saw me as the next Jane Austen— very laughably, incredibly untrue, but just goes to show: no one in this world believes in me the way you do, and I am so grateful. Thank you also to my Baba, who will always be my favorite storyteller. Thank you for the childhood library trips that made me a reader and for raising me to be curious and confident. I beam every time I make your Facebook page. I love you both.

To my sister, Aashna, my best friend and role model wrapped in one: I love you more than I can ever express. You'll always be the first person I want to talk through a new story idea with. Thank you for the care packages, life counseling, and talking me off many ledges. The only person I'd run through an airport for is you.

Thank you to Sana Sinha, my oldest, dearest friend and my most trusted reader. I am forever grateful I volunteered to be your tour guide in grade two. You are the best chauffeur, book club partner, and body language scientist a girl could ask for. I am the luckiest to have grown up with you. I love you, I love you.

Acknowledgments

Thank you to Matthew Bray, who is the reason I made it through quarantine. I am so grateful you slid into my DMs all those years ago. Thank you to Fariba Rahman for the movie nights, choir memories, and reliably sound life advice. I'm so glad we got past Disney 2019! Thank you to Audrey Im, my very first critique partner, for reading and championing the earliest pages of this book. Time is crazy. Thank you to Lina Christopherson-Jeong for the best summer of my life and for generally being one of the coolest people I know. I love you and your words. You inspire me immensely. Thank you also to Sejal Govindarao for the video call debriefs; to Radhika Gawde for being my favorite bookworm and Marathi mulgi; and to Ajay Khanna, who gets the best cousin award. Endlessly thankful!

Thank you to Sydney Sullivan for being one of my earliest readers. Thank you also to Júlia Darabont, another early reader, for being my biggest cheerleader. I love talking TV shows and writing craft with you. Thank you to Casey Rawlings and Jenna Tooley for the mugs of tea, late-night jigs, and bad British accents. We are definitely the best fake name crew in the business. I love being man-haters with you. Thank you also to Fanny Berger and Eileen Seo for the many Sproul Hall memories. I am always so grateful for you all!

Thank you to Bruin Belles, the first home I found in university. So many of my favorite college moments are with you. How incredibly fitting that Arya's safe space shares the same name.

I have been lucky enough to have some of the greatest educators this world has to offer. Thank you to Ms. Fraser for fostering my early love of reading. It was such a lovely, full-circle moment to speak to your current classroom about my career. Thank you also to Mrs. Richey for the endless support since I first shared my stories with you at age fourteen. You taught me to take myself seriously as a writer. It means so much to me to share this book with you now. Thank you also to Mr. Destro, Mr. Parrish, and Mrs. Brekke for shaping my high school experience and always believing in me. I am so thankful!

I have so much appreciation for the UCLA English department. It was my dream in high school to take the creative writing classes I've had the privilege of making my academic focus in college. In particular, thank you to Professor Simpson, Professor Huneven, and Professor Torres for an incredible workshop experience. It has been a gift to learn from you. Thank you also to all of my friends I've made through workshops, for the enthusiasm and support, especially Shalinee, Umiemah, and Ella. I am so grateful for you and your stories. Thank you also to Professor Bristow for the early encouragement.

I promise I'm winding down soon! Major thank-yous to every teacher, librarian, and bookseller who nurtured my bookworm tendencies from childhood onward. Thank you to my youth writing communities, including but not limited to Foothill Writers Group, the Tri-Valley Writers Club, YoungArts, and the Scholastic Art and Writing Awards. I found my voice as a writer in these organizations and began to dream big. Thank you to the Foothill High School Choral Program for being my favorite class of the day for four years straight and to the Senate Youth Program for the lasting online (turned in-person!) friendships. Thank you also to every person who left excited comments on my Google Drive reader doc senior year, and to every person who swiped up on my Instagram story excerpts while I was drafting and told me they wanted to read the final version—now you can! Thank you to Espresso Profeta, Kerckhoff Coffee House, and the Peet's Coffee in Downtown Pleasanton for being my go-to writing spots. Thank you to Taylor Swift and Arijit Singh for supplying my writing music, and thank you to Aditya Chopra and Karan Johar for the films of my (and Arya's) childhood. And thank you to you, my readers, for giving the story of my heart a try. I am (clearly!) very overwhelmed with gratitude and excitement that this book will be out in the world. I grew up writing this story. I have wanted this forever and ever.

Finally, I am grateful to all the past versions of myself: elementary school Arushi, who practically lived in libraries; middle school Arushi, who discovered there was nothing quite so magical as storytelling; teenage Arushi, who endured. I write for us.